JENNY IS FREE

A NOVEL

BY

Sylvia Ann McLain

BOOK TWO OF THE SPINNING JENNY SERIES

ISBN: 9781092835084

Cover and interior design by Tara Mayberry, TeaBerry Creative

For David

SPINNING JENNY:

(Noun)—A spinning machine of the nineteenth century, with multiple spindles, so that a spinner may spin several different yarns at the same time.

CHAPTER ONE

January 11, 1841

JENNY CORNELIUS, SEVENTEEN years old (she thinks), and a freed-woman for the past hour, stands at the railing of the steamboat *John Jay*, rubbing her arms and watching the Mississippi River churn behind the boat. The wind is cold and her summery dress isn't enough; she needs a cloak, or at least a shawl. But she doesn't have any of her things with her for this long journey; the dress she's wearing isn't even her own dress, and it's too small. The buttons down the front were already pulling tight when the sheriff grabbed her yesterday, but now she's glad, because nestled inside the straining bodice is the three hundred dollars Master Cornelius gave her.

Her freeing paper's tucked in there too, and that's the most important thing she has. When Cornelius handed her the paper he said, *Do not lose it*, his voice mild as it always was but with a tone that said he meant it. Not that the freeing paper looks like much, it's just a scribble on the back of a green-lined ledger page, but he wrote it, and he signed it. It says she's a free woman, and that hardly seems real to her.

When the boat pulled away from the dock at Natchez-Under-the-Hill, she looked back just once to see if Cornelius was watching. The barrooms and bawdy houses behind the dock shrank until they were small as a child's play blocks. If Cornelius was watching, she thought, the *John Jay* would look like a toy to him as it moved out to the middle of the wide river. But he was gone.

She closes her eyes, remembering what's put her on this boat. In just one day she's seen things she never thought she'd see—the inside of the Vidalia jail, for one thing. And Cornelius breaking into the jail like a madman, with fire in his eyes and a pistol in his hand, when she'd never seen him carry any weapon but a hunting rifle. The winter's been mild this year, but when he rowed her across the river she felt a cold wind on her neck, the same wind that's now making her shiver out here on the open deck.

When they got to Under-The-Hill, it was almost dawn; the sky was turning red above the bluff. She climbed out of the rowboat and stumbled in the water; then she hopped up onto the riverbank and wrung out the hem of her skirt. The *John Jay* was waiting, its boilers powered up, the ticket agent lowering his window and the boatmen waiting to pull the gangplank up. Cornelius rapped on the ticket window and the agent raised the shade. Cornelius bought her a ticket as a deck-passenger and then handed her an envelope.

"This is three hundred dollars," he said. "If you stay on the boat until you get to *Cin-cin-nati,* you'll be on free soil."

He scribbled that precious freeing-paper, gave her a last name, which he said a free person had to have, and up the gangplank she went. The boatmen threw the ropes off and the steamer slipped the dock, its engine rumbling and the stacks trailing flat streamers of gray smoke. The boat moved out into the middle of the river and righted its course, the prow heading north into the current. In a few minutes it went around a bend, and Natchez disappeared.

Now the banks are an endless line of trees on both sides. A few deckhands loiter on the deck and stare at her, making comments she can't overhear. This is the lower deck, where cotton bales will be stacked up to the rafters in the summertime. She knows it's not good to be the only woman on the deck, and besides, she looks like a runaway since she got on the boat by herself, without a satchel or a coat or a mistress, and that's a dangerous look. A gust of wind catches her hair, so she walks over to stand by the wall of the engine house, where she fishes a hairpin out of her hair and pins it back as best she can.

As long as she's on the lower deck, the deckhands will stare, so she climbs the steps to the upper deck where a crowd of men are waking to the cold morning. If she could stand behind the cabin house, she'd be out of the wind, but every spot there is already taken by other passengers with the same idea. Most of them are sleeping sitting up, leaning against the wall with their arms folded inside their raggedy coats. Some are sprawled out on the deck. These are slaves left out to shiver while their masters and mistresses sleep warm inside the cabins, Jenny knows. The slave women will be coming out as soon as it's light to empty the chamber pots into the river.

She walks to the back rail where the sternwheel churns the gray water into a spray of white lace. The world she knows is spooling away from her. Natchez is gone, and so are Cornelius and old Malachi, and little red-headed Thomas. And Esther and all the others she knew at Carefree. And Emile Coqterre, dead in this same river that's now carrying her to the north. The cabins and cotton fields of Bayou Cocodrie and everything else that's part of slave-land—it's all being swallowed up as the wheel churns.

She unfolds the ticket Cornelius gave her. It's a flimsy square of purple paper. She can't read it, but she knows it says Cin-cin-nati. Free soil.

As sunlight washes across the deck, the men along the cabin house wall shake themselves awake and rub sleep out of their eyes.

"Where's your coat, gal?" one of the men calls. He walks over to the railing and stands beside her. "Where ya headed?"

She looks up at him. He's a big fellow with a dark gentle face, wearing a ragged coat. *Slave*, she thinks. She shrugs and looks back at the river.

"Well, Vicksburg's the next stop," he says. "Four more hours."

Vicksburg? It didn't occur to her the boat would stop before it got to Cin-cin-nati. She thought it would just travel up to the free soil and then spit her out on the riverbank, where she'd fly like a bird into her new life. But the thought comes to her that she might not fly at all; if she's a bird, she might dive straight down to the water like a heron, and maybe she wouldn't come back up.

The *John Jay* looks nothing like the floating palaces she's sometimes seen docked at Natchez. Can this old boat really be her ticket to a free life? It's in need of a coat of paint and a good scrubbing. Or will she catch her death of cold out here on the deck before she gets there? She's shivering, and maybe it's not just from the cold.

She looks around as the door in the middle of the cabin house opens, and a slave woman slips out, gasps at the cold air, and goes back inside. Jenny walks over and slips in behind her. She stands just inside the door, looking down the hallway and blowing into her cupped hands.

A woman in a fur coat comes out of her cabin, pulling a scarf around her neck. She glances at Jenny. "Such a cold mornin', ain't it? The weather's made a change."

"Yes, ma'am."

The woman walks away down the hall, and then other doors open. Some of the passengers stare at her. She's not surprised, since she's a deck-passenger and has no right to be inside, and she looks like a runaway. So she goes back out.

By now some slave women are crowding along the back railing, hunched over as they watch the wheel thrash the water. Jenny walks to the rail and they shift around to make a space for her. She thinks, *When I get to Cin-cin-nati I'll sew myself a coat.* She closes her eyes and pictures the coat she'll make, the fabric she'll use, the stitches she'll take, and as always, it calms her, just to focus on her sewing.

But then she opens her eyes and thinks, *This old boat's headed in the wrong direction.*

As soon as Walker Jackson was marched onto the *John Jay* at Bayou Sara, north of Baton Rouge, and the man who captured him plopped down on the deck behind the cabin house, Walker lay down and curled himself into a ball and pulled his coat over his face. He figured if he was lucky this old steamboat would sink before it got to Natchez. It seemed like it could go down any minute, the way it sagged in the middle and rode so low in the water. It was about as sorry a steamer as you'd find on the river, but naturally this is the one that ignorant Rufus had to drag him onto. No surprise there.

But when dawn comes and the boat's docked at Natchez-Under-the-Hill, still afloat, Walker pulls his coat away from his face so he can look out. He wants to see his hometown one last time. The honky-tonks behind the dock never looked so good to him as they do now, and the long slope of Silver Street going up to the top of the hill looks like the stairway to heaven. He thinks: *I ought t' be gettin' off here.* But he faces at least another half-day on the *John Jay* until they get to Vicksburg, where a slave auction's waiting.

The chain around his ankle rubs his skin raw and he thinks again, for the hundredth time: *How could I be so stupid? To let myself get catched—snatched—back into slavery.*

Captured. Enslaved. He can hardly believe it. After he's spent half his life free. When he went to Bayou Sara to see his old auntie, he *knew* better than to go out on the country roads—

He shifts himself around. There's no use waking the man lying next to him. Rufus Hall, the man's name is, and he's as ignorant a farm boy as Walker's ever seen, puny-built and barely a man, his scrawny face bumpy with pimples. Walker can't stand to look at that pockmarked face, so he looks down at his own fine leather shoes, caked with dust, resting alongside Rufus's skinny white shank where the man's pants have hiked up. Rufus's feet are stuffed into work boots without socks, and a ten-penny chain is looped from his ankle over to Walker's, and locked tight.

He watches the Natchez passengers file on, hoping somebody'll get on who knows him, some businessman or lady who's shared her boy's clothes with him, and they'll help him. But the people coming onto the steamer are all strangers to him. Then the last passenger, a girl in a yellow dress, runs up the stairs and stands at the side railing.

Jenny.

He knows her.

Rufus coughs and snorts himself awake. He wriggles himself around until he's sitting with his back against the cabin house, his eyes still closed.

Walker sits up and shifts himself a little, not enough to rouse Rufus, just enough to make his presence felt. When he sees that the man's bleary eyes are barely open, he says, "Master Rufus, you want me to fetch you a cup of coffee? You wait here, I can bring you some."

Rufus looks at him as if he's surprised to see him.

"I bet they're makin' a fresh pot in the dining room right now," Walker says, pulling his legs up as if he's about to stand. "You take cream and sugar?"

Rufus scowls and runs his hand through his rough-chopped hair. "I ain't drinkin' coffee this mornin'. And you gonna stay chained 'til we get to Vicksburg."

"Yes, sir. Well, it won't be long now."

The sun rises above the trees. A few more women move out to the railing, pulling their shawls tight. The girl in the yellow dress is with them.

Walker stays quiet, giving Rufus time to think about the coffee, and the privy, since the need to pee gets a man moving quicker than a dry throat will. Rufus looks around, focusing on nothing in particular.

After a few minutes Walker says in a low voice, "You know, Master, one of those gals over there by the railing is a runaway. I know her. I seen her come on at Natchez. I reckon you could grab 'er pretty easy. She ain't much more'n a kid herself."

Rufus shades his eyes with his hand and looks at the women.

"We gettin' near to Vicksburg," Walker says. "You could sell 'er at the auction, then go catch yourself another one. Or find out if there's a reward out for her. There likely is."

"Which gal is it?"

"Well, I cain't really tell for sure which one it is, unless you unhook me. I'd have to go talk to her, make sure she's runnin' away. 'Course, she could just be travelin' on her own without her mistress, but that don't seem likely, do it? No, I betcha anything she's a runaway. She's got it wrote all over her."

He grins at Rufus. He knows people like it when he makes his wide toothy grin, so now he lets his teeth show wide and white. "After all, what kinda price am I gonna bring, little old dwarf-man that I am. She'd bring a lot more than me. You'll have t' unchain my leg, though. There ain't no place I can get off this boat anyways. Where you think I can go? I ain't gonna jump overboard, 'cause I cain't swim."

Rufus says nothing. Walker lets him calculate.

Then Jenny leaves the railing and walks right past Walker and Rufus almost like she's sashaying around just to show herself off. She goes inside the cabin house. Then a couple of minutes later she comes back out and finds herself a new spot at the rail, wriggling in among the women.

Rufus says, "All right. But you stay right here on this deck where I can see you." He buttons his coat and stands up. Walker stands up too, and Rufus bends down to unlock the chain.

"Hey, Jenny."

She turns around. Walker Jackson is grinning up at her. "You remember me, don't ya?"

"Walker?"

Yes, she remembers him, a little man hardly up to her shoulder, not a dwarf really, but very small. And dapper as he always was in his little coat, his dark face a network of lines. And he's right here on the steamboat with her.

"Yep, it's me all right," he says. "I seen you get on at Natchez." He elbows his way up to the railing. "I remember you when you used to be at Carefree. One time you come out to the cottonwood tree with Helene. "

"Helene got sold off."

"Yeah, I heard about that. So where ya headed?"

"Cin-cin-nati." She holds out her crumpled ticket to show him.

He whistles. "Cincinnati? How come you want t' go way up there?"

"'Cause it's free soil. My master gave me my freein' paper."

"He on this boat with you?"

She shakes her head.

"Well, I heard of masters settin' their gals free, but I never heard of one sendin' 'em so far away." He pulls a half-smoked cigarette out of his pocket and strikes a match to it. "I bet your master don't know nothin' about Cincinnati. Ain't you scared, goin' off all by yourself?"

"No, I ain't scared."

"Maybe you oughta be. It's a long way to Cincinnati. Probably four days anyway." He studies the shoreline. "That's a mighty long trip for this old tub we're on. Look at that broke rail over there, and the way the deck slopes in the middle like a sway-back old nag. I'd be surprised if this boat ain't takin' on water right now, down below. I've heard of 'em doin' that, and then, whoosh! They go straight down to the bottom like somebody pulled the plug." He puffs on his cigarette, flicking ashes out to the wind with his fingers. "We're makin' good time, though. We probably five miles out of Natchez already. It's cold out here, gal. Where's your coat?"

"Ain't got one."

He shakes his head. "You think this is cold, you ain't seen cold 'til you get to a northern city like Cincinnati. Ain't you got nothin' else with you? No satchel?"

"Just my ticket and my freein' paper." *And three hundred dollars you don't need to know about,* she thinks. She runs her fingers lightly down her bodice.

He whistles. "Your master must be ignorant as Rufus is, sendin' you up there."

"What?"

"The thing about Cincinnati is, there's runaways all over the place, and there's slave-catchers all over the place too. It's free soil, all right, but

9

it's right across the river from Kaintuck, and that *ain't* free soil, I can tell you. Shoot. Cincinnati ain't safe. You especially wouldn't be safe."

He smokes his cigarette down and flips the stub over the rail. "You think about what I said, Jenny. And while you're thinkin', I need to talk to this other gal right here." The woman standing next to Jenny turns around all at once, surprised, and then gives a hoot of a laugh. Walker has his hand on her back and he's grinning his wide grin.

Jenny unfolds her crumpled ticket and studies it. So Cincinnati's a den of slave-catchers? Cornelius wouldn't send her off to some place that wasn't safe, not after he went to all that trouble to get her out of jail. But maybe he never heard about the slave-catchers.

Suddenly the ticket, a little oblong of cheap blue paper with some letters printed on it, looks like a mighty small thing to hang her whole future on. She could be an old woman, she thinks, and back in slavery for her whole life, and she'd remember this scrap of paper, how she had to decide whether to hold onto it and let it take her to Cincinnati, or listen to what Walker Jackson says. And do—what, exactly? She turns to look at Walker, but he's laughing with the other woman, who's got a purple shawl pulled around her broad shoulders. That woman's liking whatever Walker's saying.

Jenny looks at the riverbank, and it seems to her that the boat's going mighty fast, headed north. She thinks about her brother: she'll never find him if she goes to Cin-cin-nati. He's out there in slave-land somewhere.

Walker turns back to her. "Listen, Jenny, there's a slave-catcher right here on this boat," he says in a low voice. "Don't look around. His name's Rufus. That skinny white boy in a brown coat over by the cabin house. He catched me, and he's gonna try to catch you too, if he can. But we can out-fox 'im, and we can both get clean off this boat."

The wind blows harder, moving the tired branches of the wintry trees on the riverbanks. She looks down into Walker's lined face. "How can we do that?"

"This here boat's gonna stop for wood in a few minutes," he says. "Steamboats always stop at the same woodin' place. Up ahead around the bend, we'll come to a place where there's a stack of wood higher than you. The boat'll have to stop 'cause they can't run the engines without wood. So it'll pull over and when it does, you and me can walk right down that gangplank and get off this tub."

"That slave-catcher just gonna let you walk off? "

"No, gal. We gonna use trickery. Somethin' Rufus over there ain't smart enough to figure out. Me talkin' to this other gal here, this big-hipped gal, that's part of the trick. And when the boat stops, and I give a whistle, you walk down the steps easy as you please, and just head on over to the gangplank. Don't run. And then you and me are gonna stroll right off this boat and into those woods, and nobody's gonna stop us. We'll be long gone before Rufus even notices. Then this boat'll head on out again, and we can be clean back in Natchez before it even gets to Vicksburg."

She shakes her head. "Walker, you gonna get me in trouble for sure. I cain't go back to Natchez. I got a ticket to Cin-cin-nati."

"Jenny, listen. You're thinkin' that's a good idea now, 'cause that's what your master told you to do, but you ain't gonna be thinkin' it's such a good idea when some slave-catcher's got you up on a auction block. You can make it as a free person in Natchez. I been livin' in Natchez a long time, and I can show you how you can get along there."

"I shouldn't even be talkin' to you."

"I'm your only chance, gal. We could go back to Carefree."

"But the last time I was at Carefree, nobody was there but Esther. She said Master Emile had gone stark crazy, and he sold everybody off but her. He was gonna sell her too."

"Well, she don't need to worry 'bout old Emile Coqterre now, 'cause he's dead. I remember the day they fount him in the river. We could try Carefree. I don't know what shape the place is in now, after all this time. I ain't been up there for a while." He touches her arm. "I wonder who owns it now. Let's go find out."

Jenny pulls her arm away. "I ain't goin' back, I said. I got a ticket to Cin-cin-nati."

"And I'm sayin' you can't go to Cincinnati with nothin' but a freein' paper. Come on back with me. You can always catch another boat if you change your mind. You think quick," Walker says. "This boat won't stay stopped long." He edges close to the woman standing next to Jenny and puts his hand under her shawl. The woman looks down at him and giggles.

Jenny stares at the shoreline, which is getting closer. The boat's pulling over, like Walker said. She cranes her neck to look for the high stacks of wood, and then there they are, just like Walker said, big raw saw-cuts of logs, ready to go into the belly of this boat. She thinks: *If what Walker says is true, that Cin-cin-nati's full of slave-catchers—*

It ain't what Master Cornelius told me to do, but he ain't my master any-more. I got money; I could buy my brother out of slavery.

Then a darker thought comes: *A slave catcher'd take my money faster'n you could say Yankee Doodle—*

And there ain't no way Kofi would be in Cin-cin-nati. An unwanted memory comes to her mind, of Kofi's legs pumping the air as slavers carried him off into the dark.

The boat heaves to a stop and the boatmen pull the gangplank out. The woods here are thick, with a lot of brambles.

Jenny walks over to the top of the stairs and looks around for Walker. He's talking to the white man in the brown coat. That's the slave-catcher, Jenny thinks; he looks more like a boy more than a grown man. Then Walker points to the woman in the purple shawl. The slave-catcher nods.

Jenny thinks, *I'd like to see Esther. She'd give me a coat. And I can always catch another boat.*

The slave-catcher slouches across the deck, moving slowly at first, but then picking up speed as he gets closer to the rail. Walker spins away from him and hot-foots it right past Jenny. "You comin'?" he says as he goes down the stairs, gripping the railing and swinging his feet, taking three steps at a time. His head disappears down the steps.

Jenny hesitates for a second and then opens her hand. The crumpled ticket sails off into the wind.

"Wait!" she calls after him. She runs down the steps, her arms out, balancing herself. When they get to the gangplank she's close enough to touch him; she runs down the gangplank right behind him. When they get to the bottom he jumps onto the bank and she jumps too.

"Glad you come to your senses, girl," Walker pants as they run for the woods. They both look back just once when they hear a woman squealing on the upper deck. Her purple shawl is untied and she's slapping at Rufus, pushing him away with both hands.

"Missus!" the woman squeals.

The other women on the deck are yelling and running around with their hands flapping. The door to the cabin house bursts open and a tall woman in a fur coat strides out. She stalks over to her maid and pulls the woman close to her, whacking Rufus hard with her umbrella. He puts his hands up. The woman in the purple shawls squeals louder, and Rufus backs away. Then he turns on his heel to look around the deck, and Jenny knows he's looking for Walker. He'll probably run around the whole saggy boat looking, but by then it'll be too late. Because right here on the riverbank are some cedar trees and thick underbrush, and there's a cowpath winding deep into the woods. And Walker's got hold of Jenny's hand, and they run. And even though he's a little man, he can run awful fast, Jenny notices.

CHAPTER TWO

WHENEVER HE PASSES through Cemetery Town, which he has to do whenever he heads up to Vicksburg to visit his mammy, Walker knows to be on the lookout for the gang of boys who live there. They're often out in the road playing war, crouching behind bushes, firing slingshots and pelting balls at each other. He hardly ever makes it past the cemetery which gives the place its name before they come after him, shouting, "Li'l ole dirty man, you ain't gonna outrun us!" Or else they lay in ambush, white boys nearly as big as he is. If these kids had guns they'd be dangerous, he's thought many a time, but so far he's made it past them before they can hit him with their weapons. They always stop right at the corner of the cemetery because their mammies have told them they can't go any farther than that, he guesses. But for some reason, their mammies ain't never around when the boys start in after him.

But today no kids are outside, so he can walk along the road with Jenny without watching too close. Cemetery Town is a row of dilapidated clapboard houses, each with a porch across the front with two doors opening to it, one for the living room, one for the bedroom. Walker knows exactly what those houses are like: two rooms side by side, and each room with a fireplace, and that's it. In Natchez he's been in houses just like these when he does odd jobs around town. The shutters and doors are closed up tight

15

today, gray smoke streaming from every chimney. That stiff breeze is moving the clouds fast. The air smells cold and fresh. The bare trees are swaying, restless in the wind. *They're waving their limbs just like people wave their arms when they want to flag you down,* Walker thinks. You always have to be careful when you see somebody do that, since you never know what they want. He hopes these trees aren't trying to flag him and Jenny down, knowing something they don't. But of course that can't be so.

And squirrels are everywhere, since the trees are mostly oaks. They hop chattering from branch to branch. Maybe the squirrels like the wind, he thinks. The wind will bring down more acorns, and if he went poking close to the houses he'd see lines of acorns along the sides of the porches and in piles underneath the bushes. Acorns are a five-course meal for a squirrel. But of course, he's not going to poke around close to the houses.

Ragged brown leaves skitter down the road in front of them, scratching at the ground as they tumble. At the last house in Cemetery Town, a door opens, and then slams shut. No one comes out. "Too cold for anybody to be out today," Walker says. "Let's us just head straight on down to Natchez."

Jenny walks with her arms folded and her head down. Once they left the deep woods by the boat landing and got out on the road, she didn't have much to say. He's not sure whether she's pleased to be coming back or not, and he's mighty curious about her.

She's a pretty girl, no doubt about that. Her eyelids are like little hoods over her eyes, and then every once in a while her eyes flash up, bright all of a sudden, if he's saying something important. And her lips are so full. He's glad she got off the boat with him, even though he has to trot faster than he really wants to, so he can keep a half-step ahead of her. He figures he should walk a little ahead, since he knows the way back to Natchez and she doesn't.

He tries to get her to talk; he wants to know how come her master set her free, but he won't just come right out and ask. If there's one thing he knows, a person can get all tangled up, just knowing about something. You have to be careful what you ask, because you might not want to know. He's seen lots of entanglements in his life, and he knows that a pretty girl can find herself pushed out, like any inconvenience, just sent away, here's your free paper, pack up your things, you got to go, your mistress's got fire in her eyes and your master's got a rolling pin to his head. And there's no talking back about it, just like there's no talking back about anything else. There's nothing as helpless in this world as a slave girl in a state like that.

"I tell you, Jenny, it's a good thing I saw you on that steamboat," he says as they walk down the road.

"Why? So I can freeze to death?"

"No, 'cause that old tub's probably halfway up to Vicksburg by now, and you and me ain't on it. That's a mighty fine thing. Like I said, you go to Cincinnati, you wouldn't last an hour. Slave-catchers come right in on a pretty young thing like you. And the other thing is, you stick with me, I can teach you things."

"What kinda things you think you can teach me? Except how to freeze."

"Pshaw. You ain't gonna freeze. I'd give you my coat but it wouldn't fit. Nature made me a tiny man, and that's just something I got to live with. Nature made me a slave, too, but I decided that *weren't* something I had to live with."

"I'm free too."

"So you say."

"So what you think you can teach me? I'm seventeen. I know things."

He kicks at a rock, then thinks he shouldn't have when he feels the weight of it. He wouldn't want to get his nice shoes scratched up. "Like how

17

to be free, just generally," he says. "And like you can't go 'round dressed like that."

"Well, it's all I got right now."

"It makes you look like a runaway. That dress is wrinkly, but it's fine-made, anybody can tell. And you don't even have a coat. You look like a gal that run off and grabbed one of your lady's dresses on your way out the door."

"I notice you dress pretty fine."

"I do, 'cause that's just my way. I like to look spiffy. And I can always find some lady who's got a half-grown boy, and she'll give me some clothes. There's a few ladies in Natchez who know me. And their boys grow so fast. But you gotta be more careful than me. I ain't much good as a slave, 'cause I'm so little, but you—any slaveowner's gonna think of a lot of uses for you."

She glances at him. "How come you so interested in what happens to me?"

"'Cause I can tell you're a rare bird, just like I am. There ain't that many of us freed people in Natchez, so we gotta look out for each other. And it's gettin' harder all the time, seems to me. The way it is now, they make us register with the authorities every year to prove we're of good character. They'd be just as happy to send us packin', 'cause they don't like us hangin' around their slaves. Might give 'em ideas."

"You gave me an idea, and that's how come I ended up back here."

"Well, you're free, so you better off than you'd be in Cincinnati." He looks around at the woods. "Another thing to remember, when you're in town, always try to walk on the side streets. And don't go out in the country. You safer if you stay where there's people around."

"We're in the country now."

"That's just 'cause we got no choice if we want to get back to Natchez. I'm glad we're past Cemetery Town. The kids that live there ain't nice a-t'all." He looks around.

They turn the corner and go up a little hill, before the road drops down again into a tangled swamp. A white man is standing on the side of the road watching them approach. His speckled horse stands with its head down.

They couldn't see him before because of the hill, and now there's no place to turn off the road. "What's this?" Walker says in a low voice. "Maybe his horse went lame."

They're closer now, and the man is still watching them. "Keep an eye up," Walker says in a low voice. "I ain't likin' the looks of this. Let's walk on the other side."

The man, his coat buttoned up to his neck and a bandanna tied around his head, raises his hand to wave.

"Watch out," Walker mutters.

Then all at once the man swings up onto his horse. He takes out his whip and beats the animal into a gallop right down the road past them.

"That's what I mean," Walker says. "He could'a been a slave-catcher as well as not. Good thing he wasn't. Well, it ain't far now."

They pass by some brick houses and Walker points to the church spires rising above the trees. "We're just about there."

They turn onto a cobblestone street lined with shops. One of the buildings is a butcher shop with gray-white beeves hanging in the window. A little farther on they pass a general store. A cloud moves across the sky, darkening the street, and all at once they can see into the store window. A man is standing inside, watching them pass.

"I guess he ain't got any customers this mornin'," Walker says. "Now, another thing to remember, you ain't got to worry about slaves. They won't bother you if you don't bother them. They might look at you, though. I don't think you gonna be able to keep 'em from doin' that. They look at me too, just 'cause I'm different. Just don't stop and talk to 'em. Their masters get real upset about that."

"How come you know so much?"

"'Cause even when I was just a little chap I knew I had to be smart, since I couldn't be big and strong. And then when I got my freein' paper from my old mistress, I could see right off that us free people needed somebody to help us. And if a new person comes to Natchez, just out of slavery, they especially need some help. So I knew we oughta have a leader, and I decided it'd be me. I call myself the Mayor of Natchez." He grins and glances over at her.

"Ain't Natchez already got a mayor?"

"Natchez's got one all right, but he ain't the mayor of us. He's just the mayor for the white folks. People like us, we got no governor and no president, neither. Ole Martin van Buren, he ain't thinkin' about us, that's for sure. And Governor Alexander McNutt don't care nothin' about us. I know some things about him. I'll tell you sometime. "

"I ain't interested in hearin' it," Jenny says. "Ain't we gettin' close yet? I'm hungry. Maybe Esther'll give me somethin' to eat."

"Don't get your hopes up," Walker says. "She might not even be livin' at Carefree anymore."

They turn into an alley between some bushes, and a few minutes later they come out right in front of the red-brick mansion with its four white columns.

"There it is!" Jenny says, stepping out onto the road to go across.

"Hang on." Walker puts out his hand to stop her. "We can't go blunderin' up there unless we know it's safe."

Jenny steps back. He studies the house. It's always looked dignified to him, not overdone like some big houses with their fancy trimmings. It's a stately house, and Walker admires the way it sits up on a hill in the middle of that wide lawn; it's a house like George Washington himself could've lived in. Black shutters cover every window, except for one upstairs shutter that's come loose and swings in the wind on its one hinge. That could pull right off, he thinks. But it still looks good for a house with such a sad past. He knows that out behind the house, where they can't see, is a kitchen and a slave house, a privy, and a barn. He doesn't get up to this part of Natchez much, but about a year ago this place was the talk of Natchez. Odd that it's called Carefree.

"I know Esther's in there," Jenny says. "She'll give me a coat."

"Maybe she's in there and maybe she ain't. I can't see the kitchen chimney, but it don't look to me like anybody's here."

"Quit worryin' about the smoke. Let's go."

"I hear somebody comin'," Walker says. He steps back behind a bush and pulls Jenny back with him. A woman driving a buggy goes past their hiding place and turns into the gate to Carefree. She pulls the horse to a stop and then sits in the buggy for a moment, looking up at the house, before she climbs down.

"Who's that?" Walker whispers. He studies the woman as she climbs the steps to the gallery, pulling off her leather driving gloves. "She looks like some rich lady I oughta know but I can't place her. She looks kind of familiar, though." The woman doesn't hesitate, so Walker's pretty sure she's been here before. When she goes to the end of the gallery to look across the lawn, he ducks farther behind the bush before he peers out again.

"I think I've seen her before," Jenny says. "She might've been one of Miss Stephanie's friends. She looks different now, though."

The woman strides to the door and knocks loudly.

"Now, see," Walker whispers. "I dunno why she'd knock. Everybody knows this place's been abandoned since Coqterre killed hisself. And see how nobody come to take the horse, or open the door. Let's just hold on tight right here 'til we figure this out."

The woman pushes the front door open and stands in the doorway for a moment, looking in. Then she goes inside and closes the door behind her.

"She's mighty curious about the place," Walker says.

A few moments later the woman's face appears at the window with the dangling shutter. She looks out across the lawn for a few seconds and then retreats into the dark house.

"Just hold tight," Walker says. Jenny leans against the fence, her arms folded, looking at the ground.

A few minutes later the woman comes out and climbs up into the buggy. When she drives past them she's staring straight ahead, frowning.

"I wonder what she was doin' here," Walker says as the buggy rumbles down the hill and turns onto the road into Natchez. "All right, now we can go on in and see if we can find Esther."

Jenny hurries across the road ahead of him.

He reaches out to take her arm. "Quit runnin'. You ain't goin' to a fire. We still gotta be careful."

"While you bein' careful, I'm gonna freeze," she says, shaking her arm free of his grip; but her pace slows to his. The high slope of the lawn rises before them.

They take the side-path that leads around the side of the house. Smoke rises from the kitchen chimney.

"Yep, Esther's here," Walker said. "She's got a fire goin'." He takes Jenny's arm again. "You know, you oughta be right proud, Jenny. You comin' back to Carefree arm in arm with the Mayor of Natchez." He grins his toothy grin.

In the whitewashed building that serves as her kitchen, Esther stares at the closed door. Was that a ghost who just came into the kitchen and then swift as a fox went out again? She puts her hand to her forehead. A visitor coming in so sudden, and without a word: maybe it's a sign her time's about to come at last, when she'll be sold off. At the thought, she sinks down onto the chair beside the table. Surely it won't be today. But it could be; it could be.

It started off as an ordinary quiet day. She got up early and by nine o'clock she'd already done her chores in the big house; she'd waxed the floor in the upstairs hall and polished the candlesticks in the dining room. Then she came out here to the kitchen and put a chicken on to cook. These days she tries to pass her time as she did in the old days, making her way between the kitchen and the big house, depending on the chores she sets for herself, even though the big house is an echoing empty shell and the food she cooks is for herself alone.

But then, a few minutes ago, that woman in a fur-collared coat opened the door and walked into the kitchen. She nodded to Esther and went right over to the fire to warm her hands, and then took the potholder and lifted the lid on the pot to see what was cooking. She walked around the kitchen without a word, studying what there was to see: a wooden bowl of pecans, a basket with three brown eggs, some onions, a crock of flour, a loaf of sugar. She looked at the shelves where Esther's pots and pans were stacked. She examined the spice shelf, touching each little jar and moving it ever so slightly out of its place. Then she nodded at Esther and walked out the door.

Has that woman been in this house before? Esther wonders. She looked familiar in a dim way, but Esther can't put a name to the face. But she knows her mind is foggy sometimes. When Miss Stephanie got married and they had that big wedding reception here at the house—was that woman one of the guests?

She goes over to the spice shelf and moves the tins back into a straight line. Then she sits down at the table. This intruder shook her thoughts loose, and now they won't settle just because she wills them to. The thoughts that come up are of her lost girls, and her fears of the slave market. She closes her eyes and forces her mind to fix on other things.

Lord, the things this house has seen. There was the day when Lucy Ida, the oldest slave at Carefree, ancient and frail, sat with her on the back steps and talked about where she'd come from. Lucy's mind traveled far back, as old people's minds do. South Caroline was what Lucy remembered, and those recollections didn't seem to pain her. Lucy Ida talked about her old master's ugly son who came to see her night after night, promising her freedom. But Lucy Ida died without ever having a free day in her whole life.

I don't know if I'm free or not, Esther thinks, *but I know I've been saved.* How that's happened she doesn't know, but it has. She's come out of the darkness that swallowed her up after her girls were sold off and Master Emile turned the house over to the goats. She remembers how those animals clomped up and down the stairs, traipsing over the fine rugs and pulling at the curtains and the upholstery with their teeth. Devil animals, those goats were. Master Emile was stark crazy by then, his gray hair hanging down across his face and his eyes with that fierce haunted look that a crazy man's have. He shouted at her, told her to let the goats have their way in the house, and he propped the doors open so the animals could go in and out as they pleased. It wasn't long before the whole house had their stench.

And to his mind she was as filthy as the goats, Esther imagined. He was gone almost all the time in those last months, sleeping in the woods. He the owner of one of the finest houses in Natchez, with more rooms and beds than anyone could need, sleeping in the woods. She had to save one room in the house, she decided, so she chased the goats out of the only room Emile wouldn't notice, the yellow back bedroom where no one ever slept, its only furnishings a bureau and a bed and the spinning wheel in the corner. She closed that door tight.

And then there came the day they found Emile floating in the river.

For Esther that began a time—some months, she can't remember how long—when she waited for someone to come and claim her, or to send her to the slave auction, more likely. She pictured how it would happen: there'd be a crunch of boots on the walk leading to the kitchen and the slavers would burst in with their big hands and take her away from Carefree, just like they took her daughters Helene and Theresa and everyone else here. And that's when the fog began to swallow her. Every day she climbed the stairs to the yellow bedroom and stretched out on the dusty coverlet. August and Littleton, her two little boys who died of malaria, kept her company. They'd never really left her; their ghosts had always been around, even after Helene and Theresa were born. And now they were with her every day, not sickly little boys but big strapping young men, grinning their wide grins.

"You just take it easy, Mamma," August would say, and she'd smile at him. He was always her favorite.

"I hear them clocks a-chimin'," Littleton would say, even though the hall clocks hadn't been wound in over a year. Sometimes Esther thought she could hear the chimes herself.

"Whose am I?" she asked the boys one time. "My master's dead. Ain't somebody comin' to get me?" But they didn't answer.

Months went by and no one came, and finally the fog in her mind began to clear. It started to lift on the day in November when the leaves on that hickory tree outside the bedroom window started falling. On that day she turned over on the bed expecting to see her boys hovering in the air and jostling with each other as they often did, but before her eyes they grew dim and transparent, as if she was watching them through a wavy window glass. Then they floated away, Littleton grabbing one of Master Emile's old felt hats that sat on the bureau, on his way out. The window was open, there was a breeze outside, and the boys were gone.

She sat up in the bed. Hunger, something she hadn't felt for months, was gnawing at her. And from that day to this she could feel herself coming back, her old body getting stronger and her thinking clearer.

But then today, this stranger came into the kitchen.

She sets the pot of chicken stew on the brick hearth and then goes out to her room in the slave-house. She still keeps the same room she's always had, the first one on the end at the bottom. She could take any room she wants—the slave-house is two stories tall with four rooms above and four below—but there's too many shadows in those other rooms. All the people she knew who used to live in those rooms, now sold away—they could be haunting those rooms. No, she'll stay in her own place; it's familiar. Sometimes she thinks she could use some of the things in the other rooms—a rickety table Charlie always kept pushed into a corner of his room, or a dress she knows is hanging from a nail in Daisy's room—but no, she'll just do without.

As she goes into her room she catches her reflection in a piece of a mirror propped on the shelf. She's a gaunt woman now; her neck is ropy and her eyes are huge. Her jawline is sharp. It's not the same face she once had, when her life was full. For a long time after everyone went away, all she could eat was a taste of this, a bite of that, whatever was left in the kitchen. She's eating better now, cooking just for herself, but it seems like she's going to stay rail-thin.

And as far as she knows, she has no master. She's on her own, not exactly free, but not exactly not free either. It's all right, if powerful lonely. She does what she's always done, kept up the big house and tried not to think about her lost girls or the other people who used to live in these rooms. She waxes the halls and starches the dresser-scarves, and sweeps up the leaves that pile up on the gallery. And now she even keeps the clocks wound, though why the house needs to mark the time, she can't imagine.

Thank goodness she has money. When Emile's sister Sophronia died, Esther slipped into the dead woman's bedroom and took the woman's purse. She knew the bureau drawer where Sophronia kept it; she'd pulled it out for Esther often enough when she wanted her to go buy something in town. Now the purse, holding seventy-five dollars and change, rests in a hidey hole in the wall behind Esther's bed. She buys what she needs in town, trying not to spend more than two bits at a time so as not to draw attention to herself. But whenever the butcher has goat meat, she makes an exception, buying a *chevon*, a goat roast, so she can cook it up in her skillet. Remembering how the animals once roamed through the house, she feels it's a kind of revenge. Every evening she sits out on the back steps and looks down to the pond, where the ducks settle. Lucy Ida comes to mind.

Right now, shivering a little, she pulls off her shawl and takes her cloak from where it's hanging on a nail and puts it around her shoulders.

The fire in the kitchen will be dying down soon, and on this cold day the kitchen will get chilly pretty quick.

She goes back out to the kitchen and stirs up the fire. She thinks she'll just sit at the table and enjoy some chicken stew. She won't let herself think about her unexpected visitor. Then the door behind her swings open, bringing cold air into the kitchen, and before she can get up to close it, she hears a girlish voice.

"Esther, it's me!"

CHAPTER THREE

ESTHER KNOWS SHE'S HEARD that voice before, and at first she thinks it's August, that he's come back out of the ether to visit her again. But he would've murmured "Mamma," almost too soft to hear, not "Esther!" and the sound of his voice wouldn't cause the birds in the tree outside the window to flutter up like they did just now.

And then in marches Jenny, looking almost like a ghost herself in Miss Stephanie's yellow wedding dress; and right behind her is Walker Jackson, that little busybody. Esther claps her hands to her face.

"Esther, I come back!" Jenny says, putting her arms around the older woman.

"Keep your voice down," Walker says.

"My lord, Jenny," Esther says. The last time she was grabbed tight like that was the day her girls were sold off, and then it wasn't a friendly hug. She steps back and sits down hard on the chair.

"I got my freein' paper, and Walker and me got off the boat and come here!" Jenny says.

"What boat?" Esther asks.

"Steamboat named *John Jay*," Jenny says. She slaps her arms. "We come here 'cause it's so cold outside. I gotta warm up." She goes to the fire and holds her skirt out wide to make it billow up.

"What on earth was you doin' on a steamboat?" Esther asks.

Jenny turns around. "Well, I was headed for the free soil. But then I run into Walker, and he told me I better come back here."

Esther looks at Walker. "Was you goin' to the free soil too?"

He rubs his hands together. "Naw. But I run into Jenny here, and I told her if she goes to free soil she'd get catched before she hardly got off the boat. Cincinnati's crawlin' with slave-catchers. So we changed our plans, like a person sometimes have to do, and off we got."

"Walker got catched, down by Bayou Sara," Jenny says. "And that slaver drug him on the boat, but him and me got away. We figured there wasn't any place to go to but here." She frowns at Esther. "You look awful skinny. I almost didn't know you."

"Well—I ain't been eatin' much." Esther looks at Walker. "That slaver ain't gonna come *here* lookin' for you, is he?"

"Nope. He's still on the boat. And it sailed away." He swings his arm out in a wide arc. "He's probably clear up to Vicksburg by now."

"Well, I want to know, 'cause there's been lots of trouble here, and I can't take any more," Esther says.

"What's that you cookin'?" Walker asks.

"Why don't you have a seat?" Esther says to him. "Jenny, I can't hardly believe I'm seein' you. And you so grown up. Did Master Cornelius treat you good out at his place?"

Jenny shrugs. "I don't know. There wasn't nobody there but him and Malachi and me. Mal's so old he couldn't do much. We just worked in the cotton, and shoo, that was hard work. I didn't like it. Then Cornelius got to thinkin' he'd come back to Natchez to live. But he never got to, because the sheriff come and took me to jail. Cornelius had to get me out of there 'fore they hung me."

Walker sits down at the table with his hands folded in front of him. "I couldn't see lettin' Jenny go up north. Somethin' smells so good. Is that chicken?"

Esther looks at Jenny. "Why was you in jail?"

" 'Cause I beat up a white woman."

Walker whistles. "First I heard of that."

"You know better'n that," Esther says in a low voice.

"Yes, I do know better," Jenny says. "But considerin' she was a thief who stole my money, it was more than I could take. You think you could find me a coat to wear?"

"You ain't got a coat?"

"Nope. Sheriff come awful quick and grabbed me, and he didn't care if I was gonna freeze to death or not. It ain't like he was gonna wait while I packed my satchel." She rubs her arms.

Esther stares at her for a moment, then gets up. "I'll go see if I can find one. Walker, why don't you bring us in some more logs. We need to stir up that fire."

As she goes up the back steps into the big house, Esther turns around and looks back at the kitchen. Yes, that's Jenny all right, that same girl she remembers, but heavens, what a start, the way she burst into the kitchen with Walker Jackson, of all people, and on the same day that strange woman paid her a visit. She's still quivery about that.

She turns down a side hall to Sophronia's bedroom, where the woman's tall black chiffarobe stands against the side wall. Esther turns the key and the chiffarobe doors swing open, and the fragrance of tightly-packed clothes floats out. Well, there's no reason Miss Sophronia's old clothes should go to waste. Sophronia hardly ever wore any of her dresses; the woman hardly ever set foot outside her bedroom and she just wore a dressing gown most of the time. And to think every one of her dresses was sewn up in a New Orleans shop by a seamstress trained in Paris.

She reaches for a honey-colored coat with a velvet collar. This will do for Jenny, even though the girl can't wear it out on the streets of Natchez; it's way too fine. But when Jenny came into the kitchen a few minutes ago, Esther saw her chapped complexion, her tangled hair. What was Cornelius Carson thinking, to put her out in this weather in only that cotton dress?

When Esther gets back to the kitchen she says, "This coat's too nice to wear out in town, but as long as you ain't goin' to town, you might as well wear it. It's plenty warm."

Jenny stands up, beaming, and shrugs her arms into the coat. She folds the lapels up, wrapping one side over the other. "I love this," she says, putting her face down into the soft fabric.

"Well, you better not love it too much, 'cause it ain't yours. And it's way too big on you. You never grew tall."

Walker comes back in carrying three split logs. He drops them on the hearth and squats down to poke at the fire. He puts two logs on the fire, and the last flame winks out.

"You better get some light'ard," Esther says, and he goes back out.

When he comes in with the wood, she says, "Y'all are hungry, I guess. I made chicken and dumplings. It's about done."

"I ain't ate nothin' since yesterday," Jenny says. "Walker ain't neither."

Walker sets the pieces of light'ard on top of the other logs in the fireplace.

"You know that ain't how you build a fire," Esther says.

"Best I can do right now," he says. "It might catch."

Esther pokes at the chicken with a fork. "Hand me those bowls, Walker," she says, pointing to the shelf where she keeps the dishes. "I was cookin' this to last me all week, but now you're here—" She ladles the stew into the bowls and sets them on the table.

Walker doesn't wait for Esther to sit down before he starts to eat. "This is real good," he says. When his spoon scrapes the bottom, he hands the bowl back to Esther.

"If there's any left after today," she says, leaving the thought unfinished as she fills his bowl again. "I sure am havin' lots of company for one day."

"You sure are, Aunt Esther," he says. "If you ever lonesome, you just remember, you always got Jenny and me. We're just about as surprised as you are." He dips his spoon into his bowl again.

Walker eats fast, and when he's finished he leans back in his chair to look at the two women sitting there, one young and fresh, swaddled in a fancy coat Esther got for her out of the big house, and the other one as old as any woman he's ever seen, old as his mammy in Vicksburg. Esther's smaller than he remembers, when he used to see her around Natchez. He heard a rumor, after Emile Coqterre died, that somebody was still living up at Carefree; but then after a while he didn't hear any more about that. Now here she sits at the table quiet as a haunt, except when she's telling him what to do. And he sees that Esther's looking at Jenny, and thinking about her, who she is and why she's come here. And Jenny's eating her chicken and dumplings and not thinking about anything but herself.

"Now that Jenny's got her freein'-paper," Walker says, "maybe she could stay here with you, Esther."

Esther looks up from her bowl and touches the corners of her mouth with her apron. "Well, there's lots of rooms in the slave house with nobody in them. I don't think it'd matter if Jenny moved in. Nobody's here to tell her she cain't."

He waits for her to mention him moving in, but she's looking down into her bowl again. So he says, "I got me a place. It's in the alley behind the Saint Vigilius church. Kind of a shed, really, but nobody bothers me there, so I figure I'll go back to it. It's by a cedar tree, and I can build fires in the alley when I need to keep myself warm. But I lost my freein' paper."

Esther looks up. "You lost it? How'd that happen?"

"Well, I didn't just lose it. It was snatched away from me when I got catched down by Bayou Sara."

"And just what was you doin' down there?" Esther asks.

He stretches his legs out under the table. "I went down there to see my old aunt, but I ended up runnin' into a slave catcher. Bad news for me."

Jenny eats the last of her stew and then reaches into her bodice and pulls out her freeing-paper. She lays it in the middle of the table. "This is what Master Cornelius gave me. It says I'm free. He said don't lose it."

Walker stands up to look. "That don't look near as nice as the one I had."

"That's all you got?" Esther asks Jenny.

"Yep."

The paper lies on the table like a relic. The pale green paper is creased up on one end, and Jenny smooths it down with her fingers, but it folds itself back up again. "There's some lines on the back," she says.

Walker looks at the paper and whistles low under his breath. "The one my ole missus gave me looked a lot better than that. That's just scribbled."

"He only had a minute to write it," Jenny says. "The boat was goin'."

"Mine came from a lawyer," Walker says. "It even had a stamp from the county." He squints at the paper on the table. "I wish I could read it."

"I can't read it neither," Jenny says.

"Me neither," Esther says with a little hiccup. "I never seen one of those before."

"Where's that old master of yours now?" Walker asks Jenny.

She shrugs. "I don't know. He said he was goin' to Texas. So I guess he's on the road."

"I wonder if I could copy these letters," Walker says. "I can't write, but if I could trace these letters for Esther, and then I could make another copy, all three of us here in this kitchen would have papers. I could try holdin' this up on the window glass and tracin' it. I did that once for my missus's grandbaby, li'l Jimbo, just to keep him entertained. He was a mess, li'l Jimbo. I traced him a picture of a cow."

Jenny studies the paper. "You think you could trace this?"

"It'd be worth a try. But I'd need to find the right paper. Not too thick."

"There's some paper in Master Emile's desk, "Esther says. "I could get you some of that." She frowns. "But listen, Walker, if you copy this, that ain't gonna work. These papers would all have Jenny's name on 'em. If anybody asked you for your freein' paper, they'd know your name ain't Jenny."

"It'd be better than nothin'," Walker says. "Which is what you and me have got now."

"If you get caught with a made-up freein' paper, you'd be in trouble for sure," Esther says. "You'd get whipped."

"I still think it'd be worth a shot," Walker mutters. He can see how Esther likes to be bossy sometimes. She was known around Natchez for that, he remembers.

Esther shakes her head. "Well, you ain't usin' my window for it." She looks at the fireplace. The light'ard is blazing. "Tell you what, Walker, why don't you come stay here in the slave house? I got lots of jobs you could help with."

"'Cause I ain't a slave, that's why," Walker says. *That sounds sharp,* he thinks, but he can't say what he's thinking. *Esther, you think you're free, but you ain't. Somebody died who was your master, but that means somebody else is your master, and they gonna come get you. And when they do, I ain't gonna be around.*

"I better go back and see if my place is still there. I'll just move back in if nobody ain't tore it down. There's some big bushes around it, so it's mainly hid. Nobody's bothered me there yet. You know where that church is?"

Esther nods.

"Walker's the mayor of Natchez," Jenny says, folding her paper and slipping it back into her bodice. "If we have any trouble, we can just run and get him."

Walker looks at her. Jenny's not making fun of him for being the mayor; her face is serious. That's a relief, in a way; nobody likes to look foolish. But Jenny's not a girl who makes fun much; he noticed that when they were walking back to Natchez and he tried to make a joke about this or that thing they passed. She didn't laugh.

Esther looks down at her hands. "Child, a slave don't usually have time to run. A slave gets catched quicker'n lightnin,' and you never know about it ahead of time. One day you're thinkin' it's just a day like any other, and then before you know it you hear some commotion and they start haulin' away—." She stops. The thought comes too close to what she's lost.

"Don't you lose that paper, Jenny," Walker says. "If you keep it safe, it *might* keep you safe." He buttons up his coat. "Esther, you reckon you could find me a hat to wear around here somewhere?"

"I expect so," Esther says, and a few minutes later Walker walks down the lawn whistling, with Emile Coqterre's good beaver hat pulled low over his ears.

After he leaves, Esther and Jenny go out to the slave house. "Pick a room quick so we don't have to stand out in this cold too long," Esther says. "You can have just about any room you want except for mine."

But when Jenny walks over and pulls open the door to the room next to Esther's, Esther wishes she hadn't said that. This was the room that once belonged to Helene and Theresa, and that door had stayed shut since the day her girls went away. From that day to this, Esther thought if she opened it a wave of pain would wash out from the empty room and drown her. But now she doesn't have time to be swept underwater, because Jenny barges right in and goes over to the back wall, where one of Helene's dresses hangs on a nail.

Jenny holds the dress out to study it. It's a pale green dress, summery style, with ribbons sewn in a neat row down the front to hide the buttons. "I made this dress for Helene," she says, brushing the skirt out. "I remember it. And I made that one for Theresa." She points to a gray dress lying across the foot of the bed. "Both of these'll fit me good. I can let the hems down if I need to." She piles them over her arm. "Let's go look at the other rooms."

They walk back outside and Esther opens the door to the next room; this room once belonged to Daisy and her children, and Esther could swear it still has the smell of sour milk. Back then, Esther was glad there was a room between her and Daisy's noisy kids. But now, a year later, many's the silent night she wishes she could still hear those little chaps giggling and chattering as she tries to sleep in her room at the end.

Jenny looks into the room and shakes her head.

The door to the last room is hard to push open; it sags a little on its hinges, so it scrapes along the floor. This room belonged to no one in particular. A narrow bed in the back corner is covered with a faded quilt, and a small grimy window up high on the back wall lets in a little light. Jenny walks in and looks around.

"I'll take this one," she says, turning to Esther with a bright smile.

Esther shakes her head. "This ain't the best room. It's too far from the kitchen, and it's got this outside wall. It'll be awful cold. Let's go upstairs and take a look at those other rooms."

"No, I like this one. It's got nails and a shelf and everything." Jenny goes to the back wall and hangs her dresses on the nail there, one atop the other. "I might put in another nail."

"You'll have to air the place out and shake out that quilt. It's dusty as anything," Esther says. "Well, if this is the room you want, I guess you can have it. Now, take off that coat so I can put it back in the chiffarobe. I'll bring you a shawl."

Jenny folds up the collar. "I'm gonna keep wearin' it. I like it."

"You can't wear it in town," Esther says, her voice firmer than she intends. "A slave girl can't go around dressed like that. But you can spread it out on your bed if you get cold at night. This old quilt looks pretty thin."

"I ain't a slave girl anymore, and I want to keep it," Jenny says, buttoning the top button. She runs her hand over her hair. "I need to get me a hairbrush and some hairpins. Is there someplace I can buy 'em?"

"Sophronia had some hairpins in her dresser," Esther says. "Ain't no use spendin' money if you don't have to. I'll go see if I can find 'em."

As she goes again up the back steps to the main house, Esther thinks, *Lord, this girl's got so much to learn. That Miss Priss is hardly a grown woman, and she's got no idea how to get by, especially since she's free. But she's not going to listen to me. What do I know about being free, anyway? I'm fifty years old, and I've never had a free day yet.*

She comes back out with a handful of hairpins and a crocheted shawl draped over her arm. Jenny shakes her head. "Those ain't the right kind of hairpins. I like the wide ones. I'll go buy some." Esther tosses the hairpins onto the quilt and spreads the shawl out on the bed.

"And I don't want to wear that shawl. It's ugly. Just point me to the store. I'll go by myself. I might stop in and see Walker while I'm out."

"I better go with you."

"You don't need to. I can find it by myself." She turns and goes out the door.

Esther walks outside and watches as Jenny strides across the lawn and down the road that leads into Natchez, a small figure in a fancy coat, her yellow skirt bouncing about her legs.

Everything will be all right, she tells herself. The world she's known her whole life is still here; the big house is the same as it's always been, even though the shutters are starting to sag at the windows, because the bolts need tightening, and that one shutter's about to pull right off. That job needs a man's strong arm, and it's been more than a year since there was a man living here. Off to the left is the broad lawn with the drive that leads up from the road. It's all still here. And over there's the kitchen, where in a minute she'll go inside and stir the fire back to life, and then rinse out the coffeepot and make a fresh pot of coffee to get herself through the afternoon. Just like she's always done.

But things will be different now because Jenny's here, and she'll be sleeping under the same roof. And Jenny's a free girl, not the skinny kid she was when she stayed here before, but almost a grown woman, and with no more sense than a wild goose.

Well, one day at a time, she thinks as she walks over to the kitchen and opens the door. The wind's still cold, but in the kitchen, her own place, the fire is sputtering, because that's how light'ard is, it blazes up fast but then dies just as fast. But the room is warm. The logs are starting to char, and licks of flame are still running around them.

CHAPTER FOUR

IN THE PARLOR of the Elenora House, a mile to the west of Carefree, John Landerson looks up from his newspaper as the nursemaid Delphine tiptoes into the room. The baby, Cyrus, nestles in the crook of her arm, asleep. The floor creaks as she walks across the rug to lay the baby in his cradle. John smiles; he likes Cyrus, his last baby, with his pretty features, his sober expression and his tiny balled fists. He seems more lively than the other boys, a trio of little chaps with runny noses and mouse-colored hair. Or the one girl, Lissy, with her nervous stammers. Cyrus seems cut from a different cloth altogether. He smiles often, is easy to please. When John carries him up to the nursery at night, the baby's head bobbing at his shoulder, it's a comfort to feel the warmth of the heavy little lump.

"I believe he'll take a good nap this afternoon," Delphine whispers. John nods at her and watches as she goes out the way she came. They're lucky to have Delphine, he thinks. Her own baby girl's not yet a year old, and Delphine's as attached to Cyrus as she is to her own child, little Ruby, who's sleeping in a basket in the kitchen right now.

His wife Elenora is uninterested in the children, and he doesn't know why. Over the nine years of their marriage, there's been a change in Elenora. When he married her, he valued the intelligence in her homely features, the refinement that told of a proper upbringing, her strong common sense. She still has those qualities, but as the babies came one after the other, five in seven years, Elenora turned restless. For himself, he's proud he could sire so many kids so quickly—he even brags about it sometimes—but what's a delight to him seems to be a weight to his wife.

Today he came home from his office for dinner to find Elenora gone. He doesn't think she should drive around town by herself, but he figures she won't be out long on such a cold day.

Little Frank, two years old, toddles into the room. The boy flops down on the floor to prance his toy horse across the rug, making clip-clop noises. Delphine comes back in and takes the boy's hand and leads him up the stairs, Frankie hanging onto his horse with one hand and climbing the stairs with crab-like steps.

Then the room is quiet. John leans back in his chair and folds his newspaper, listening to the crackle of the fireplace and the soft breathing of his favorite child. He's always been proud of this room: the scarlet and purple hues of the French rug on the warm oak floor, the golden hue of the damask wallpaper, the heavy forest-green curtains. It's a room he designed by himself for his bride, and Elenora loves the room too. And up on the roof, there's a cupola, something he insisted on having. It's a feature that makes the house distinctive even in Natchez, a town with more than its share of grand houses. It's the second cupola that's been built up there. The first one was knocked down in the ferocious storm that swept through here seven years ago, the same storm that took pretty Stephanie Coqterre out of the land of the living. Stephanie would have loved this room. He pushes that thought away and closes his eyes.

A few minutes later he hears Elenora's quick footsteps on the marble floor of the hallway. She comes into the parlor, pulling off her coat.

"Is Cyrus fed?" she asks, walking over to peer into the cradle.

"Fed and sleeping," John says. "Where were you?"

"I drove up to Carefree." She unpins her hat. It's a plain black hat, not feathered and ribboned like the hats that are fashionable now. She could get the milliner to sew on some flowers or bric-a-brac, John knows, but that doesn't seem to be her style these days. She took up this severe style of dressing right after Cyrus was born.

"Carefree? Why'd you go up to that old place?" he asks.

"I was just curious about it, I don't know why. Something must've made me think of Stephanie Coqterre. I wanted to get out of the house, and well, anyway, I went. The bushes are all grown wild around the place, so you can hardly see the house from the road. But nobody answered the door, and I figured the house was vacant. So I let myself in."

"You were trespassing. I'm glad the sheriff wasn't around."

She picks up her hat and brushes the sides with little slaps of her palm. "Dusty," she says. "I didn't figure the sheriff would be there. Anyway, here's the thing. The place is a wreck. Clean as a whistle, the floors all polished and the beds made up, everything dusted, but the house is ruined inside."

"Ruined how?"

"Well, all that beautiful furniture they had—you remember—is shredded to pieces. You remember how fancy it was. Now the stuffing's pulled out of the sofas and chairs, and the curtains are ripped apart. It's strange."

John picks up his newspaper again. "Well, everybody in Natchez knew Emile Coqterre was cuckoo before he died. I'm not surprised his house would be a wreck."

"But there's still one slave there. Esther."

"I heard Emile sold off all his people," John says. "Maybe Esther somehow got left behind." Cyrus begins to fret in the bassinet and John gets up to lift the baby to his shoulder. "Is that cold wind still blowing?"

"It is." Elenora gets up to stir the fire. The logs fall to one side and send a spray of dancing sparks onto the hearth. She watches them wink out.

"I'll tell Marcus to get some more wood in here." She walks toward the hall, but then she stops and looks back at John. "But I wondered—since Emile's dead, and Stephanie's gone, who owns Carefree now? How come nobody's claimed it? Is it just gonna fall down?"

"It's odd you bring that up," John says, patting the baby's back. "I know who owns it, and I wrote him a letter, just last week. I don't know if it'll reach him, though. I've heard he's left the area."

At mid-afternoon Sheriff Willie Haynes is galloping down a backcountry road toward Bayou Cocodrie. The cold weather bothers his rheumatism more than it used to, and now that he's on the far side of sixty he'd rather be back in Vidalia in his warm office. But he won't let his aches and pains keep him off his horse when there's work to do. It's just that this Halloran business is taking more time than it needs to. But that's always how it is with people like the Hallorans; he's learned that from his years as sheriff of Concordia Parish, and he knew it instinctively when he first laid eyes on Pless Halloran, just yesterday, that this Halloran business would be a time-consuming mess.

And sure enough, this is the second time in two days he's been out to Bayou Cocodrie on Halloran's behalf. Yesterday the man charged into his office in Vidalia spitting mad and pounding the desk, ranting about his wife's broken nose, her swelled-shut eye, her bruises. It seems Miz Adelaide got the worse of a fight with a slave girl. Willie didn't know the Hallorans, it wasn't a name he'd heard before; but from the looks of the man, they weren't much in this parish. Here and there you saw people like them, hard-pressed farmers scratching out a living from a few arpents of soggy land. But the Hallorans are white as buttermilk, so the black girl would pay for Adelaide's beat-up face. Pless Halloran insisted on it, and after Willie heard the story he agreed.

44

So Willie rode out here and arrested the cold-eyed slave girl, Jenny. She didn't even try to cover up her crime, just sat on the side of her bed in the ransacked cabin and looked up when he came in, almost like she was expecting him. She said nothing, even when he roped her ankles and wrists and pushed her onto the horse. And she was silent the whole way back to Vidalia.

And Willie figured he'd done what he was supposed to do, by law and by custom. But by daybreak the girl was gone, stolen right out from the jail by a man with a gun. Who was, Willie feels sure, the man who owns this farm right here in front of him, Cornelius Carson.

Willie knew it had to be Carson who pulled his own gun on the deputy and took the girl. In the dark the deputy didn't get a real good look, other than to note that it was a tall man wearing a hat. Willie suspected the deputy was half-soused anyway. But no man pulls a gun on an officer of the law in Concordia Parish and gets off scot-free.

This morning, trying to figure where the girl and Carson could be, Willie rode out to the Hallorans' place to see Adelaide's injuries for himself. Hallorans' cabin was about what he expected, a shoddy little house built right onto the ground with no foundation, and starting to sag to one side, like such houses always do. And of course trash was scattered about the yard—an old chair, a broken bedstead. A pile of logs, not stacked.

Adelaide was sitting in the front room when the sheriff walked in. Her grown daughters, scrawny as woods foxes, wandered in and out of the room, pretending to be busy at some task or other but watching Willie out of the corner of their almond eyes.

Adelaide's face showed the beating she got. After he got a quick look at her injuries and jotted down a description in his notes, he rode the five miles to Carson's cabin. Which is where he sits now, staring at the Carson place and thinking he should retire from this job. When he was here yesterday, there was only the girl Jenny and an old uncle on the place.

Carson was nowhere around. Today the place seems deserted, although a few animals are still out in the field.

Willie dismounts and goes up to the porch. The door to the cabin stands open.

"Hello?" he calls, not expecting an answer and not getting one. When he goes inside, he can tell that the place hasn't been deserted long. The jars of flour and beans, the bowl of eggs on the shelf, the milk in a crock, tell him that. When he walks into the bedroom, he sees that the bed's neatly made. The room is tidier than you'd find in most cabins in these parts, but the dresser drawers are standing open and empty.

When he glances over at the bed he sees something you wouldn't ordinarily find out here; three daguerrotypes are lying on the quilt. He picks them up and studies them. These small gray images must be the faces of the people he's looking for. Here's Cornelius Carson staring back at him. And in the second image, the slave girl Jenny—he recognizes her in an instant—holding a small boy. Carson's boy, no doubt. The other picture is of the black man Willie saw here yesterday. Carson would have taken Jenny and the boy and the old slave when he left. When he went to—where?

They could all have gone over to Natchez-Under-the-Hill to jump a steamer, but that doesn't seem likely. Carson might've put the girl on a steamer at Natchez but he wouldn't have gone himself if he didn't have the old man and the boy with him.

Willie drops the picture of the old man on the quilt and goes outside with the other two images. He stands on the porch studying them. Yes, that's the girl, no question about it. Now he has an image of who he's looking for, something he's never had before. There've been times when he's tried to make a sketch when a victim describes a perpetrator, but he's never been much of an artist, and the victims were never sure he had it right, once they saw his drawings. His sketches had never yet helped him apprehend anyone. But here in his hand are true likenesses of the two people he seeks, and he knows their names.

He feels a cold determination set in. Now he's a man on a chase. Most of the time the crimes he has to deal with are so petty, widows complaining about neighborhood boys breaking their flowerpots, or kids stealing peaches from a tree that isn't theirs. It's the rising blacks who make Willie's blood run cold. Last year, when a slave named Lafayette took up his fists against his master Jake Turley, a big planter in these parts, Willie was keen to hang the man, and he did so in a double hanging the next day, along with a murderer who belonged to the Murrell gang. There are no good murderers and no good violent slaves, and Willie was glad to rid the world of both of them. He keeps a yellowed newspaper in his desk drawer with an article about Nat Turner and the murders he committed in Virginia. Willie can't let that happen here.

He walks back to his horse and buckles the pictures into his saddlebag. When he looks up he sees a woman walking up the road. She walks with her head tucked down into her cloak, but she strides along with a pace that shows she's walked this road before.

Willie waits until she's nearer, and then he calls out, "Ma'am, do you know the people who live here?"

She stops.

"This place belong to Cornelius Carson?" he asks.

She nods.

"You know where he is?" Willie asks. "I'm sheriff of this parish. I need to know."

"If he ain't here, I guess he's gone," she says.

"You don't know where he went?"

She shrugs. "I couldn't say."

He studies her. She's a tall, rangy woman, not young. A neighbor lady. He won't get any information out of her. He's seen that purse-lipped suspicious look in country people before.

He looks around. A cat slinks across the yard.

The woman turns around and walks away down the road. He swings up onto his horse. There's no more he can learn here.

Where would Carson have gone? He would've tried to put as much distance as he could between himself and Vidalia. The slave gal could handle the kid, and he and the old man could drive. Willie can see how they could've made a breakaway.

Carson could've gone straight over to hop a steamer in Under-the-Hill, heading either north or south. Or he could have disappeared into Mississippi. Either way, it's clear he's abandoned his homestead. He'd likely go to—where? To the south is nothing but swamps. Out to the west is Avoyelles Parish. More swamps. And then even farther west, Rapides Parish. And beyond that—Texas.

Willie doesn't know what direction Carson went. But if there's one thing he does know from his years wearing the badge, it's that criminals have a way of circling back to the scene of their crime. Willie's seen it happen. He's heard of murderers mingling with the crowd at a funeral, just so they can watch whoever they killed get lowered into the ground. To make sure they're really dead, probably.

He has a long ride back to Vidalia, and it'll be dark when he gets there. He'll take the pictures back and tack them up on his office wall where he can look at them every day, to remind himself he's looking for this white man and that black gal. And even if right now he can't figure out where Carson went, all he really has to do is wait. Justice, in his mind, is a sharp sword, always at the ready, and sooner or later it'll fall, even if it has to gather some dust in the meantime.

CHAPTER FIVE

WALKER SITS ON THE LOG outside his shack in the late afternoon, his eyes closed. The fire he built an hour ago is almost out, and his soup has simmered down to a low boil. The aroma, when he gets a whiff of it with the breeze that's still blowing, smells fishy, and good. It's getting dark and one star has popped out between the clouds. Under his heavy eyelids he sees the star for one minute, but then the next minute it's gone.

When he hears the scrape of footsteps in the alley, he opens his eyes. Jenny is striding toward him, still wearing that big old camel-colored coat.

"Hey, Jenny," he says, shaking his head to clear it. "What're you doin' out?"

"Just lookin' around, tryin' to learn the town again like I used to know it." She sits down beside him on the log, her knees up under her chin. "And I been to the store. I bought these." She pulls a hairbrush and some hairpins out of her pocket to show him. "This your place?"

"Yep. It ain't much, but it's what I got." He feels ashamed for Jenny to see his shack. He built it himself, but it's not near as nice as he could've made it if he'd been able to get hold of some decent lumber. As it is, he had only enough wood to make two sides out of some rough-cut boards he found thrown away down a ravine. He angled them against the fence so they wouldn't fall down and he braced them with some short-cut boards. But that still left the front open, so he strung a rope across the opening and hung a blanket on it. He's embarrassed that at this moment the blanket's pulled open and Jenny can see everything he's got.

"That your bed?" She points to the tangled-up quilt in the corner.

"Yep." He picks up his spoon and stirs his soup, then pours some of the gray broth into a cup.

"What's that you eatin'? You ain't still hungry, are you?" she asks.

"This here's fish head soup. And no, I ain't hungry. I'm still stuffed with that chicken stew Esther gave us. But somebody left me some fish heads in my bucket right here, so I figure I better cook 'em up before they spoil. I'd offer you some but this ain't no fine food like Esther'd make." He puts the cup down and looks at Jenny. "You think you oughta be wearin' that coat when you out in town?"

"I gotta keep warm."

"This cold spell ain't gonna last long. But the thing is, people see you out and about, they gonna want to know who you are, some strange girl they ain't seen before. And you wearin' that fancy coat that used to be Miss Sophronia's. They'll think you stole it."

"Well, the storekeeper didn't think I was strange," Jenny says. "He just took my money and was happy to take it. He's probably from the North."

"Could be."

"I got some dresses too. Esther let me take two dresses that used to be Helene's and Theresa's."

"You sure you want to be wearin' them girls' dresses? They was two sad young gals, what happened to 'em."

"I'll wash 'em and they'll be all right. And I'd wear Sophronia's clothes if Esther'd open up that chiffarobe, but she probably won't." She stands up to warm her hands over his fire. "So. What you plannin' on doin' now that you're back? You gonna make those copies of my freein' paper?"

"I been thinkin' about it," Walker says.

"I think you oughta try it. What harm can it do?"

"It could get us arrested. Or worse. How'd you like the inside of that jail you was in?"

"I didn't."

"Keep that in mind."

"Well, I've still got it right here." She pats her chest. "In case you change your mind."

When he doesn't say anything else she says, "I'm gonna head on back now 'cause I gotta fix my hair. I can't go 'round lookin' like this." She looks up at the gray wall of the church that looms above the fence. "You ever see anybody from in there?" She hooks her thumb back toward the church.

"Sometimes. Once in a while the priest sends me some of the food they have left over, which I appreciate. I keep hopin' they'll bring me some leftover wine, but far as I know they drink that theirselves. But they ain't told me to move on out. I guess they figure a little ole dwarf-man can't do no harm, and it's better to give their scraps to me instead of some mangy dog." He looks up and down the alley. "It's gettin' late. Ain't you pretty tired? Esther's gonna be wonderin' where you at."

"I ain't sleepy yet," Jenny says, folding her collar up.

"Well, now you know where my place is, you welcome to come visit when you want."

"That's good, 'cause you about the only person left in Natchez I know, except for Esther."

She walks away down the alley, her skirt swinging under the long coat, and Walker picks up a brick and sets it in the dying fire. Then he sits down again to finish his soup. What he showed Jenny just now was, you eat when you got food. You stock up. Because there'll be other times, like yesterday, when you don't have a thing. So when somebody leaves you some fish heads, don't let them go to waste. Of course, up at Carefree Jenny won't have to eat fish head soup. Esther'll cook plenty of food, and she must've bought that chicken she stewed today; he didn't notice any chickens pecking around the place.

He scrapes at the ashes with a stick; then he sits back, looking up. Bright stars mean a cold night. And the moon's coming up too.

The day's left him dog-tired. And what an awful day it's been, maybe the worst of his whole life. He'll always have bad memories of it. A day like today can make him afraid, deep down in his bones. He'll never be able to forget how Rufus dragged him onto that steamboat, him howling and wailing so loud Rufus said he was gonna throw him overboard if he didn't shut up. And how close he came to being up on an auction block for only the second time in his life. By now the big-hipped gal and the lady with the parasol and the rest of the passengers on the *John Jay* would be halfway to Memphis; but Rufus probably got off at Vicksburg. That scamp would've been awful mad once he realized that Walker had vamoosed right off the boat.

He thinks about his mammy; she's in Vicksburg too. She misses him, her oldest boy, even though she had other children after him, seven in all, and except for him they're all living in Vicksburg. But she always told him he was her favorite, because he was her first. He rubs his hands together to warm them.

He's been in Natchez over ten years, ever since Missus Blanchard moved here to live near her brother. Missus Blanchard was the most sociable person he ever knew. She had no children of her own but before you knew it she was right in the middle of everything here in Natchez; every cotillion for the debutantes, every wedding reception, every baby shower. She was right there with the other ladies, planning and organizing, making sure the occasions were done right. There were so many details for Missus Blanchard to see to. That's how the smart people of Natchez got to know him, since he was helping her with all of it. Then she said he could buy himself out of slavery, and that took him five years. After that it was only natural that he took responsibility for the freed slaves around town, since he already knew so many of the society people and he could help the free people find a job or a place to live. He began to think of Natchez as his home more than Vicksburg.

But that doesn't mean he doesn't miss Vicksburg every once in a while. He misses his mammy and his brothers and sisters. But here in Natchez he's got responsibilities, and the free people here look up to him. They count on him to see to their well-being. Up in Vicksburg he wasn't anything but a dwarf man riding around town on his mammy's horse; a person of no particular importance. But here in Natchez, with all the free people there are in this community, he is somebody. That's why he calls himself the mayor.

But he needs to go see his mammy. His birthday's coming up in a few days. Maybe he'll get to Vicksburg then. He likes to get up there every few months, and he's overdue. He tries to imagine what it must've been like when he was a babe, forty years ago, when his mammy was young. He can't really picture her any way but old, like she is now, but she had to be young back then.

"You was a seven-months babe," his mammy told him the last time he visited her, "and we put you in a little box by the fire to keep you warm. It was cold the night you was born, and the wind was just howlin' outside." *Cold like tonight*, he thinks. "But me and your daddy Vinson, we watched over you like a hawk. You was my first-born, and I couldn't stand to think I'd lose you. But I knew you was goin' to make it. I felt like I just *willed* you to live, day after day. I had plenty of milk, and you was always hungry. Missus Martin couldn't make me leave you, tiny scrap of a babe as you was, so I brought your box into the big house and kept you in the kitchen while I cooked. Your daddy was still here with us then. That was before all the trouble later on. And once I seen you was gonna grow and plump up like a regular baby, only littler, I got so happy. Vinson too, we was both happy. Missus Martin even gave you some little bootees she made. They just flopped on your little feet. But I was just as proud of you as if you'd been a big baby. Prouder maybe."

Vicksburg. He pictures his mammy creeping about her little one-room cabin behind the house on Washington Street where Missus Martin still lives. He hates to think his mammy, frail as a bird, has to go up and down those big stairs every day carrying the old lady's dinner tray and her chamber pot, and has to wash her hair and soap her white limbs, and all the time saying nothing but "Yes, ma'am." His mammy was always a quiet woman. That hump on her back is getting bigger all the time. Yes, he needs to go see her, next chance he gets.

He folds a rag over the warm brick and takes it over to his bed. He pulls the quilt one way, the top blanket the other way, and then he brushes it smooth; some leaves have blown in, with the wind. He takes off his shoes and dusts them with the back of his hand before setting them along the back wall of his shack. Then he closes his curtain and lies down with the brick at his feet.

He rolls onto his side, pulling his quilt tight, and thinks about the free people of Natchez. Every night before he sleeps he runs a list in his head, to keep track of them. He sleeps better when he knows he's fulfilling his responsibilities. The oldest one is Doda Jefferson, who must be about 80, her face as wrinkly as a crazed china cup. Her toothless mouth's caved in on itself. And there's Doda's daughter Eula, who lives with her. Eula says her mammy was a beauty in her young days, but Walker can't picture it. They live for free in the back of a livery stable run by the man who used to own them, a Mister Farnley, on Monroe Street. There's Oakwood Jackson, no relation to him, a bent-over man who has a bad leg and lives in a room in the basement of the Presbyterian Church; it has an outside door so Oakwood can come and go as he pleases, if he can limp his way up and down the steps. But Oakwood can't work with his bad leg and his bent back, and he ain't got a family to take care of him, so Walker brings him food from time to time, and in between times it seems like Oakwood's doing all right. He's not starving anyway. Maybe the church people help him out some, but Walker would bet the Presbyterians don't really know Oakwood's living there.

There's Pete Adams, a handsome young man, and his wife Reena, a good-looking gal herself. They live in a little house in some woods just south of town, and they both work for pay at the dry-goods store. Walker wonders about them, how two such likely people came to be free. But he can't come right out and ask them. Maybe someday they'll tell him. There's Martin Jones and his wife, Dorcas, both too old to work. They live in a cabin not far from the Forks of the Road, which is close to the slave auction house of Franklin and Armfield's, and that's not Walker's favorite neighorbood. There's Jack, Rudy, and Tom, three old brothers who live in a shack behind a house just outside of town. In the summer they grow a big garden, rows of beans and peas and corn, in the backyard. There's Terry Bones and his wife Lucy, who live in a little house built into the side of a gulley on the east side. They smile big but don't say much, and Walker doesn't know them as well as the others; but he knows they hire out for odd jobs around town.

There's newcomers too: out by the Saint Catherine's Creek there's an encampment of new-freed slaves living in tents. Walker's not sure where they come from, or how long they'll be here. He might try to get to know them in the next few days, go out there and introduce himself. They need to know they can rely on the Mayor of Natchez. But if they look like rough characters, he'll try to talk 'em into moving on down the road. He's not looking for trouble.

But then he thinks: *Jenny*.

Of all the free people here, she ought to have it the easiest, living with Esther at Carefree. But already today she's running around town wearing a fine coat she oughtn't be wearing. It'll be an easy life for that girl if she'll behave herself, but he can see there's going to be trouble unless he can get her settled down. But who could she settle down with? There's no suitable single man among the freed men in Natchez but him, and he's way too old to take on a high-spirited wife. The only young men she'll run into here in Natchez are slaves, and there's all kinds of trouble in that.

For the first time, he thinks maybe he should've let her go on to Cincinnati.

But then he thinks, no, he's heard too much about that place. And being a small man, he knows what it's like when you're easy pickings. Any man could catch her, especially gullible like she is. He didn't have any trouble talking her into getting off the steamboat with him, and him practically a stranger to her. Who knows what story she'd fall for when some slick-talking stranger sidled up to her the minute she stepped foot off the boat in Cincinnati. She's going to be the biggest problem he's got, unless those strangers living east of town turn out to be trouble. Well, he'll figure something out for Jenny.

He wishes he had a better place to live than this shack. The priest could make him move out any time, and just today Esther offered him a room in the slave house. He said no, because he likes to keep his distance, but now, feeling the hard ground under his bed, he thinks maybe he could change his mind on that. There'd be two women at Carefree now, Esther and Jenny, and they might appreciate having a man around to help with the work. Even a little man can lift and hammer and carry wood for the fire better than a woman can. Esther'd try to boss him around the same way she thinks she's going to boss Jenny around, but she won't get far with Jenny, and she wouldn't get far with him either. He could just do what he felt like doing. Yep, one of these days he might haul his pack up to Carefree and tell Esther he's come to claim a room. One of those upstairs rooms, he thinks, and as far away from the two women as he can get. A mayor should have something better than a shack in the alley. He'll have to think about that.

He is so, so relieved to be back in Natchez, and safe. Moving his feet so his toes wrap over the edge of the warm brick, he tucks his head down into the folds of his blanket, and snores.

As Jenny walks up Main Street, past the row of shops, she watches her reflection walking along with her, in pieces, one moment moving toward her, showing her profile, and the next minute retreating. The moon casts a cool blue light on the street. In the Cocodrie her only mirror was a shard she found dropped by the side of the road; it was no bigger than the palm of her hand, but she'd propped it up on her shelf in the little house there so she could see at least part of herself, even if all she was doing that day was going out to the cotton fields. But here she is, Jenny top to bottom, walking up Main Street in a fine coat like any Natchez lady.

She looks up ahead, her attention caught by the yellow flare of a match scratched against a lamppost. A man is standing at the corner holding the match into the bowl of a clay pipe, and watching her. She walks more slowly, then stops, not sure whether to pass him or not.

"H'lo, Jenny."

She remembers that voice. It's Marcus, one of Master Landerson's slaves. When she gets close enough she sees it's him all right, but he's a lot older now than she remembers. He looks like a man, not like the skinny boy she remembers. His face is filled out and he doesn't have that jumpy look he used to have.

"Marcus?"

"That's me."

"What're you doin' out here on the street this time of night?"

"Oh, I'm just out here havin' my smoke. I come out most every night, just before I have to go see to my master's horses. Master John don't care if I take a little break. Come on over here where I can get a good look at you. My eyes ain't so good anymore. I remember you was at Carefree. Where you been keepin' yourself? It seems like you went away all of a sudden."

She stands a few feet away from him. "I did go away all of a sudden, 'cause my master come and got me and took me across the river. But I'm back at Carefree now."

"You at Carefree? I didn't think anybody was left up there but Esther." He squints at her, pulling his eyes into slits.

"Now it's Esther and me." She looks away; the street's getting dark in a hurry.

"Why'd you come back?" he asks.

"I got my freein' paper. And I was gonna go up north, but I met up with Walker Jackson and he told me I oughta come back here. So I did."

"You got your freein' paper. Ain't that somethin'? Well, if I was free, me personally, I'd rather be in the north than in this slave country. Who was your master? I don't remember 'im."

"Cornelius Carson."

"I never heard of 'im. He still live around here?"

"No, he ain't here. He said he was goin' to Texas, so I guess he's on the road. I don't know how long it'd take him to get there."

"It'd take a week anyway. He ain't never comin' back?"

"Prob'ly not."

"Well, you stuck here with us for good, I guess. Good thing you got Esther to take care of you. She's steady, that woman is. She'll look out for you."

"Walker Jackson says he'll look out for me, too. He told me he's the mayor of Natchez."

Marcus chuckles. "Walker's goin' around sayin' he's the mayor? Well, if he is, that's good to know. He ain't the mayor for the white folks, I bet. But I guess if Walker thinks he's the mayor, he could do it good as anybody."

"You still with Master Landerson?"

"Yep. We live at the Elenora house. My wife Delphine's there too. We got a little baby girl." Smelling of sweet smoke, he moves closer to her and rubs the sleeve of her coat.

She pulls her arm away. "You look different, Marcus. What's happened to your eyes?"

"I don't know. They started gettin' blurry about a year ago. That's why I'm squinty-eyed."

"Can't you get some glasses?"

"Where'm I gonna get 'em?"

"Can't Missus Landerson get you some?"

"She could do a lot of things she ain't doin'. I'd have to be plumb blind, bumpin' into the walls, before that woman'd notice anything about me. That's some fine coat you wearin'. I like the way it feels."

"It was Sophronia's." She steps away from him, folding her arms. "I got to get on back. It's gettin' too dark to be out."

"You come see me again, Jenny," Marcus calls. "I come out here most every night."

She walks across the street, watching a dim reflection of herself walking toward herself, in a shop window. When she glances back over her shoulder, Marcus is still standing there watching her, his pipe cupped in his hand. She hardly remembers him, but he was nice to her when she knew him before. And she feels sorry for anybody who can't see right. She brushes her sleeve down, where he rubbed it.

When she gets to Carefree she walks around to the kitchen. Esther's not there, but the fire's still going. Esther's probably gone into the big house to wind the clocks. Jenny remembers how Esther used to do that job every night, going from clock to clock, twisting the key on each one.

She sits down and folds her arms on the table. The warmth in the room washes over her and suddenly all she wants to do is sleep. She rests her head on her arms. The fire makes little popping sounds, and then she's asleep, caught in the snare of a dream. For an instant she sees a woman standing behind a window, the glass washed with rain.

"Abena," Jenny thinks she hears the woman say, but in her dream there's no sound.

She startles awake, but the dream's gone, and the only sounds are the pops from the fire in Esther's kitchen.

CHAPTER SIX

IN THE RECTORY of Saint Vigilius Church, Adrien Jean-Pierre takes off
his jacket and tosses it on top of the chest next to his bed. He unlaces his
shoes and with one foot nudges aside the schoolbooks that have tumbled
from his shelf onto the floor. His small room is as disorderly as it's possible to be with just a few possessions. The books are unread; he packed
them only at his papa's insistence. They'll still be unread when he goes
home to France, whenever that may be. When he moves his candle around
the clutter to find his socks, it shines on a white triangle of dust in every
corner. For most of his eighteen years his mother or a servant took care
of his housekeeping, but now it's fallen to him, and he's failing at it. No
one comes to his room anyway.

He goes to the window and pushes the curtain aside. In the darkness
he can just make out the alleyway behind the rectory, where a low fire is
flickering out. The only sounds are some dogs barking, out in the street.

He knows the alley; his high window looks right out onto it. A dwarf-
man's built a shack there out of some boards. The three-sided structure
reminds Adrien of the crèches he used to see in front of churches in France,
at the blessed Christmas season.

The dwarf-man comes and goes. He was there again this afternoon,
and a pretty woman in a fine coat came to visit him. She sat with him

for a while, talking. There's a story there, Adrien thinks, but it's one he doesn't understand.

As he doesn't understand so many things here. He's been here two weeks, but he feels he hasn't gotten his sea legs yet. When Uncle Louis summoned him to America, he didn't know it would mean coming to this steamy outpost in America. It wasn't what he pictured when he accepted his father's plan to send him to America so he could consider his future. Or so he could at least escape the gendarmes who'd pounded on the door in the middle of the night, to answer questions about a body found in the alley behind the house. There'd been other missteps, pilferings and vandalism, and a knife held to the neck of a teacher at the Latin school. But this time his knife had been all too true in its aim, and a boy who tricked him out of his girlfriend lay dead. Papa looked the other way for the other crimes; he paid the fines and covered up the scandals, but this time Adrien saw his father's shocked face when the gendarmes burst in. And his father paid like he always did, but Adrien knew this time was different. By dawn he was on the road riding like thunder to the port at Andernos-les-Bains, his schoolbooks packed in his saddlebags. A tall ship was waiting.

The trouble he was in was Papa's fault, Adrien thinks; what did he expect, trying to bring up a yellow Creole in France, a boy with an accent that still sounded like Martinique. He should've known the boy would be taunted, pushed aside, bullied, his whole life. After the final thing, Papa said you go to your Uncle Louis in America, he's a priest, he'll take you in; so Adrien came to Natchez. He'll never be in the church himself; he knew it wasn't for him, that path, but Father thought America would help him escape his troubles in France, and maybe someday he might even return to the cloister.

That's just an old man's dream, Adrien thinks. It's true he's always been awestruck by the vast cathedrals of Europe, their soaring gilded ceilings grounded by ranks of burning candles, their statues of somber saints looking down on the sinners below. Papa gave him only a pittance to make his way with in America, but he knew Uncle Louis would take him in. "Saint Vigilius in Natchez" is what Father wrote on a note he stuffed into Adrien's satchel. For all Adrien knew, Saint Vigilius might be as grand as Saint Patrick's in New York City, or even Saint Louis Cathedral in New Orleans. He, Adrien, may not be headed for the priesthood, but he wanted to see America and he didn't want to hang, so he wasn't going to turn down the money his papa handed him as the gendarmes carried a body out of the alley on a board .

Uncle Louis has made him comfortable enough, giving him a room in the rectory. There are only himself and Louis in the whole building. But Saint Vigilius is a sinking church, Adrien thinks; the congregation is just a few old souls. He leans on Uncle Louis to make introductions and show him the ropes, how things are done here. It helps that Uncle Louis speaks French, but it hinders too. How can his own English improve if he speaks only in the comfortable language he already knows? His own French is sprinkled with Creole, from a boyhood spent in Martinique. You don't so easily erase your first language, especially when it's the language of your mother. And when others look at him, he knows in a split second they can see the planter father, the slave mother, a common tale. But less common is his father's choice to bring the boy to France for upbringing. Father tried to make Adrien into a Frenchman, but he won't be going back to France anytime soon.

He turns away from the window. He's restless tonight. He pulls on a coat and takes his candle and goes out onto the gallery. Perhaps Louis is still awake and would like some company. He's learned to appreciate his uncle for his knowledge about the area and for his patience with the parishioners. He's Father Louis Maercru to his parishioners, their kindly pastor. His uncle is fleshy and he has a mild florid face, but he can also have a sharp look sometimes. Adrien's seen it more than once. A fierce expression will cross the man's face; his eyes narrow, the lines beside his mouth deepen. The look passes quickly, but it's there. Adrien thinks this must be the result of many years spent shepherding his wayward flock.

And what kind of place is Natchez, anyway? Protestant, largely; Presbyterians have an imposing church just two blocks from here. A splendid new cathedral, St. Mary's, serves most of the Catholics.

And the population is so restless; never has Adrien seen such a scrabbling, merchant-minded people. Not in France, and not in Martinique either, where what he remembers most are slow steamy days that smelled of sugar cane. But he was very young then; how much could a boy remember, from the age of eight?

Down at Natchez-Under-the-Hill, the steamboats come in day after day, their stacks billowing, and the people who get off the boats seem to be thinking of one thing: commerce. Money changes hands faster here than he ever saw in France—at least faster than in the village of Lormont where he spent the later years of his boyhood and became a man. In Lormont a water wheel mill rumbled at the river below the hill. The families who lived there had been rooted in the village for centuries; and except for the Revolution and its Terror, which was a break, they seemed resigned to what they knew best: poverty and want. And the Church kept them watching eternity. But here no one seems part of any family larger than their own, and underpinning everything isn't poverty, as in Lormont, but riches, and slaves, and that endless striving.

The light from his candle jumps against the brick wall of the gallery. When he comes to the last window he looks in and sees Louis sitting in his big armchair next to the fire. Adrien raps on the door and when he hears what he usually hears, a cordial *"Entrez!"*, he opens the door.

"Adrien, come, have a seat," Louis says, motioning to the chair on the other side of the fireplace. "Move the cat."

The yellow cat molds himself into the back of the chair cushion and won't be forced, just pushed. He clings to the cushion until Adrien puts both hands under his belly and sets him on the floor.

"Mon chat doesn't appreciate all I did for him," Louis says, "rescuing him from the alley." He holds up the wine bottle for Adrien to admire. "I sent Quincy into town to buy this today. And I must say, it is exceptional."

Adrien pictures the lanky slave Quincy striding back to the rectory carrying the wine bottle. Quincy has a wide smile, and he stops and bows whenever Adrien passes him. But whether the gesture is genuine or a slave's put-on, Adrien's never sure. He's never sure about any of the slaves he encounters.

Louis pours a glass for Adrien, who sips it and then rolls the stem of the glass between his fingers, twirling it slowly.

The old priest smiles at him. He's feeling genial tonight, Adrien thinks.

"What's on your mind?" Louis asks.

Adrien holds up his glass and studies it. "Well, I was thinking earlier tonight—I wish I knew the town better. I hardly even know my way around the streets."

Louis nods. "We can fix that. I'll take you with me on some pastoral calls." The firelight gleams on his bald head.

"I'd like that," Adrien says. He looks around the room. His uncle's room is as simple as his own, but it has a fireplace which his doesn't have, so it seems finer, more welcoming. The cat has slunk away to the corner of the rug and curled up, licking his paws.

"Of course, I see people at mass, but I wonder what their lives are like. What would you say they're like, the people here, generally?" Adrien asks.

"Oh, I'd say they're like people everywhere. No different. Just some richer—much richer—and many poorer. Every Sunday in mass you'll see every human quality." He looks at his wine, then at the fire. "If you saw the things that I see, you'd be surprised. Just when you think you've gotten to know someone well, you find you don't know them at all." He raises his arms in a wide Gallic shrug. "But really, people here are just like people anywhere else."

"But people everywhere don't have slaves," Adrien says. "I remember slaves in Martinique, but I was just a young boy. You hardly see them in France. But here there are so many. Hundreds. Thousands. I wonder if it doesn't change the people, make them different." An image dances in the firelight, of the white-clad slaves who sit in the balcony at every mass. He sets his glass down on the table beside his chair, and a plum-colored reflection dances on the waxed surface.

"Well, it changes the slaves, I'm sure of that," Louis says. "You and I both know, no human being wants to be unfree. It's not a natural state. I think it eats at their souls from the moment they're born until they meet St. Peter. And when they do meet the Almighty, the first thing they're going to ask is, 'Why'd you make me a slave?'" He sips his wine. "As for the whites, they just get used to having all the help. It's the easiest thing in the world to get used to."

"The blacks don't just accept their slavehood then?"

"Absolutely not. But the whites like to think they do. It's how they justify it. And you know the slaves wear masks. Their faces don't tell what they're thinking."

Adrien is quiet for a few moments, thinking he's asked too many questions. He watches Louis savor the wine. It's kind of a vinegary wine,

Adrien thinks; he doesn't find it either satisfying or soothing, nothing like the full-bodied wines that grace even the poorest tables in France. The thought comes to him that Louis could be his future, if he'd chosen to continue with his studies. When he looks across the room at the portly priest smacking his lips at the inferior wine, is he looking at himself in twenty years? At the thought, he sips his wine again.

"I've learned to be careful what I say," the older man says, "and I urge you to be careful also. The white people here are very afraid. That's what you need to remember." He clears his throat. "The *Liberator* comes every week; how it shows up here I don't know, but it does. You've seen it?"

"I saw it once," Adrien says. "It was blowing down the alley and I picked it up. Then I realized, that's not the *Picayune*. I looked at it."

"You may read it if you want to, but you'd best hide it afterwards. You don't want to be seen with it. It calls for abolition with such a strident voice. It drives the people here mad. They see their whole world coming down around their ears, because all their wealth is tied up in slaves and land. These fine houses, these brick streets, that mighty river—Natchez is the center of their world. Their roots, such as they are, are here. And the abolitionists want to tear it all down."

The men sit in silence for a few minutes, looking at the fire.

"I'm counting on you to teach me," Adrien says. "Not just by what you say, but as I watch you with the people. You're a university to me." He finishes his wine.

Louis holds the bottle out to him but Adrien shakes his head and stands up. Louis empties the bottle into his own glass.

"Well, if I'm your university, you'll learn things they wouldn't dare teach in a real university," Louis says. He raises his hand with a drowsy "Bon soir."

"Bon soir."

Adrien steps over the cat, but when he opens the door the cat runs out anyway. Louis raises his hand in dismissal of the animal, and Adrien goes out to the gallery and walks back to his room. The wine, sorry as it was, has lightened his steps. When he gets to his room he folds back his blanket, and then goes over to stand at the window again. He can't see anyone out there now, and the fire in the alley's gone out; a thin trail of smoke rises into the black sky. It reminds him of the fires he used to see in Lormont, back home in France. But there, people crowd around any fire they can find, to warm their hands and backsides. And the fires burn all night.

The young man from the church brings food more regularly now, and Walker is happy about that. Every couple of days the Creole brings gumbo and rice, red beans and rice, smothered chicken and biscuits, just the kind of food Walker likes. The cook in the rectory must overcook all the time, Walker thinks. And the young man who brings the food usually stays to talk for a few minutes.

He comes down the alley silent as a cat, so Walker is always a little surprised when he looks up and sees him standing there with a bowl of food. If he wore regular heavy shoes like most men do, Walker would hear him crunching on the gravel before he gets here, but he wears soft-soled shoes the color of doeskin, more like slippers than shoes; Walker hasn't ever seen a man wear that kind of shoes before. Walker doesn't like anyone creeping up on him like that.

Adrien, his name is, and he dresses fine, in a jacket with a velvet vest and a silk cravat the color of claret wine. He says his uncle is the priest at the church.

"I used to be a Caribe from Martinique, but I'm a Frenchman now," he says. His smooth light skin and straight black hair had already told Walker he was a Creole. Adrien says his Papa sent him here so he could figure out what to do in life.

He sent you here because you're running from something, Walker thinks.

And when Adrien pointed out his window, which looks right out onto this alley, Walker thought, *If you had your window open, we could hear each other snore.* And that's when he decided he'd take Esther up on her offer and move in to the slave house. He doesn't need anybody watching him that close.

And it wasn't long before Jenny showed up when Adrien was there, and five minutes later they both were looking like two people who were waiting for something. Walker's seen that look before. He tried not to look at them, but while he ate the good food Adrien brought him, Adrien and Jenny drifted farther away down the alley together. Not that Walker's paying much attention to them, since the gumbo's the best food he's had all week, but he watched them out of the corner of his eye. They moved down the alley without looking back at him at all. Sometimes that's how it is, he knows; two people meet each other and first thing you know everybody else disappears. He's seen it happen before, especially with young people. Adrien and Jenny are in their own circle, and he's left out of it. He doesn't like it much.

Adrien Maercru has a secretive way about him, Walker thinks. He walks with a springy rolling gait, and he claps his hands in front of him when he walks, like he's slapping the air.

Walker thinks, *One day, maybe tomorrow or the next day, Jenny'll come down here, and you'll show up, and y'all can talk a big talk, right out here in the alley. And Jenny's so pretty, and you with your skin so smooth and light, and your hair so straight and dark. You can't be much older than she is, and she's hardly more than a kid. And y'all can drift up and down the alley together like two angels, both beautiful, both young, and nobody will see you behind all these fences. And you for sure won't see anybody else. You'll only see each other.*

Walker feels a chasm of sadness yawning in front of him. He hates for Jenny to fall in with this Adrien. Walker's kind of thought Jenny belongs to him, since he rescued her off that steamboat and brought her back to Carefree. But he's just been kidding himself. She really doesn't belong to him, and never will.

Every day Jenny goes to the alley, and every day Adrien shows up. Walker doesn't want to talk to Adrien much and he usually says he has to run some errand when Adrien shows up. Walker's slowly getting himself moved into the slave house, taking the room on top of Esther. It's a lot better place for him than the alley.

Today when Jenny comes to the alley, Adrien is carrying a black jacket on his arm, and he shows her the missing button on the jacket. When he hands her the jacket he kisses her.

Later, sitting on the side of her bed, she thinks about how his kiss felt, his lips against her lips, how it surprised her. He put his arms around her when he did it, and she liked that. He looked deep into her eyes. Then he kissed her again, his tongue probing her mouth quickly. He ran his hands up and down her arms.

"What do you do when it's summertime? Isn't this hot?" she asked him, fingering the weight of the jacket.

"I sweat," he said, and kissed her for the third time.

"Esther has a button box," Jenny said. "I'll find one that matches."

Now, sitting on the side of her bed, she puts the garment up to her nose and breathes deeply. Yes, it has his scent. Her heart sings. This is new. She looks through the button box and then threads her needle and bites off a length of black thread. She pierces the needle through the fabric. The day has brightened, and it seems like a fine spring morning.

He could love me, she thinks. *Maybe he already does.*

Can I love him back?

When she returns the button box to Esther, she sees the older woman looking at her curiously, the way she's smiling so wide, so happy. She can't help it.

CHAPTER SEVEN

Friday, January 15
Natchitoches Parish, Louisiana

MALACHI, SIXTY YEARS OLD as near as he can figure, and bone-weary from traveling, lies wrapped in a blanket on the hay-strewn floor of a barn, listening. The night is full of sounds: somewhere far away a panther screeches; an alligator hisses as it glides through black water. These noises don't bother him much as long as they don't come too close. They're the same sounds he used to hear night after night back on Bayou Cocodrie.

Through the half-open door of the barn he can see the window in the log house where Cornelius and Thomas will sleep tonight.

As he watches, the light in the window suddenly gets brighter; somebody's turned up a lamp. He rolls onto his side, trying to find a more comfortable position.

He hopes this trip is nearly over. The journey's been much harder than either he or Cornelius thought it would be. After four dreary days of travel, they're close to Texas. He wonders where they'll end up, in that new country.

When they started out four days ago, Mal wasn't surprised that his time in the Cocodrie was over. As soon as Adelaide Halloran got her nose punched in by Jenny, Mal knew a major change was headed their way. What kind of change he didn't know, but when Cornelius showed up without Jenny and told him to get packed, he wasn't surprised.

"I'm a wanted man," Cornelius said, but he didn't give him any particulars. And what happened to Jenny, Mal couldn't bear to imagine. They cleared out of the cabin as fast as they could, threw their clothes and everything else they could fit in the buggy, drove to the McKees' place to get little Thomas, and off they went. Cornelius was dead set on heading west.

Texas will be a whole new life, Mal figures, and not one he much wants to blunder into. But he knows Cornelius is running from the law; Texas is where a man heads to if the law's looking for him. Thomas, two years old and a wiggle-worm if there ever was one, whimpered and sniffled throughout the drive. Mal thinks Thomas didn't want to leave his home on Bayou Cocodrie, and Mal didn't either.

After the first day, when the road took them past the same kind of wide cotton fields they knew in the Cocodrie, they drove up into some hills, where the piney woods were thick and the road was narrow and dark. If they ran into danger, it would come at them out of these forests, Malachi thought as they rattled along. He saw that Cornelius was thinking the same thing, watching hard to left and right as he drove. Who knew what could be hiding in the woods? It wouldn't be Indians, Mal felt sure; the Choctaws were all gone. But murderers, or thieves with skin as white as a cream pudding: they might be lurking anywhere in that wild country.

Mal wondered if they looked unusual, a white man in a wide Spanish hat and an old gray-haired slave hanging on to a little red-headed boy. But the few people they passed just nodded at Cornelius and kept driving. No sheriff's posse tailed them, as far as Malachi could tell. That was a relief. Now they're so far from the Cocodrie they're probably safe from the authorities back in Concordia Parish. Mal was glad when the road dropped down into bayou country again, where there were clearings and streams and the woods didn't hem the road so close; this kind of country was more familiar to him. And then an hour ago, when Cornelius came to this house next to the road and stopped the wagon, Mal was glad they wouldn't be driving in the dark.

He wraps his blanket tighter.

How many years has he been with Cornelius? he wonders idly. Ten years, at least. And he feels himself getting older by the day; lots of times when he wakes up in the morning his old bones hardly want to get moving at all. He thinks back to the place he was born. "Virginny," he mumbles, a name that's meant only one thing to him his whole life, and that's home. When he was a little chap no older than Thomas is now, he lived with his mammy and his brother in a cabin on the side of a hill in Albemarle County. Back then he didn't know what kind of world he'd come into, or that he was born to be a slave boy. Little Malachi hadn't learned it yet.

Well, he learned it soon enough. He learned it for sure the day he was sold away from his mammy and his brother to pay off a gambling debt his master's oldest boy ran up. Sold off to the cotton fields in Alabama, and that's where he grew up. And he'd never have made it there if some of the women hadn't taken him under their wing, talked to him, sewed him some clothes when his own fell into rags, saw that he ate something every day. He was just a boy named Malachi, snatched away from his mammy and his brother at only twelve years old and turned into just one more field hand on a big plantation. No one knew about the cabin on the hillside in Virginny. No one asked.

He sighs. Well, he married a wife in Alabama, later on. Lula was a big girl with welcoming eyes. They were married ten years, and then he was sold away from her to a cane plantation south of New Orleans. And then later on he was sold one more time, to this young man, Cornelius Carson. And now he's on the run with Cornelius and Thomas.

It was Jenny who started all this trouble, yelling and punching Miz Adelaide, and yanking her hair. And then Adelaide got loose and ran out of Jenny's room squealing. When Mal tiptoed over to Jenny's room to see what happened, there was Jenny, sitting on the side of her bed, holding her empty money-bag. It draped over her hand like the pelt of a dead animal.

"She stole my money, Mal," Jenny said.

"You gonna be in trouble now," Mal said, but Jenny didn't run. She just sat there and waited for the authorities to come. And that didn't take long. He remembers how Jenny's eyes flashed when the sheriff came and hauled her off.

And Cornelius wasn't there to save her.

He was supposed to be driving up to Slocum to take Miss Hattie's dresses to her sisters. He said he'd be back by dark, but it was nearly noon the next day before he showed up, and he didn't have Jenny with him.

"Get your things together, Mal," Cornelius said. "We're headed for Texas." Leaving Malachi to wonder, what kind of crime can a white man do that would make him run for Texas? Well, a white man can do any crime known, but knowing Master Cornelius, it couldn't be just any crime. But what about Jenny? The question still nags at him.

This evening a woman welcomed Cornelius into her house, which didn't surprise Malachi; a handsome man gets doors opened for him anywhere, even if he's carrying a restless toddler. Maybe especially if he's carrying a toddler. Now through the window he can see Cornelius sitting in a chair, his head bent down. He's probably reading something, Mal figures. Miss Phony McKee handed Cornelius a book when they swung by the McKees' place to pick up Thomas.

Cornelius looks up and stares across the room. Mal's seen him do that many times when he's reading—read awhile, then look up and stare off in the distance, then go back to the book. Sometimes he laughs when he's reading, and Mal always wonders about that. Is there something in the book that's funny?

Sleep seems closer. Mal watches the window through half-closed eyes. He hasn't asked Cornelius about Jenny because the man seems so panicked with the run they're on, and with Thomas being hard to handle. As they drove along, the two men passed the boy back and forth, and while one kept Thomas occupied, the other took the reins. It left both of them tired.

But Mal still wonders: Where's Jenny?

Maude O'Donnell was a bride five years ago when she first saw the home her husband Bill was bringing her to, but she knew from the moment she saw it that there'd be more money in running a hotel than in tending a scrabbly twenty-acre farm. It wasn't enough land to do more than run a few cows and raise a little garden. The log house was a rectangle front to back, with two large rooms, and being right on the road, it was bound to be a likely stopping place for passers-by. Travelers couldn't miss it, she saw right off, especially after she had Bill put up that big sign that said "Lodging." And sure enough they pull their wagons in, night after night. She doesn't mind sharing her house with strangers if they open their wallets, and usually they're so relieved to find a place that'll take them in for the night that they don't quibble about her price, sixty cents for a room, a meal, a bed.

Some travelers do look shady, though; it's usually young men traveling alone, with darting eyes and nervous grins, and when those types show up Maude's glad she doesn't have a teenage daughter prissing around. What are these men running from? They never say, of course. Well, whatever it is, Texas is the place to go to, right close by. Get across the Sabine River, a few miles to the west, and you're in another country; the law can't get you. She knows not to ask questions, just let the men eat their viddles and bed down, then be gone by sunrise. Texas can have them.

If the men look too shifty, scary, Bill gives her a signal they've agreed on—he turns his head and coughs a dry cough to the side—and she cuts her price some and points them to the barn. Or if they have noisy children, they can sleep on the hay with the cows. Or if they come with slaves, which most don't, the slaves can sleep in the barn.

Cornelius Carson has a red-haired boy who's most unhappy to be traveling, but Maude's made an exception for him; he needs a woman's touch with that boy, she can see it. The old slave could go to the barn, but the look of relief on Carson's face when she reached for the boy told her that her help was needed, and his pay would be proportionate. That's all she asks; that her pay be proportionate.

He hasn't said what he's running from, though; not that she would expect him to.

All Cornelius asks tonight is a resting-place better than the shacks they've stayed in the past few nights, especially since this chill has set back in. The owner of this lodging house, Bill O'Donnell, made him feel welcome, shared a good meal with him, and his missus made up a bed for him in the corner of the room. She set a dresser drawer on the floor for Thomas and padded it with quilts. Now the boy sleeps there where they can all keep an eye on him.

Cornelius stretches his long legs out and gazes at the fire. Outside the wind is cold, but in here there's warmth and a golden glow cast by the fire. It's a homey room, filled with the aroma of the dinner that was eaten at this table an hour ago. There's hospitality here, offered by this farmer whose work boots are propped by the fire. His wife sits close enough to Thomas to look over at him every few minutes, to make sure he's still sleeping well, while she knits. Cornelius didn't like sending Mal out to the barn to sleep, but because of Mrs. O'Donnell there was no question about it. If it had been just the men here, Mal could have slept inside, but with a white woman here—no, he'd have to go out. But at least the old man would be sleeping out of the wind.

Bill sits down at the table opposite Cornelius and pours a glass of whiskey for himself and his guest. "You're headed for Texas, I take it?" Bill asks. The whiskey gleams amber in his glass.

"I am. A fresh start."

"I never been over there myself. I do see people headed that way, all the time. They come down the road near every day. Lots of 'em stay with us for the night. What is it you think you'll do over there?"

"Set myself up, I guess. You can see I've got my boy to raise." *He's curious,* Cornelius thinks. *Well, I'm an odd sight, a single man travelling with a baby and an old man.*

Bill clears his throat. "Maudie here's a Scotswoman," he says. "She come out here with her family about 20 years ago. I met her in Baton Rouge, and I knew soon as I seen her she was the one. It took me awhile to convince her of that, though."

"I wasn't sure I wanted to marry such an old man," Maude says.

"She knew a good thing when she saw one," Bill says, and Maude chuckles.

"Where's your boy's mamma?" Maude asks Cornelius.

"She died about a year ago."

"Good thing you got a helper, with a boy that age," she says.

79

"Yes, ma'am." Cornelius downs the rest of his whiskey. "Mal's getting old, though. I been thinkin' I might free 'im, old as he is, once I get to Texas."

"Free 'im?" Bill says in a low voice, looking at Cornelius. "You look like a man who'd know better 'n that, to free a slave. It don't matter how old he is."

Cornelius shifts in his chair. "Well, I promised my mammy I wouldn't keep slaves. It's an old promise, but I aim to keep it."

"You an abolitionist? If I'd known that, I'd a' told you to keep drivin'. I don't hold with havin' free blacks wanderin' around."

"Bill, calm yourself," Maude says. "What Mr. Carson does ain't your business."

"No, it ain't." He stares hard at Cornelius. "Well, you in for a surprise, Mr. Carson," he says, taking another drink to drain his glass. "You get to Texas, remember, you ain't in the good ol' United States anymore."

"Yes sir."

"They got laws there, and their laws say you ain't allowed to free a slave."

Cornelius stares at the man. "It's the law?"

"So I been told. And it's a good law, you ask me. Free blacks wanderin' around, they give ideas to the ones that're still slaves. Can't have that. No sir."

Maude says, "Bill, keep your voice down. You'll wake the boy."

Cornelius looks from one to the other, an old couple infected with slave-holding ideas; they who obviously own none. Well, he learned long ago to mind his own business. And someday he'll learn to mind his tongue, too.

Bill clears his throat. "Well, like Maudie said, it's a good thing you got the old man to help with him. A young'un that age, they take a lot of watchin'."

"They do."

"Where you say you come from?"

"Georgia, originally. Then after that I had a place over in Concordia Parish, a little farm. But that's done with now. "

Maude sets her knitting down. "I'm puttin' a stop to all these questions. Bill, let Mr. Carson get some rest. He's bound to be tired out."

"Awright," Bill says. "Turn down that lamp, will you, when you turn in? "

Cornelius stands up. "I will. Good night, sir." He nods to Maude.

Bill's questions brought a chill into the room, but it leaves the room with them. When the bedroom door is closed, Cornelius reaches into his saddlebag and pulls out the book Euphonia McKee gave him as a parting gift, Fielding's *Tom Jones*. He turns up the lamp and leans back in the chair. Good old Phony. She knows he likes to read.

As the book falls open in his hands, Cornelius sees there's a folded letter stuck into the pages like a bookmark. Euphonia must have put the letter in there so he'd be sure to see it. He knows the postmistress at the settlement on Bayou Cocodrie sometimes hands letters to country people to take to their neighbors in case the neighbors don't make it into town very often.

He holds the envelope to one side so he can study it. He's seldom seen his name written in such a careful script and on such fine cream-colored paper. In the upper left-hand corner is the return address: J. R. Landerson III, Esquire, Natchez. He's never seen that address before.

But he knows that lawyer. John Landerson was a dandy at the wedding reception held at Carefree when he married Stephanie. That August day in 1833 seems like it belongs in some other man's life.

Well, a letter from a lawyer demands attention; you can't ignore it, whether it's good news or bad. And whatever the message is, it doesn't mean he's going back where he came from. He's put miles and rivers between himself and the Cocodrie, and the closer he gets to Texas the safer he feels. No matter what the law might think, the life he left back on Bayou Cocodrie was decent enough. He pulled his weight, worked his farm, brought in his cotton. It wasn't really a happy life, though, with two young wives in their graves. And the one part that wasn't decent, when he pulled a gun on a sheriff's deputy in Vidalia, well, that could be justified.

He unfolds the letter. If he doesn't like the message he can burn it. There's still a fire going in the fireplace.

Jan. 5, 1841
My Dear Sir:

A matter of importance concerning the estate of the late Mister Emile Coqterre, Esquire, of Natchez, requires your attention at your earliest convenience. I apologize for the delay in notifying you. My late father, who had this office before me, was himself ailing at the time of Mr. Coqterre's death, and he filed the relevant document away in a back file. When I took over this office, after Father's passing, I at length came upon said document.
Please contact me at my office upon your next return to this city.

Yours truly
Your most obed. servant,
John H. Landerson III, Esquire, Attorney at Law

Cornelius reads the letter again. Would he really have some business with Emile's estate, after all this time? Landerson must be referring to Emile's will, and that might mean an inheritance. But that's unlikely, given Emile's contempt for him. He remembers the sharp-featured Frenchman with hostile eyes. Emile never really thought of him as a son-in-law, just as an interloper who stole his daughter away. When Stephanie died, Emile took her body back to Natchez instead of letting Cornelius bury her on his own land. He even swapped out the pine coffin Cornelius provided for a fine mahogany one with silver handles. All to try to undo Cornelius's marriage to Stephanie, to turn back time.

He folds the letter and slips it back into the pages of the book, and then stares into the dying fire. This lawyer has summoned him, but the sheriff in Vidalia might have other plans. From here there's no ready route back to Natchez except through Vidalia. But he might be able to slip through the town; he remembers the smell of whiskey on the deputy's breath, and how dark the night was.

But going back would be a reversal. It would change everything, and if a man has a destiny he'd better go for it, Cornelius thinks. That's what brought him to Louisiana in the first place, back before he met Stephanie; he was following his destiny.

But what's in this lawyer's letter might be a different destiny. The hard part is knowing which destiny to aim for. This travelling's been rough on him, Mal, and Thomas. He hadn't realized, when he started out, how wearying it would be for all of them to be out on the road, day after day.

And tired as he is, he can't shake the feeling that something in his destiny has gone awry. When he came to Louisiana, he was alone, but he was young and free. He's still a young man, but he's not free; he's got an old man and a boy in his charge.

He still feels alone, though. Just not free.

Malachi is up and ready to go by daybreak. He harnesses Tearose to the buggy and then sits on the porch step with a bowl of oatmeal that Maude cooked. He knows that Cornelius, inside the house, will be feeding Thomas a few spoonfuls of the same oatmeal.

When Cornelius comes out of the house bundling Thomas against the early morning chill, Mal climbs up into the buggy and reaches for the boy. Thomas, still sleepy, sinks into the crook of his arm.

Cornelius gets a blanket out of the back of the buggy and hands it to Malachi to tuck around the boy. Mal thinks, *I've got to find out.* Lying in the barn last night, with the hard floor beneath him and the animals prowling outside, he couldn't get the memory of Jenny out of his mind. Now he thinks, *He's got to tell me what's happened to her. It's not right, him not telling me.*

Cornelius climbs up and takes the reins. They drive out to the road where the pine trees end, and Cornelius pulls the horse to a stop. They sit like that for a few minutes, while the sun breaks through the clouds to the east and Cornelius looks both ways down the road.

What's the holdup? Mal wonders. "At least the wind's laid down," he says. "It'll be easier drivin' today."

When Cornelius doesn't say anything, Mal decides that now's as good a time as any to get his question answered. He takes a deep breath. "Master," he says in a low voice, "there's something I need to know. Is Jenny dead?"

Cornelius looks over at him in surprise. "No, she ain't dead."

"That's good." He nods. "Very good. Well, where is she?"

"I sent her to the free soil."

The free soil. The words sound so strange, coming from a white man's mouth. The very words Mal's said to himself a thousand times, and he'd practically decided it couldn't be a real place. But here's Master Cornelius, saying the words right out loud.

The free soil. Where is it? How far away? He starts to ask Cornelius, but he sees the man is thinking about something else. Cornelius is looking up and down the road both ways, but Mal can see nobody's coming.

Then Cornelius says, "Mal, let's go to Texas," and he shakes the reins. "It ain't far now."

CHAPTER EIGHT

FIVE MONTHS IN TEXAS was enough to tell Mal that Cornelius wasn't going to settle in Texas permanently. It's too different from what they all know, Mal figures, and Cornelius is not a man who can work for hire. Mal could see the discontent growing in Cornelius's eyes as he went out every morning to work for pay, wrangling cattle for a man named Henry Parks, and coming back in the evening sweaty and tired.

The place they rented was good enough, a cottage just on the edge of town, and set behind some trees. Missus Grenward, who ran the hotel in Pine City, owned it; but after her husband died she wanted to rent the house out and live in the hotel so she could manage it better. And the house came with furniture. So Cornelius took the big bedroom for himself and Thomas, and Mal took the smaller bedroom at the back of the house.

But it didn't look to Mal like Pine City would ever amount to much; it was just a scrub-pine hamlet with a road running a quarter mile between a row of false-front stores, a few houses, and the one hotel. That was it.

He hoped Cornelius would get himself a wife here. The girls in town are good-looking enough, and there's plenty of them around. The store-keeper's got two daughters who eye Cornelius pretty hard when he and Mal take Thomas to the store for a sweet. One's a tall brown-haired girl with straight hair falling down her back—her name's Corinne—and the other one has black hair and a tipped-up nose. Her name's Joanna. For sisters they don't look much alike. Those girls brighten right up whenever Cornelius comes in to the store, and they make a fuss over Thomas. When the boy runs over to press his nose against the glass case where the taffy's laid out on a tray, the girls come right out from behind the counter, their skirts swishing, to talk to Cornelius. They laugh big and tease him, but he stays pretty quiet. Many a conversation that starts inside the store could continue on that sidewalk out front, but so far, Cornelius hasn't stuck around to talk with the girls. He just walks off down the sidewalk holding Thomas by the hand, with Mal walking behind.

It's because he was shell-shocked by what happened with the sheriff, Mal thinks. A man as upright as Cornelius, to suddenly find himself on the receiving end of a warrant, and to have to send Jenny away where they'd never see her again, well, that would upset any man. It's plain Cornelius is not really looking to make himself a life in this foreign country, Texas.

Corinne and Joanna can both find themselves another man without much trouble. But Cornelius ought to be thinking about the future, Mal thinks.

When he turns down his bed at night, Mal likes to look out his window; now that it's summer, the velvet sky is sprinkled with diamonds. It usually takes him a while to get to sleep. Tonight, just before he'd normally drop off to sleep, he hears a sound outside his window, not that he pays much attention to the night sounds; he's used to them. But this is a heavy sound, like a crunch on pine needles made by a man's boot. And then some of the stars go black all at once, and it's not the shape of a cloud that's done it. It's a shape of a man's head and shoulders, rising.

Mal rolls over and stands up. When he looks out the window again, the stars are all back where they belong.

If someone's tom-peeping, he has to tell Cornelius. Thomas, sleeping in the other bedroom, can't be left unprotected. Looking over his shoulder at the window, Mal tiptoes out and goes to the front room, where Cornelius is reading a book.

"Master, someone's out there," he whispers, pointing toward the back of the house.

"Out where?"

He points. "Out by my window."

As Cornelius gets up and goes out with a candle to check, Mal feels unsure whether he'd seen something or not; maybe it was just a thought that passed by, not a real sight.

Cornelius comes back a few minutes later shaking his head. "I didn't see anything," he says. But, still, he looks around the room, frowning at the door and the window, and Mal knows it'll be a while before he settles back to his book. He goes back to his own room, thinking he won't get to sleep so easily now. That open window's more than a way for him to look out at the sky; it's a hole in a wall that can let anybody look in. Or climb through, if they want to. He lies awake well past midnight, listening. He knows Cornelius is listening too.

Sometimes a widow woman's not exactly what she says she is, and her husband's not exactly dead. Which is what the men learned the next day when Missus Grenward showed up at dawn, banging on the door. She wore a wrinkled housedress and her gray hair was unpinned, and there was excitement in her wrinkled face.

It turns out Mister Grenward scampered off to New Orleans on a whim one day, not having drowned in the bayou after all, just having abandoned his skiff there. Now he's turned up and today Missus Grenward's standing in their front room giggling like a schoolgirl, and she wants the house back. The woman's excitement is kind of pitiful, Mal thinks; what kind of warm welcome home should a man get if he just up and took himself away for half a year? But then Mal never did understand white women much. He's sure he won't be sleeping under that open window and smelling the piney-woodsy smell of Pine City much longer.

They spend the day packing up to clear out of the house. After supper Cornelius sits down at the table and writes a letter. This tells Mal there's something else in the wind; it always is when Cornelius writes a letter. Mal remembers that from the years on the Cocodrie.

The next morning they're on the road back to Louisiana. Cornelius stops the buggy at the hotel to mail his letter, and then they drive eastward toward the Sabine River, him holding Thomas and Cornelius driving. But by evening it's pouring rain and they have to take shelter in the first place they come to, an unpainted cabin that might hold promise because there's a lamp burning in the front window, bright on this dark afternoon. The white-haired woman who answers Cornelius's knock doesn't much want to take in lodgers, that's plain, but with the rain pouring from the roof and thunder crackling overhead, and seeing the small boy huddling in a blanket in the slave's arms, she takes pity and tells them they can stay in her barn. She holds out her wrinkled hand for the fifty cents she says the charge will be. Cornelius pays her and then he and Mal duck under the water cascading from the roof and step around what puddles they can as they pick their way around the side of the house. The barn looks more substantial than the woman's cabin, its roof sloping up on two sides to a higher pitch in the center. When they push the barn door open, the sweet smell of hay, the scent magnified by the humidity, permeates the air. A brown sky hangs low even as the rain slackens.

Cornelius drives the buggy into the stable and unhitches Tearose so the horse can graze on the hay there. Then Mal and Cornelius sit on hay bales in the center of what was once a stall, Thomas sobbing into Cornelius's shoulder. Mal reaches for Thomas and peels off his wet clothes and dries him as the boy stands dejectedly, his breath catching with every sob. Mal takes dry clothes from the satchel and dresses him.

"It's all right, Thomas," Mal says. "You gonna be all right, little man." But he hates to see Thomas crying, and this is the hardest he's cried in a long time. He spreads the boy's wet clothes on a hay bale, hoping they'll at least partially dry overnight.

Cornelius fishes into his pack and brings out a piece of soft caramel candy he'd bought at the store earlier, and Thomas quiets as he sucks on the sweet. When it gets dark, Cornelius lights a candle, being careful to set it high on a board away from the hay. In the flickering light the rafters of the barn cast shadows at odd angles over their heads. Seeing how Thomas is afraid of the looming shadows, Mal holds him and tells him a story about a robin who lived in a warm nest up high in a tree; he makes his voice into a high "cheep-cheep" as the bird would sound. A cow lows in a stall at the back of the barn.

As the candle drips down and the night outside takes on a milky darkness, the rain stops and the bayou animals begin to screech. Cornelius has no more candy to offer Thomas, but he pulls out a loaf of brown bread he'd bought at the store in Pine City, along with some cheese and a jar of molasses. He carves a sliver of cheese and gives it to Thomas, who nibbles at it, and Malachi holds the water flask to the boy's mouth. He spreads a blanket on the hay for Thomas, and after the boy falls asleep, the men eat bread and cheese. Cornelius pulls a whiskey flask out of his pack.

"That'll get us through," Mal says when he sees the flask, and the men pass it back and forth between themselves, saying little.

When the candle burns low they lie down on blankets, both of them sleeping poorly because they wake to check on Thomas every hour or so. But the boy, curled up against Cornelius, sleeps better than they do.

The next morning is sunny, but dripping wet. Yesterday's downpour has moved out but reminders of it are still with them, big drops falling from the leaves with every passing rustle of wind. The ground is a bog. Going outside to pee by the side of the barn, Cornelius hears the birds twittering in the trees around the barn, happy for the rain and for the clear summer day that's followed it. But the road will be soft as pudding, he thinks. Maybe that sun will dry it some.

After Mal feeds Thomas and they pack up their satchels, they climb up on the buggy and pull out, Cornelius steering the horse along the higher ground where he can, hoping the buggy's wheels don't get sucked into the mud. Out on the road they pull their hats down to shade their eyes against the sun, and Mal puts a hat on Thomas, even though the only one they can find in their packs is a slouch hat and way too big, but the boy likes it and decides he'll wear it all the time.

Four days will take them back to the Cocodrie.

The Sabine River in flood is a mighty sight, Malachi thinks that afternoon as Cornelius stops the buggy on the riverbank and they watch the gray-brown water surge past. The water reaches halfway up the trunks of the trees on the opposite bank and disappears into the tangle of underbrush. Sunlight glints on the swirling surface. The ferry won't be running until the water goes down.

"I guess this flood'll set us back," Cornelius says. He looks around at the few log buildings that form a settlement near the crossing: the ferryhouse, a hotel, and a couple of cabins; off to the north are split-rail pens in a clearing cut from the scabby pine woods, with dozens of miserable cattle penned inside.

Cornelius gets down from the buggy and goes over to talk to the ferryman. "He thinks it'll go down pretty quick," he says when he comes back. "Maybe by tomorrow. Let's see if we can get a room."

They drive a quarter mile back the way they came, to a building with a sign over the door that reads "Hotel."

"We're a pretty muddy group," Cornelius says. "But maybe they'll take us."

"I expect they've seen mud before, bein' this close to the river," Mal says.

The woman who takes the fifty cents Cornelius pays for a room scowls at Malachi, who stands behind him holding Thomas. She points toward the stairs. "Second room right." As they walk toward the stairs, she says to Mal, "You keep that boy quiet."

The floor creaks as they climb the steps and clump their way down the hall. The room is only big enough for a narrow bed and a weathered chest. A water basin and a pitcher sit on the chest; a long crack runs down the side of the pitcher and the flower design painted on its bulbous side is almost scratched away. The bedspread might have been white once; little balls dance along its fringes. Somebody must have traded that fancy bedspread for a night's lodging, Mal thinks; it's out of place here.

"At least we'll be dry," Cornelius says to Mal. He peels back the bedspread and pulls out the ragged quilt underneath and hands it to Mal, who folds it in half and spreads it on the floor. Cornelius hands him the one pillow.

When they go downstairs for dinner, the dark-eyed woman behind the counter is younger than the woman they saw earlier, and a good-looking woman at that, Malachi thinks. Her dark hair hangs long and straight down her back. Her lips are painted red. She fixes her eyes on Cornelius and when she brings the bowls of what she says is jambalaya to their table, she stands close to him and her bosom presses against his arm. He glances up at her and doesn't lean away.

After they eat, the men take Thomas for a walk down the length of the town. They try to stay on the wooden sidewalks when they can, although the boy likes to stamp the water with his feet and after the first puddle they decide to let him do it; it's easier than trying to hold him back. His shoes are already sopping, but at least the weather's warm. They stop by the pens to look at the cattle.

"Where you think these cattle're headed for?" Mal asks.

"Alexandria," Cornelius says. "Slaughterhouse."

"No wonder they're mooin' so sad," Mal says.

When it's almost dark, they go back to the hotel. Cornelius takes a candle from a stand near the stairs and they go upstairs, but not before Mal sees Cornelius glance back at the dark-haired woman behind the counter.

Later Mal has Thomas settled in the bed asleep and himself lying on the pallet next to the bed, his hand up on the boy's chest, when Cornelius answers a light tap at the door. Mal recognizes the voice of the woman who'd served their dinner. Cornelius glances back at Thomas and then steps out into the hall, easing the door closed. A few words are murmured, which Mal can't make out, and a moment later he hears footsteps as they go down the creaky stairs.

When Cornelius returns, after midnight, he brings the smell of whiskey in with him. He steps quietly around Mal's pallet and slips onto the bed to lie pressed against the wall on the other side of Thomas, who's taking up most of the bed and who doesn't stir.

Three more days, Mal thinks, if that ferry runs tomorrow.

Euphonia McKee, an intended bride, is standing in the front room of her parents' cabin, watching Cornelius pace back and forth with his whimpering child. He glances at her from time to time but she can't read his expression. What is it he's seeing when he looks at her? It can't be beauty; she didn't even primp herself up this morning. She put on her brown calico dress and combed her hair in its usual style, parted in the center and pulled tight to a bun at her neck. She's thirty-nine years old, eight years older than Cornelius, and while no lines are yet etched on her long face, she knows she has the mature look of a sensible spinster.

When Cornelius drove away from the Cocodrie back in January, she thought she'd never see him again. The letter she received from Texas earlier today had shocked her. Then an hour later he arrived, clumping across the porch in his high boots and then standing in the doorway with his hat in his hand. Her parents were delighted to see him.

He came into the room addressing her parents first, as was proper. He's decided not to stay in Texas after all, he says. He has some business to attend to in Natchez, and he plans to make his home there. And he asked if he might have their daughter's hand in marriage.

They reacted as she knew they would, her mother clapping her hands to her face in surprise, beaming, and her father reaching out to shake Cornelius's hand. They'd grown fond of him during the years when he was their neighbor here, his hundred arpents almost abutting their land along the bayou.

Then Thomas began to wail, out in the buggy, and Cornelius went out on the porch to see about him. The boy wriggled and arched his back and Malachi set him on the ground. When Thomas saw Cornelius, he charged over to the porch and Cornelius picked him up and brought him inside.

The three McKees are standing in the living room looking at him. The summer air is glittery with happiness.

"Do you need your land back?" Amos asks. "I can deed it back to you."

"No, it's yours now. It's your pay for keeping Thomas after Hattie died. I'll deed it over to you, first chance I get."

"We've missed little Tommy since he's been gone," Margaret says. "He felt just like my own child. 'Course right now he won't even look at us. He's forgotten us already." She pats the boy's back as he rests his head on Cornelius's shoulder.

"We'd better let y'all talk," Amos says, and they retreat to their own bedroom at the back of the house. But Thomas refuses to let Margaret take him, and he won't go back outside with Malachi either. He wants only Cornelius, at this inconvenient moment.

Now Euphonia watches Cornelius pace up and down with the boy's arms locked around his neck. After a few minutes she sits down and gazes out the door at the green fields beyond the barn, the landscape she's look at for most of her life. When Thomas is quiet at last, his eyes closed, Cornelius eases him down onto the sofa. He pulls up a chair in front of Euphonia, their knees almost touching.

"Phony, I have some money," he says in a low voice. "I've only got one slave, Malachi, since I freed Jenny, but we can get more help with Thomas. I want you to come with me to Natchez."

She holds him in her steady gaze. "Why were you in such a hurry running out of here last winter?"

"I got scared, I guess. Not just for me, but for Thomas and Mal, too. I'm by myself, and if anything happens to me—well, the truth is there's probably a warrant out for me in Vidalia. I had to break into the jail there to get Jenny out. She beat up Adelaide Halloran."

Euphonia's eyes get wider. "A warrant?" She glances away. Then she says, "Well, I certainly heard about Adelaide. It was all the talk here after you left. She paraded that broken nose of hers around the settlement like a war trophy."

"That wouldn't surprise me." He reaches into his pocket and pulls a letter out. "But just before I got to Texas, I found that letter you stuck in the book you gave me. It's from a lawyer, and it has to do with Emile Coqterre's estate. I'm not sure if there's anything in it for me, but I figure I need to go see. And regardless, I plan to live in Natchez from now on. I can find work there."

He unfolds Landerson's letter and hands it to her.

"How will you get through Vidalia if there's a warrant out for you?" she asks after she reads it.

"I don't think anybody'd recognize me. It was dark when I went to the jail, and the guard was drinking. And I sure don't plan to dilly-dally getting through that town."

She frowns. "Where *is* Jenny?"

"I put her on a steamer headed to free soil. Cincinnati." He leans forward. "Well? May I have an answer?"

She studies his face. He's browner and thinner than when she last saw him. The angle of his jaw is sharper. Texas must have done that. She looks over at Thomas. Cornelius is expert at handling this restless child, but the boy needs a mother, that's plain enough. Was that what spurred Cornelius here? It can't have been easy for him, travelling for days with the boy and only Malachi to help with him. She knows Thomas well from the months he lived here with her family, but it was her mother who was the nursemaid to the boy, not her.

She says, "I'm thirty-nine years old, Cornelius. I've never been with a man."

He grins. "You danced with me at the frolics."

"I did."

"I'm a good dancer."

She smiles. "You are. By the way, there's something I need to show you." She goes to the sideboard and pulls the drawer open. "The day you left, I went over to your cabin to get the animals. And I could see you left in a rush, the way things were. But this was lying on the bed." She hands him a photograph.

The image of Malachi rests in his palm. He stares at it. "Where are the others?"

"What others?"

"There were three in all. I put them all on the bed when I left. There was one of me and one of Jenny with Thomas."

"This was the only one there."

He frowns.

He's tired, she thinks. She won't trouble him by mentioning the sheriff who was there that day.

"I'll probably never see Jenny again," he says. "It wasn't a very good picture of her, anyway, and Thomas wouldn't hold still, so he came out blurry. This one doesn't favor Malachi much."

She sits down again. "It's Malachi I need to talk to you about," she says in a low voice.

He looks up. "What about him?"

"It's not about Malachi himself," she says, "but I swore long ago I would never spend my life as a slave owner."

"But you own slaves, right here on this place!"

"Mother and Father own them. I don't. They own fifteen, four families in all. And I am telling you I will never own a single one."

He takes her hands, pulling her to her feet. "And here I thought it was something about me personally you couldn't stand, just to find out it's Malachi. Well, I've been thinking I need to free him one day anyway. I didn't know you had those views. Have you been reading *The Liberator* or something?"

"Only when I can get my hands on it."

"Did that paper turn you into an abolitionist?"

She shakes her head. "No, that's not what did it. I've held those views since I was ten years old, when Pa took me to the slave auction to buy Celia and Jim. He told me to wait in the buggy, but I didn't. I went over and stood in the door and watched. And after I saw what went on in that place, I swore I'd never own a slave. Or marry anyone who did."

"Euphonia, you have got yourself a deal." He dances with her across the room. "I told you I'm a good dancer," he says. He plants a kiss on her mouth. "Do you want to live dangerous? Let's do it today. I bet we could find a preacher who'd marry us."

She stops dancing and pulls away from him. "I'll do it if you promise me you won't get arrested. I don't want to be married to a jailbird."

"I ain't gonna hide like a rabbit in a hole. But like I said, nobody's gonna recognize me. That sheriff's probably got better things to do than chase after me, with people murderin' each other right and left like they do in Vidalia. I'd be of low importance to him. So let's go live dangerous."

He's smiling, and she knows that something momental is happening at that moment. She'll be a wife, and her life will assume a new shape. Thomas rolls over on the settee, his arm hanging off, and Cornelius goes over to move him back from the edge. Then he walks back to her and kisses her again, a real kiss this time.

Yes, she thinks.

CHAPTER NINE

ON SUMMER AFTERNOONS all Natchez winks in the sunlight; the tiny leaves of shrubs along the fences catch the sun, and every bush drones with insects. The shrubs reach halfway up the houses, so every house is half-buried in green, and pulses with that thrum.

It's a place of many memories for Cornelius. Natchez proper was where he bought Jenny, and Under-The-Hill was the place where he freed her. Natchez Improper.

The town still looks familiar to Cornelius, even though it's been more than a year since he rode up Silver Street. The last time he was here was the day he brought Jenny to Carefree to get her away from Hattie's fists. But when they got there, they found only Esther living on the abandoned place, so they went back to the Cocodrie that same day. By the time they got home, Hattie was dead.

Jenny. He thinks about her in passing every day; she flits across his thoughts like a Cooper's hawk against a blue sky. He wonders what's become of her, in her freedom. Did she make it to Ohio all right? He remembers how she looked that night, running up onto the *John Jay* in the dark. It was a relief to see her go up that gangplank, even though he had to break the law to get her there.

But he won't let himself worry about Jenny, because she'll make her own life. He can't feel self-righteous about freeing her, either. If his mother were here she'd scold him for that; she told him not to keep slaves in the first place. Jenny's like a phantom who once worked with him and Mal in the cotton fields, and now she's gone.

It's Malachi who talks about her. "I wonder where li'l Jenny ended up," the old man said more than once as they drove back from Texas. "I bet she'll do all right. Make something of herself."

"Oh, she'll make it all right," Cornelius said, but he's not dwelling on what's happened to Jenny. He has to consider the here and now. Right now he's a man with a new wife, on his way to a lawyer's office to see about a will. Which might make him luckier than most of the men in Natchez, at this moment.

This morning was a whirlwind. Mal said he wanted to stay in the Cocodrie for a few days, and he'd just as soon sleep at his old cabin, so Cornelius drove him over there. The McKees said they'd keep Thomas for a day or two, a honeymoon gift, so Euphonia folded her dresses into a satchel, hugged her parents goodbye, and then she and Cornelius tiptoed out while Thomas slept. Before noon they were on the outskirts of Vidalia and driving up to a house where a preacher lived who'd marry them. The McKees knew the man, and they recommended him. And in no time at all—eleven minutes by the clock on the preacher's wall—Cornelius and Euphonia Carson were husband and wife.

He glances over at Euphonia, who fans herself with her hand. Because of her, his life has transformed today. She's willing to step into an unknown future with him. And she's told him she won't own slaves, which suits him. He's proud of her for standing her ground on that. A man can do worse than marry a principled woman, he thinks. His father had.

Up ahead is wreckage. A storm passed through Natchez back in March—Cornelius read about it in the New Orleans *Picayune,* the newspaper having miraculously shown up at the hotel in Pine City, and only a week out of date. Hundreds of people were killed, the downtown destroyed; that explains the swarms of workers on the streets today. He can see that the storm wrecked some blocks, leaving others untouched. New buildings are being framed up and rise skeleton-like along the streets. The staccato sounds of hammering are everywhere. It surprises him how quickly the town's being rebuilt, but then Natchez has always been known as a town in a hurry. He wonders if Carefree was damaged, but the track of the storm doesn't look like it veered off to the east.

He pulls the horse to a stop in front of a red-brick building. A bronze plaque fastened to a low wall at the curb reads, "John H. Landerson III, Esquire."

In the baking heat they walk up the brick path to the door. The air is fragrant with the blossoms of two magnolia trees that tower over the porch. A black man in a formal coat answers Cornelius's knock. He says, "Master Landerson's at dinner right now, sir, but he'll be back soon. You're welcome to come in and wait, you and your missus. Y'all come in out of the sun." So they step past him into the cool of the office.

John Landerson walks into his office worrying a piece of steak out of his back tooth. A slow afternoon stretches before him. He doesn't much like this small-town lawyering business, but Father handed it over to him, a prospering practice, so what choice did he have? He had no appointments for the afternoon when he looked at his calendar this morning, but now he's surprised to see that he does have clients after all. And he's even more surprised when he sees who it is.

He remembers Carson from many years ago. He shakes Cornelius's hand and motions toward a comfortable wing chair for Mrs. Carson, and then goes into the back room where his law books fill two bookcases against the back wall. He slides into his chair behind the desk, surprised that Mrs. Carson has come into the back room with her husband and sits in the chair beside him, her cloth bag in her lap.

"Ma'am, may I offer you a cup of coffee?" John asks. "That big chair over by the window is the most comfortable one. You'd enjoy your coffee there. William?" he calls to the black man, who appears in the doorway. "William, fetch Mrs. Carson a cup of coffee."

"I'm comfortable where I sit now," Euphonia says. "I'll sit here if you don't mind. And no thank you for the coffee, it being so hot today."

"Yes, ma'am, it is hot."

John folds his hands on the desk and studies the Carsons. People come to his office on all sorts of legal matters, and he finds it helpful to understand them. The law tells its tales, that's certain; there's a story going back centuries behind every legal thing, but the stories are often as dry as the paper they're written on. What intrigues John are the breathing people the law touches, or the ones who once were breathing. Which is everybody, sooner or later.

Cornelius Carson is a man whose face he knows, and he's about to become one of the wealthiest men in Natchez by the stroke of a pen. And his wife, who John's never seen before, is a tall plain woman in a calico dress and a country bonnet. The three of them are sitting here in this office this afternoon for one reason only, because Emile Coqterre was the loneliest man in Adams County.

John reaches around and pulls a file drawer open. "I'm glad you made it back here, Mister Carson," he says. "I wasn't sure my letter reached you."

"It got to me, but I wasn't in a position to return until now," Cornelius says. "Thank you for notifying me."

John nods. "You know, I always felt sorry for Mister Emile, the way all his family died on him. I guess you were the closest thing to a relative he had left." He pulls a large yellow envelope from the desk drawer. "But he did have a will, filed right here in this office, but as I wrote you, I didn't know about it until a few months ago. I find things stuck away in the wrong file all the time." He opens the envelope and slides a document out onto his desk. He reads it over.

He looks up and says, "If you'll permit me, I'll read it out loud. That's the custom."

He begins to read in a soft voice.

Last Will and Testament
August 23, 1833
In the name of God Amen

I Emile Coqterre of Adams County Mississippi being of perfect mind and memory do make and ordain this my last will and testament. My worldly estate I give and bequeath in the following manner. It is my will that my son-in-law Cornelius Carson, husband of my daughter Stephanie Coqterre Carson—John pauses to clear his throat—*enjoy the use of the plantation I own in Rapides Parish, Louisiana, together with the one thousand arpents of land belonging there to during his life. I further bequeath to him my son-in-law my livestock, all my household furnishings and utensils, my farming utensils, and my growing crop and all my corn. I further bequeath to my son in law Cornelius Carson the house in Natchez, Adams County, Mississippi, known as Carefree, together with its outbuildings, household furnishings, and*

kitchen utensils. I further bequeath to said Cornelius Carson all my
slaves, numbering over one hundred, situated both at Rapides Parish,
Louisiana, and at Natchez, Adams County, Mississippi. I further
bequeath to my son in law Cornelius Carson all my ready monies in
my account at the Planters' Bank, Natchez.

/S/ Emile Coqterre
Witnesseth: Josiah Hargraves, Esq.   Dr. Herman Brice

When he finishes reading, the ticking of the clock is the only sound
in the room. Then he says, "He made this will right after you married
Stephanie." He hands the document to Cornelius. "It would be best if I
kept the original here in the office, in case there are any questions about
it. Although I don't think there will be, given the circumstances. I can
have my secretary make you a true copy. He's here now."

Cornelius hands the will back to him and John gets up to go into a
back room. When he returns he says, "It will only be a few minutes." He
sits back down and folds his hands on the smooth surface of his desk.

"You know, Cornelius, I think Emile saw himself declining, with his"—
he glances at Euphonia—"his illness. And he wanted Stephanie to be taken
care of. Of course, when she died, the next relative was Miss Sophronia, his
sister. Had there been no will, it would have gone to her, as a single woman.
But he favored Stephanie over her." Sunlight comes through the shutters and lays stripes across the oak desk. "And of course Stephanie herself
couldn't inherit, as a married woman. So it went to you, as her husband."

John glances at Mrs. Carson; her only reaction to the windfall that's
come to her husband, and ergo to her, is a nervous motion her hands
make, to straighten the wings of her bonnet. Well, John's seen all kinds of
reactions to bequeathments made in wills; there's not a human emotion

the prospect of money doesn't bring out. But for himself, he'll get the probate fee, file the documents, and Carson can make of it what he will. Eight years ago Cornelius wooed pretty Stephanie Coqterre right out from under him. He himself would have made a perfect match for her, and if his parents hadn't sent him to France in the fall of 1832 the marriage would likely have happened, and she wouldn't have drowned in that flood. But that was a long time ago; she's been dead nearly six years. He has to let it go. This is all business.

The secretary, a thin young man in a black suit, comes back in with the documents. John lays the original on the desk and places the copy beside it, running his finger down each line in both documents, comparing them. "All correct," he says. He folds the copy into a heavy envelope with the word "Will" embossed in black letters and hands it to Cornelius. He returns the original to its folder.

"You'll have a big job out in Rapides Parish, I expect," John says. "The place may have been neglected the past couple of years. Emile had an overseer out there, but if the man hasn't stole you blind, I'd be amazed. But you'll find out. You'll probably be away from Natchez much of the time."

"I imagine so," Cornelius says. He and Euphonia stand up. "First we have to go see about the house. Do you know if it was damaged in the storm?"

John remembers Elenora's visit there a few months ago. "Not to my knowledge. Most of the damage was downtown."

"We saw the rebuilding. It must have been bad," Euphonia says.

"Well, the town was busy with funerals for a week or so."

"Mercy."

John opens the door. Euphonia walks out and stands on the sidewalk. The men shake hands and Cornelius steps though the door, putting on his hat.

John watches as they walk out to the street. He doesn't understand this couple, but they'll have a lot to talk about between themselves, this man who stole Stephanie away from him, and his quiet wife. Ordinarily he wouldn't give them a second thought; any day he might pass them on the street without a sideways glance. But since they'll be moving into Carefree, and Natchez isn't that big a place, he's bound to get to know them, his new neighbors.

They climb up into the buggy and Euphonia pulls her bonnet off and fans her face with it; the heat hangs like a shroud out here in the street. Cornelius turns to look at her. She's never seen him wear that look of astonishment before.

She wonders: What will this bequeathment mean? It will change everything. She came here a wide-eyed bride, unconsummated, with an eager husband. Did Cornelius suspect the lawyer would hand him Emile's entire estate? That riches would fall on their heads?

She pulls the pins from the bun on the back of her neck. Her hair is damp and she shakes her head to let it fall down her back.

"A hundred slaves, Cornelius?" she asks. "What on earth—?"

He reaches over and covers her hand with his own. "Phony, I told you I wouldn't keep slaves, and I won't. But it may take some time to free so many. Don't worry about it. Let's just go see our new house. Carefree." He shakes the reins and they drive up the street.

"It has a splendid name, Carefree," she says in a low voice. She looks into the windows of the shops they pass.

"Don't expect too much. I'm sure the place is a wreck," Cornelius says. "Emile stabled his goats in it."

"*Goats?*"

"Goats." He smiles as he turns the buggy onto Jefferson Street. *Goats?* she thinks. *Surely not.*

A little man like Walker Jackson learns to stay away from trouble; he's spent his whole life ducking, and crouching, and watching his back. If you're small and a freed man, you're especially careful. *'Cautious' is my middle name*, Walker's's thought many a time, *if I had a middle name.* It's how he's always lived his life, and so far it's worked out all right, although he did have that close shave down by Bayou Sara back in the winter. And that came from not being cautious enough, right at that moment.

In the four months he's lived at Carefree, he's learned the sound a buggy makes when it comes onto the property, that low scrunch of iron wheels on the gravel drive. Visitors don't come to Carefree much, which suits him fine, and when they do it's usually Esther who takes charge, directing the intruders to where they need to go, or giving vague answers to any nosy questions they bring up. The intruders almost always turn around in the drive, realizing they've made a wrong turn, and they head on back down into Natchez.

Except today this driver doesn't stop; the buggy rolls right on up onto the grass in front of the gallery.

At this moment Esther's gone into town to do her kitchen shopping, and Lord knows where Jenny is, so it's up to him to head off any snoopers. He lopes over to the big house and goes up the back steps and through the main hall to the front door. Whatever the people in the buggy think their business is here, he'll head them off at the front gallery.

By the time the driver climbs down from the buggy, Walker is standing on the top step, a little winded. "Can I help you, sir?" he asks.

The intruder puts his hand up to help his lady down. "Is Esther here?" he asks.

"No sir." Walker makes himself stand tall as he can, seeing that this man has got to be two feet taller than he is. "If you have a message for Aunt Esther, I'd be happy to pass it on to her when she gets back. She went into town a little while ago."

"She still lives here then. I was hoping so. My name's Cornelius Carson."

Walker stares. This is the man Jenny's told him about, her master who put her on that steamboat and ran off to Texas. But here he is, big as life, and obviously not in Texas.

"How do y' do, sir," Walker says, with a little half-bow.

"And who are you?"

"My name's Walker Jackson."

Cornelius's face creases into a puzzled frown. "Are you stayin' here? I thought it was only Esther living here."

"I'm stayin' here; yes, sir. I'm a free man, and I've lived around Natchez for more than ten years now. I was in need of a place to stay, and Aunt Esther told me I could come stay here. She's a good-hearted woman, Esther is. So I took a room out in the slave house. I help out by keepin' up the place." *And y'all need to head on back down that drive right now,* he thinks. *Shoo.*

Cornelius looks around. "I'm the owner of this place now. Is anyone else staying here?"

You're the owner? Walker thinks. *Do I tell him about Jenny, or just let him find out later?* But if he doesn't tell, Carson will find out anyway, and then he'd know Walker hid something from him. That wouldn't do.

He clears his throat. "Well, sir, the big house is empty. Nobody lives in it." He grins his toothy grin. "There's just one other person livin' out at the slave house. Her name's Jenny."

"Jenny?"

Mrs. Carson stops fanning herself.

"Yes, sir." He knows Carson's going to want the whole story about what happened with Jenny, but that doesn't mean Walker has to be the one to give it to him. Jenny can tell her own version, when she shows back up. She's been spending way too much time in town, in Walker's opinion. "She's been here since wintertime. It's been a good thing for her, living here with Esther taking care of her. She's a young girl, so she needs somebody to look out for her." *Which you wasn't ever gonna do*, he thinks.

He sees how Cornelius takes this news, holding his hat by the brim and shifting it a little. "Is Jenny here now?"

"I couldn't say where she is, right this minute. She kind of comes and goes like she wants. She's a free gal. Now Aunt Esther, she's been taking real good care of the place. After Master Emile died, none of us knew who owned the place, so Esther decided the thing to do was just keep it up real nice 'til we found out. You'll be pleased when you see how she's got the inside tidied up, best as she could, what with the goats. She goes in every day to scrub and clean, just like when Master Emile was livin'. Would you like me to show you 'round the house?"

"I know the place," Cornelius says, reaching for his wife's hand.

Walker steps aside as the couple go through the front door. When the door closes behind them, he whirls around and plops down on the top step, his hands up on his face and his mouth open wide, but he doesn't make a sound. *Won't Esther be surprised?* And Jenny—what'll she do when she finds out who owns Carefree now? When he ran into her on the *John Jay*, she was even afraid to get off the boat because it wasn't what Carson told her to do. But now she just goes around doing what she pleases, without a by-your-leave from anybody. She's forgotten how she had to do what she was told, back when she was in slavery. People always want to forget that slave life quick as they can, and forgetting it can get a person in trouble pretty quick.

Won't she be surprised?

He hops up and sprints down the drive toward the road that goes into Natchez. He was aiming to go into town today anyway, and he thinks he'll just go ahead and do that. He'd just as soon not hang around this Carson fellow 'til he figures out how this is all going to work out. He might even run into Jenny or Esther in town, and won't he have some interesting news for them?

"The goats did all this damage," Cornelius says as they go into the parlor. He hates for Euphonia to see the place this way, but it can't be helped. In the past few minutes, since leaving Landerson's office, he's begun to think of himself in a different role than that of an east Texas cattle wrangler. Now, standing in the parlor of his new house, it's plain that Emile got his revenge on the man who would own this house after him. He knew his heir would be his hated son-in-law.

The curtains aren't quite closed, and the afternoon sun throws a wedge of light across the floor. The rug used to glow in deep hues of scarlet and purple, but now it's dull and the fringe is pulled off. The stuffing's been pulled out of the sofa, and bits of horsehair dance across the floor. The bottoms of the heavy velvet curtains are shredded, and the golden tassels chewed off.

"Is there anything a goat won't eat?" Cornelius asks.

But the French tables along the wall are buffed to a mellow glow, and the silver candlesticks that sit there are polished to a sheen. Esther's worked to keep the room clean, he thinks, but she couldn't fix what the goats did.

"This was Stephanie's house?" Euphonia looks around.

"It was," Cornelius says. "I wanted to bring you in the front door so you could see the place at its best. These front rooms used to be the nicest rooms in Natchez, but you can see the damage. We'll have to make a lot of repairs."

Euphonia walks around the room, taking it in. Then she faces him. "Cornelius? Did that man mean what he said? That Jenny's living here?"

"It's a surprise to me," he says. "Maybe it's somebody else who has that name."

"What if it is her?"

"What if it is? She got on the boat, that's all I know. Maybe she decided to get off the boat and come back here. But she's free, so I reckon whatever she does now is up to her. "

"And all this time, with the house sitting empty, Esther's been living by herself in the slave house?"

"Far as I know. Where else would she go? As for Jenny—"

"Is Jenny old enough to decide for herself what to do?"

"She must be seventeen or eighteen. I never knew exactly how old she was, and I don't think she knew either."

Cornelius walks to the window and pushes the curtain open so he can look out onto the lawn. "You know, Emile wasn't right in the head," he says. Then he looks around at Euphonia.

"Is the whole house torn up like this?" Euphonia asks.

"Let's go upstairs and see the rest of it," he says, taking her hand.

Upstairs the hallway smells of wax, and the sun casts a mellow gleam down the floor of the hallway. A door stands open to a bedroom. Euphonia walks in and looks around, and Cornelius follows. He remembers this peach-colored room, but it looks different now, forlorn, not like it looked when Stephanie was alive. Her silk counterpane is still spread on the bed, but it's ragged along the edges where the goats chewed. Her big chiffarobe sits like a dark monument against the far wall, just as he remembers. The room seems stuffy. He steps back into the hall.

"That was Stephanie's room," he says.

"Goodness." Euphonia goes into the next room, which overlooks the side yard.

"This was Emile's bedroom," he says. The bedspread here is smeared with streaks of mud, but the top of the dresser's been waxed to a sheen. "It doesn't look like Esther cleaned in here much."

They walk down the hall toward the back of the house. Cornelius opens another door.

Cornelius remembers this room too. The yellow bedroom is where he changed his clothes for the wedding reception. The bed, the chest of drawers, the old spinning wheel in the corner—he remembers those. The goats haven't been in here.

Euphonia turns to him with a smile. "This can be our room," she says, putting her arms around his neck. He notices the dimples that deepen alongside the corners of her mouth when she smiles. She'll be a city woman now, he thinks. Her homemade dresses will give way to city dresses. In the soft light of this room, her face reflected in the mirror of the dresser, he notices her big eyes, her wide mouth and strong jaw. It's an interesting face, if not a beautiful one.

He puts his arms around her and moves close to her, breathing in her warm musky aroma; her face is soft against his neck. Euphonia who likes to read racy books. Who swears she'll never own any slaves.

Except now she does. He'll have to make good on his promise when he has time. He can free Esther and Malachi, but then there are the hundred slaves in Rapides Parish, a more complicated problem. For now it can wait.

He reaches out and unties the ribbon on her dress. She pulls her hair around over her shoulder and stands still as he unbuttons her bodice. Then he kisses her long and deep.

He pulls her back and they tumble onto the bed together, her head on his arm. *Wife*, Cornelius thinks. And taken more properly than either Stephanie or Hattie, as befitting a man who owns the finest house in Natchez. She tastes salty and both of them are sticky, from the heat; but the late afternoon is quiet and there's even a little breeze. He knows Esther won't come into the house unannounced. The bed smells a little dusty, and the sound of a hollow chime echoes from some far-off room.

Wife, he thinks again. There's deep pleasure in that word.

CHAPTER TEN

A HOUSE LIKE CAREFREE always comes with ghosts. They huddle in the rafters; they chatter in the cobwebby corners of closets, waiting for the day they can claim the house again and roam freely like they did before this couple showed up. Who are these people anyway? Oh, just two fools, practically strangers to each other, who've yoked themselves together man and wife. They've moved in with their needs, their fears, their cautious and privileged lives, and committed the act of marriage. The ghosts want them gone. They will be, soon enough.

Euphonia, a half-day's bride, is sitting on the edge of the bed in the upstairs bedroom, thinking, *well, that's settled. I had no need to fear him.* The fear rattled around in her head all during the drive here. It was there when they left the preacher's house in Vidalia, and when Cornelius drove the buggy onto the ferry, and when they came up the hill to Natchez; but it's gone now. Cornelius is worldly, a man who's already had two wives, and she's never even had a beau before. And he wasn't really a beau; a beau would court you, would bring you presents, would take time to make you love him. Cornelius was just a man she knew, a neighbor who'd gone to Texas, running from the law like so many other men. And then he showed back up and she married him. But he wasn't a beau.

"Beau": a strange word, she thinks. It reminds her of a song her Grannny Taylor used to sing. Granny said she used to sing it when she was a girl, back in South Carolina. And then she'd warble away in her trembly old lady's voice, and she'd wave her hands from side to side, conducting herself:

The needle's eye, it doth supply
The thread that runs so true.
I stump my toe and down I go
How many beaux have I let go
Because I wanted you?
Because I wanted you?

But no beau came for Euphonia. She was always waiting for the right one to come along; her mother and the women of the Cocodrie said he would, sooner or later. She didn't know if Cornelius was the right one or not. How would a woman know? But when he pulled off her chemise and she lay down on the soft bed with him, in the afternoon heat, she found she melted into him as naturally as anything she'd ever done. And it didn't hurt, and afterward she found only two drops of blood on the bedspread, red as rubies but no bigger than pinheads. Pain and blood were her fears; wouldn't they be, for any woman? But those fears were groundless, she knows now. Why would anyone think otherwise?

If he's the right one, she thinks, her heart will let her know, sooner or later.

She admires his keen intelligence and high principles, yet in many ways he's a stranger to her.

At first she thought he wanted her as a mother to Thomas; certainly the red-haired scamp will need constant shepharding, and he's obviously too much for Malachi. But the way Cornelius looked at her, she thought, no; it was her he wanted. And she took the leap, thinking he was her best option –maybe her last option—before spinsterhood swallowed her up for good.

He gets up and pulls on his trousers. She reaches for her chemise and slips it on, thinking he might like her to have a prettier one instead of this plain one she brought from the Cocodrie. She sees him looking at her reflection in the mirror, and then he walks over and kisses her.

"We should go downstairs," he says. "Esther will be wondering about us. She'll be wanting to light the lamps."

"You're going to free Esther, as you promised?"

"Of course. I keep my promises," he says. He bends to kiss her again.

"When she's free, do you think she'll stay here?"

"I hope so. This is her home. We can pay her wages, and she can live in the slave house. Only we can't call it the slave house anymore. We'll have to call it—I don't know, behind Carefree, or something."

"How about Care—*full?*" She giggles. "Because with Esther and Malachi living here, and that little man we met, and Jenny, that's four free people. The slave house will be filling up with free people."

He chuckles. "If Jenny's living here, and if it's the same Jenny I know, we can call it—Care Less. I put her on that steamer and told her what to do, but she obviously couldn't have cared less what I told her."

She pinches him lightly on the arm, and they both laugh. She goes to the dresser and opens the top drawer. She takes out a hairbrush and then puts it back. "Whose room was this?"

"No one's that I know of. It was always empty, a guest room. That old spinning wheel came from Stephanie's mother."

"My mother has one of those old spinning wheels, too. She wanted our slave women to use it, but they didn't like it. It was too slow."

"You can buy cloth goods in the store," Cornelius says. "We'll get rid of that thing." He looks out the window, where the hickory tree throws a canopy of shade. "This is a good room for us. It's north-facing. The sun won't ever come in."

"We could put Thomas in that bedroom at the front," Euphonia says. "We have to get someone to watch him. Could Esther do it?"

"I doubt it. She's too old. It should be someone young, since he can be a handful. We'll make that our first order of business, finding a nursemaid. I hope Esther does stay, though. She knows the house." He looks down at the stream-bed that runs along the side of the house. "Some people call their slave house a Dependency. We could call it that."

"Dependency. That sounds right."

He buttons his shirt. "I'll have to get out to Bayou Boeuf as soon as we get things settled here. I'll write to the overseer out there, first thing."

"And my place will be here. Running the house."

"You won't have to do it alone. We'll hire whatever help we need. Esther can probably be our cook. She's probably tired of having all the responsibility herself. And don't worry about the furniture. We'll get new. I'll have to look at Emile's bank accounts, but I imagine we'll have more than enough to fix this place up."

"How will I meet other women?"

"Don't worry about that. Once the place is up and running, people will come out of the woodwork to meet us. They'll be curious as all get-out. Are you gonna miss living in the Cocodrie?"

You will, you will, the ghosts chatter, but to Euphonia it's only the sound of the hickory limbs brushing against the side of the house.

"No. I've been waiting all my life for you," she says, reaching up to put her arms around his neck.

120

The sun is setting when Cornelius walks down the back steps to the kitchen. A flock of crows circle overhead. They loop and swirl and then vanish into the trees at the bottom of the hill. He stops outside the kitchen door to watch them, thinking he doesn't want to startle Esther. He knocks lightly on the door, then pushes it open.

"Esther?" he says.

She's standing at the fireplace, her back to the room. When she turns around her face is glistening.

"Good evenin', Master," she says.

"Good evenin'."

She smiles, and he sees how gaunt she is now. Her wrinkles are sharp carvings in her face, and one tooth catches on her lower lip, so her smile is lopsided. She looks so old now, he thinks; but she can't be more than fifty. He remembers that her daughters were half-grown when he used to come here to visit Stephanie. He glances around the kitchen. Her cooking's done for the day, her pots washed and sitting upside down on a towel.

"I want to let you know that I'm moving into the big house. And my wife, Missus Euphonia, too. And my son Thomas. I figured Walker Jackson might've told you. The house came to me in Mister Emile's will."

Esther pulls her apron over her head and reaches up to tuck her hair back under her tignon. "Yes sir, Walker told me, just a little while ago," she says.

"Miss Euphonia is already here, but we left Thomas with her parents over in Louisiana. I have a servant, too. Malachi. They'll be coming here in a day or two. We'll need to find Mal a room out here in the—Dependency."

She walks to the table and sits down. He pulls out a chair and sits opposite her.

"I s'pose you heard about Jenny livin' here, too," she says.

"Yes, I heard that. I was surprised." *Well, that question's settled,* he thinks; *same Jenny.*

"Well, Jenny's been a surprise to most everybody ever since she showed up."

"It's kind of you to look after her. And I know you stayed here by yourself after Mister Emile died, and that had to be hard. But I need to tell you something. Miss Euphonia and I—we don't hold with keeping people in bondage, so I'm gonna put you free. I'll get the papers made up so it's official. You'll be free."

Her mouth falls open, and she puts her ropy hand up to cover it. She looks at him hard for a minute. When she speaks her voice is soft and husky. "Sir, at my age, to be free. Can that really be true? That is somethin' to take in."

He's surprised at the quiet way she takes the news. "I'll take care of it as soon as I can," he says. "And I'll be freeing Malachi too. There won't be any slaves at Carefree. But I hope you'll stay on here. I can pay you a money wage."

Minutes pass. He glances at her, but it seems intrusive to stare. He can't read her expression. She sits in silence, first looking down at her hands folded in her lap, then gazing around the kitchen. Finally she says, in a voice that's almost too soft for him to hear, "I thank you for that. I always knew you was a kind gentleman, even back when you was courtin' Miss Stephanie. Back then we was all slaves here. Every single one. And then they was all sold off but me. But then Jenny came and she showed me her freein' paper. And then Walker showed up, and he's free. And now you're sayin' I'll be free." Her voice drops to a whisper. "Well—"

"Miss Euphonia will need some help with the big house. If you can stay on to do the cooking, we'll pay you a wage. We'll hire someone for the housework."

"Yes sir. I hope Miss Euphonia won't mind my doin' things my usual way. She might have other ideas, but if I can please her, I will."

"Oh, you'll be a big help to her. She'll have a lot to deal with, coming to a new place."

He stands up. "That's settled then. I'll get your freein' paper made up as soon as I can, after I get Thomas here." He walks to the door. "When you see Jenny, tell her I need to talk to her."

He goes out the door, leaving a whirlwind behind, but there's no one but Esther to feel it.

She can't sit still. She lights a lantern and walks out of the kitchen. Then she stops on the brick walk and looks around. Everything is as it should be, the house in front of her, the little kitchen off to the right, and to the left the spire-pierced skyline of Natchez. Nothing's changed, but yet it all has.

How will I steady myself? she wonders. This is a new world. She walks across the lawn in front of the house, not stopping until she gets to the place where the hill drops down to the streambed. She turns around and looks up at the house, a black rectangle at the crest of the upsloping lawn. In Master Emile's old bedroom upstairs, a candle flickers past the window where the shutters aren't closed tight.

This big house with its four white columns has been the center of her whole long life. And all these years it's looked so calm, so quiet, day after day, just sitting here by the road that runs down into Natchez. On the day Mister Emile decided to throw himself in the river, the house was perched up on the hill, just like it is tonight; and before that, it sat watching, just like it is now, when the slavers came to take her girls. On the day that happened the camellias were blooming just like they are now, and the moss was sweeping down out of the trees just like it is now.

It's like that clock in the hall downstairs. Once you've wound it, it chimes and you can't stop it. Jenny used to say it sang. It keeps on ringing the hours 'til it runs down. You can't stop time. Now her girls are off in slavery somewhere, but their mammy will finally be a free woman.

It's her girls that should be free, she knows, because they have their whole lives ahead of them. Their mammy's an old woman who's worked her whole life without money pay, just glad to have a decent place to work and a roof over her head. All those wasted years; most of her life's been taken up with hard work, and never has she gotten a penny in pay.

Free. She should be running up and down, shouting "Hallelujah!" and waving her hands in the air. But instead she's standing all by herself in the dark in front of a house that wasn't ever hers, watching lightning bugs spark. Sadness has sat like a stone on her heart for so long, it's hard for her to move it away. Out here on the lawn, under a glittery wheel of stars, she's just an old woman, and her heart hurts.

But then she looks out at the road that leads into Natchez; it's a light-colored band going down the hill. It hooks up with the next light-colored band, she knows; that's Madison Street. And Madison Street comes to Canal Street, and that runs into Silver Street that goes down to Under-the-Hill, where boats come in at all hours. She thinks, it's all mine now, the whole world. And she laughs, putting her hands over her mouth to cover her big maw so her missing teeth won't show, even though there's no one out here to see.

Oh, glory be.

CHAPTER ELEVEN

THE NEXT MORNING Walker comes in to the kitchen and pours himself a cup of coffee. He sits down at the table.

"What's up, Esther?"

Esther, scrambling eggs in her iron skillet over the fire, looks around at him and presses her lips together. She thinks it's a silly thing to say, "What's up?" but it's something he must've heard somewhere and he says it a lot now.

He scrapes two spoons of sugar from the loaf into his coffee, then reaches into his shirt pocket for a cigarette.

"We got us a new master here at the house," she says. "Master Cornelius Carson. I knew him when he was married to Miss Stephanie. He's got a new wife."

Walker lights his cigarette and then sits in a cloud of smoke. "I know. I met him yesterday," he says. "Tall fella."

Esther dollops a spoonful of eggs onto a plate and hands it to him. The yolky smell rises in the moist air and mingles with the ashy smell of the cigarette. Walker balances his cigarette on the side of a saucer and picks up a fork.

She sits down and leans close to him. "But here's the thing: he told me his missus don't hold with keepin' slaves. Cornelius is gonna put me free."

She's never seen Walker look surprised before, but she's surprised him this time. His mouth drops open and he sets his cup down. He's speechless, which is a first for him. Then his face crinkles into a smile. He leans forward and puts his hand on top of hers. "I'm glad for you, Esther, I really am. You'll be just like me."

"I ain't never gonna be just like you. Don't wanna be, neither," she says, pulling her hand away. When he grins, his teeth look like brown pearls, she notices. *See, you didn't know my big news*, she thinks, and she has to swallow a giggle.

"That's most unusual," Walker says. "I never knew a white woman who didn't hold with it, 'cept my old mistress Alcie Blanchard, and even her I had to buy my way out. Took me five years."

"Didn't she have other slaves beside you?" Esther asks.

"Yep. A whole kitchen full."

"Did she free them, too?"

"Nope."

"Maybe she let you go 'cause you just wasn't worth much," Esther says.

"That could 'a been it." He chuckles.

"But I'm gonna keep on livin' here," Esther says. "Cornelius says he'll pay me a money wage if I do the cooking and such. You better ask him if you can keep on livin' here, too, since you ain't exactly got permission. Tell him you a handyman. He might like that. And he says he's gonna get a better freein' paper for Jenny than the one she's got, which as we know ain't much. If she ever shows back up. Where is Jenny, anyways?"

Walker taps his cigarette into his saucer. "Well, I ain't mentioned this before, but Jenny's been keeping company. Her and her man are spendin' a lot of time at my old place on the alley."

Walker ain't likin' that, she thinks. He's kind of sweet on Jenny himself, but he's just too shy to announce it. She moves the sugar loaf closer to her cup.

"Keepin' company with who?" she asks.

"Some guy," Walker says. "He's a Creole. Frenchman. Somethin'. At first I thought he was a priest, but he ain't. He just cleans out the Saint Vigilius church. That's a far cry from bein' a priest. Anyway, he brung me food ever now and then when I lived on the alley, and 'course it wasn't long before he run into Jenny, 'cause she was there botherin' me all the time. And I could tell there was gonna be somethin' up between 'em, right off. That's one reason I moved in up here. I didn't need to be watchin' no ro-mance firin' up."

"You could 'a told me about this sooner."

"The reason I didn't mention it is because I figured may be I wasn't seein' right, and I sure didn't want to say somethin' that might not be so. But you know as well as I do, you can *try* to think you ain't seein' right, but nothin' can make you think somethin' ain't happenin', when it's happenin' right there in front of your eyes." A long minute passes. Walker stares across the room, dragging on his cigarette. "Gonna be a hot day," he says.

"Jenny better be careful. She'll get herself in trouble," Esther says.

"There ain't nothin' careful about Jenny," Walker says. "And there ain't nothin' we can do about it neither."

"Good thing he ain't a priest. That's probably illegal or somethin'," Esther says.

"It's somethin'," Walker says.

"Well, when you see her, tell her to get herself back up here," Esther says. "Her master's showed back up and she can get herself a real freein' paper if she comes back."

"He ain't her master no more. And he ain't yours neither. You gonna have to get used to that," Walker says.

"I'm already used to it. There ain't really been nobody lookin' over my shoulder since Emile died."

"I guess I could go see if Jenny's down at my old shack," Walker says. "She don't sleep here much, does she?"

"Not much." Esther shakes her head. "Would you tell me, Walker, how come trouble's always around, and everything happens at the wrong time? Here I found out I'm gonna be free, and I oughta be shoutin' 'Hallelujah!' I'm thinkin' it, though, on the inside. But the first thing I can think is, my girls is out in slavery somewhere, and why couldn't he get here sooner, and free us all? Why'd that old clock just keep tickin' and he didn't come and free us back then?"

" 'Cause y'all wasn't his property back then, that's why," Walker says. "Emile was still livin', and that old coot wasn't gonna free nobody. He was just gonna sell y'all off, and that's what he did. If he hadn't killed hisself, he'd 'a sold you too."

"Maybe one day I can find out where my girls is."

Walker stubs out his cigarette. "I hope you can. I think I'll ask Cornelius if he can help me get a new freein' paper. Since he's handin' 'em out right and left."

After Walker goes out, Esther washes the two dishes and sets them upside down on a towel, and then scrapes what's left of the eggs to one side of the skillet in case Jenny shows up hungry. Then, thinking now's as good a time as any, she goes into the big house to meet the new Missus Carson. Normally she would've gotten to her chores in the house by now, but with Cornelius and his wife here, she's got to figure out when's the right time to go in, and when it's better to wait. The dew is drying on the grass by the time she ties on a clean white apron and walks up the back steps. She smooths down her skirt as best she can; she feels self-conscious, having to go introduce herself to this stranger. She's so bony now, in her fifties; when she goes up the steps she knows her legs wobble underneath her skirt, showing the angles of her bow legs. Not that there's anybody out here to see.

The new wife is sitting in the dining room slapping through a stack of Miss Josephine's doilies which Esther knows were in the top drawer of the sideboard, as of yesterday.

She taps lightly at the door. "Miss Euphonia. Excuse me, ma'am."

Euphonia looks up. "Yes?"

"I'm Esther, ma'am."

Euphonia scrapes her chair back and stands up. Esther sees that the woman is making a quick judgment, just as she herself is. Missus Carson is no beauty like Miss Stephanie was, but she's decided not to keep slaves, and that's a recommendation. What that means for a person working for her as a free woman, Esther's not sure.

"I'm glad you came in," Euphonia says. "My husband tells me you're the one who kept the place up after Mister Emile passed."

"Yes ma'am, I am." Esther says. But then she thinks, *Emile didn't just pass, exactly. He killed hisself. He's the only person I ever knew who did that.*

"I don't know if my husband mentioned it to you, but we're going out to the Cocodrie today to get Thomas. He's two years old."

"Yes, ma'am. He told me about your son."

"He's not my son. He's Hattie's boy. She was the second wife."

Esther thinks, *What kind of wife would say that, to make sure a house-maid knows that her little stepchild wasn't her natural-born son?* "I didn't know Master Cornelius had a second wife," Esther says. "I only knew Miss Stephanie,"

"Hattie died over a year ago. I'm the third wife. Mister Cornelius hopes you'll stay on as a cook. Is that all right with you?"

"Yes'm. He said he'd pay me a money wage, which I'll be most grateful to have. It's right kind of you to keep me on," Esther says. "And I should say, ma'am, I respect you for sayin' we all got to be free here. It means a lot." She looks down at the floor where a morning sunbeam is tarnishing the wooden planks. "Can you tell me how much that money wage might be?"

Euphonia frowns and looks out the window.

That camellia bush out there ain't gonna give you the number, Esther thinks.

Euphonia says, "Um. Two bits every day. Paid on Friday."

The amount sounds small. *I should've asked Cornelius,* Esther thinks. But she says, "Thank you, ma'am. I'll do my best to keep things runnin' like they always has. You can see the state everything's in, with the furniture and all. That's from the goats. I think pore Master Emile just wanted the place tore up because there was so much sad here."

"We'll get new furniture." Euphonia walks over to the door that leads into the hall. Then she faces Esther again. "The other thing is, we've got to find some girl to watch Thomas. What about Jenny? Could she do it?"

"Jenny? I can't rightly say she could do that job. She ain't settled down enough for that. She's spendin' a lot of time with a young man." Euphonia's eyebrows go up, but Esther thinks, *Jenny'll have to tell her own stories.* "I imagine Walker might know somebody," Esther says.

As Esther goes out the back door, she props it open with the needlepointed brick that Miss Josephine made as a doorstop, to bring in the cool morning air. Then she goes to the back gallery and stands on the top step listening to the birds that are setting up a chirp in the trees next to the house. The sky is a blue crystal, shimmering with humidity. *This is a pretty morning,* she thinks; *Lucy Ida used to love a morning like this.*

It's good to remember Lucy Ida. She and Lucy used to work and talk, hour after hour, waxing and cleaning in the big house. Lucy Ida lived to be ninety-two. Esther doesn't think she can match Lucy Ida in her long life, but she might. She has a lot of her life yet to live, as a free woman. Freedom is something Lucy Ida never had.

Even so, the day seems a little darker than it should be, because of the two bits.

But at the same time, there's a big space in her mind that's bright as this sunlight, even with the two bits, because she's free.

The fresh morning breeze comes in to the parlor and brings in outdoor sounds: birds, a dog barking, the gentle rustle of leaves. Euphonia sits down on the wooden side chair in the parlor and puts her hand to her forehead. Is two bits right? She hadn't known that Esther would ask her right out about the pay, and she ought to know what it should be. But she just said the first thing that came into her head. Pay too much, and the people in Natchez will think she's extravagant, and her free woman housekeeper might put on airs. Already she feels she's made a mistake.

Can Carefree ever really be her home? She'll be living in what used to be Stephanie's house. Cornelius's first wife walked these halls, slept in these beds, probably sat in the parlor just like she's sitting now. And she'll be thinking about the second wife all the time, too, because Thomas will be here. And Hattie didn't just die; she was murdered, and nobody knows who did it. Euphonia didn't feel like explaining that to Esther.

The other wives in Natchez knew Cornelius when he was married to Stephanie. And those women will be slaveholders, every last one of them, and she won't be; that'll make her an oddity. They'll talk.

She spreads her fingers out and looks down at them. They're chapped from that strong soap they use out in the Cocodrie. Starting tonight, or as soon as she can get to a pharmacy, she'll rub them with balm.

She looks around the parlor. This room was beautiful once, although with the shredded furniture and the ruined drapes it's hard to picture how splendid it must have been. The goats spared nothing; they would have even climbed the furniture. She pictures them picking their way along the backs of the sofa and chairs with their dainty hooves. They might even have jumped up to walk along the mantelpiece and nosed the portrait hanging over it. That woman's pretty face may have been kissed by a goat.

It's her house now, and she'll see to it that the room is transformed, not just repaired. There'll be new colors on the walls, new upholstery fabrics, new rugs—everything will be different.

Cornelius comes in and holds out his arms to her. She stands up to kiss him. Her thoughts of faceless strangers and their judgments fade.

"How do you like the parlor?" he asks.

"I'll love it once it's repaired," she says. "And I met Esther. She came in a few minutes ago. We worked out the terms for her pay."

"Good."

"Cornelius, I was wondering; who are the people in these paintings?"

He looks around. "Well, that's Josephine Coqterre, over the fireplace. Stephanie's mother. And the other one's old Emile himself."

"Do you ever feel like they're watching you? I've heard of paintings like that, where the eyes follow you around the room."

He chuckles. "They're not watching us. They're dead." He kisses her. "In a little while let's go get Mal and Thomas. Right now let's go upstairs. Everything else will keep."

As she goes up the stairs ahead of him, she glances back to the parlor, thinking, *Those paintings are going into the attic, first thing.*

CHAPTER TWELVE

OVER THE ALLEY the full moon rises, and lightning bugs are blinking everywhere. Adrien sits up to try to grab one and gives up.

"You need a jar," Jenny says.

He lies down again next to her and fumbles with the bows on the front of her dress. He nuzzles her neck and breathes deeply. She smells of camellias and roses.

"What's that you're wearing?" he asks.

"Perfume," she says. She puts her arms around his neck, her eyes sparkling. "French women wear it, so I knew you'd like it."

"I didn't know you were rich enough to buy something like that."

"I'm rich enough. Cornelius gave me money. I've still got most of it."

The yellow cat minces in to the shack, mewing. Adrien sits up again and reaches for it. It nestles in his arm for a moment and he puts his face down close to the cat's face and talks to the animal in baby talk, French words Jenny doesn't understand. The cat swipes his paw at him and then bounds away, disappearing between the boards of the fence behind the shack.

"Uncle Louis kicked the cat out because he scratched the rug. I'll have to bring him some scraps." He lies down again and puts his arms under his head. "So how are things up at Carefree?"

"I had a big surprise this morning, something Esther told me. I would've told you sooner but you had other things on your mind." She sits up and smooths her skirt down primly. "My old master Cornelius is back, and he's moving into the big house. He inherited it."

"I thought he went to Texas."

"He did. I thought so, anyway. But he must've decided to come back. I don't know why Emile would've left the house to him. He hated him."

"Do you hate him, your old master?"

"Nope, I don't hate him. Esther says he's got a new wife, and I know her. Miss Euphonia McKee from the Cocodrie. She was our neighbor out there."

"My papa's got a new wife too, and she hated me. That's why I came to Natchez."

They watch the moon rise higher, turning silver instead of gold.

"I wish I could be with you all the time," Adrien says.

She leans against his arm. "Don't wish that. Anyway, you can't be. You've got a good room and a job at the church."

He looks away, frowning. "I don't know how much longer I'm gonna do it. Uncle Louis's been good to me, but I think he's starting to depend on me, so I know he'll want to keep me here. I don't think Saint Vigilius will be here much longer, anyway. It's just a few old souls. The diocese might close it down and everyone will go to Saint Mary's. And anyway, people are talking about us. The old gossips are probably jabbering right now." He runs his hand over his hair. "All right, I tell you what we'll do. Uncle Louis wants me to go to New Orleans to help at the cathedral for a couple of weeks, so I'll go. And while I'm there, I'll see if I can find some kind of arrangement for us."

"What do you mean, some kind of arrangement?"

"A job. A place to live."

"A job sweeping the church?"

"No. Something better. There's good money in New Orleans."

"I might not want to go there. The last time I was there I was a slave girl."

"You're not a little slave anymore. And things'll be better for us there, because we can live together and no one will pay us any mind." He pulls her back down to lie beside him.

Jenny puts her hand out toward the sky, pointing at the moon. "If you could touch that big moon, what do you think it is? Something hard, or soft?"

"It's soft. Just a balloon full of air."

"My brother Kofi's probably watchin' this same moon as we are, wherever he's at. He's somewhere out in slave-land, doing some slave-work, and then this moon comes up, and I bet he's lookin' up too. Maybe he remembers me."

"Maybe he's in New Orleans," Adrien says.

"I doubt it."

⁂

The next day Jenny opens the door of her room just as Cornelius and Malachi walk around the corner of the slave house. She blinks. The two men look like ghosts to her. Cornelius looks older, she thinks. It's been half a year since she saw him last, and even in that length of time a person's looks can change. He's browner and his jawline is sharper. And Mal looks smaller than she remembers; his shoulders are more stooped. But it's him, all right.

She runs her hand across her hair and smooths her skirt down. She's wearing a biscuit-colored cotton dress she stitched for Theresa long ago. Little tucks run along the bodice where the buttons are almost gaping open. Her bosom seems to be swelling into the bodice tighter than it was the first time she put this dress on. *Maybe I'm eating too much,* she thinks, although she knows she hasn't been. Or maybe she's just growing. A girl has to grow, but she knows she's not getting any taller.

Both men grin when they see her. "Look what the cat dragged in, Mal. Come out here, Jenny, where we can get a look at you," Cornelius says.

She steps out into the sunlight.

Cornelius walks over to her. "So you decided not to go to Cincinnati," he says. "How'd you end up back here?"

She takes a deep breath. "It's a long story, sir. How'd *you* end up back here?"

He chuckles. "Long story."

"Mine too."

"It's good to see you." He looks at the slave house. "Can you help Mal pick a room out here?"

"Yes sir."

He starts to walk away, and then stops and turns around. "By the way, you still have that freein' paper, the one I gave you?"

She nods.

"I need to get you a better one. A proper one. I'll go to the lawyer and get one written out and file it with the county clerk." He turns to Malachi. "And listen, Mal, my missus doesn't hold with keeping people in bondage, so I'm gonna get a free paper for you, too, and one for Esther. All three of you."

Jenny looks at Mal, who stares at Cornelius as if he hasn't heard properly. So Mal will be free, and this must be the first he's heard of it. She wonders if Cornelius's taken to drinking strong whiskey. Most men wouldn't give away all their slaves; they cost so much in the market. But Mal was a field hand, and there won't be much call for that here.

She turns back to Cornelius. "Could you get a freein' paper for Walker Jackson, too? He's already free, but his paper got stole away from him, and now he's afraid to go anywhere for fear he'll get catched. His old mistress is dead, so he can't go back to her to get another copy."

"Who'd he belong to?"

She shrugs. "Some ole lady."

"Have him come talk to me. I might be able to help. You still got any of that money I gave you?"

"Most of it."

"Keep it in a safe place, will you? And don't tell anyone you've got it."

"I keep it in a hidey hole."

He looks at the open door behind her. "That your room?"

"Yes, sir. This one right here. Esther's down at the other end, and Walker's upstairs, on top of Esther. I guess Mal could take any other room he wants."

Mal stands with his hat in his hand. He's still barefooted, Jenny notices.

Cornelius says, "Mal, maybe you'd like an upstairs room. That way it'd be men upstairs, women downstairs."

Mal steps back and looks at the front of the building. He says in a hoarse voice. "No, sir. I'd rather be downstairs. Maybe in that room next to Jenny, like we was out on the Cocodrie. I don't want to go up and down them stairs all the time. My knee's so stiff."

"Well, you pick the one you want, and put your things in it. I've got to go get Miss Euphonia and Thomas settled in the big house."

As she watches Cornelius walk away, Jenny thinks, *owning something as big as this house changes a person, the way they look, the way they talk.* When they all worked in the cottonfield, you couldn't tell much difference between him and them, when the sweat was running down his face just like it was theirs. And Miss Hattie always screeching about how Thomas cried too much, and how she had to work too hard. Cornelius had trouble then, with his farm and his wife.

But now he's got a new wife, and Miss Phony's gonna be a whole different kind of wife than either Stephanie or Hattie. And Cornelius'll be different now. He'll wear his big hat and a string tie, and people'll tip their hat to him when he rides down the street.

"Come on, Mal, let's pick you a room," Jenny says, and she opens the door to the room next to Esther's. "This is the best one. It's closest to the kitchen in case you want something to eat. Or if you get cold in the winter, you'll be close to the fireplace." They go inside. "Or there's that other one, next to me, but you don't want to be close to me. I might be too noisy."

"What kind of noise would you make, gal?"

She shrugs. "I snore pretty good. I remember you do too." She goes to the door and looks out to see if Cornelius has gone inside the big house. "Mal, you're gonna be free!" she whispers, leaning close to him.

"I can't imagine it," Mal mumbles. "If I knew Cornelius to be a hard drinkin' man, I'd 'a thought his brain done gone pickled. And old as I am. Just to think."

"Don't worry," Jenny says. "You're gonna be right here by me. He ain't gonna put you out."

"If he did, I sure couldn't outrun any slave-catchers, old as I am," he mumbles.

She reaches over and puts her arm around him, realizing he's crying. She pats his back gently as she would an infant. Because in a way that's what he is, she thinks. An old old man, new in freedom.

Later that night, Esther walks in to Jenny's room and sits on the side of her bed. "Jenny, did you want somethin' to eat?"

Jenny, nearly asleep, opens her eyes. Esther's taken her apron off, so she must be finished in the kitchen for the day. She shakes her head. "I ain't hungry."

Esther stands up. "Well, if you want to eat, you need to keep yourself here when its mealtime. I can't keep the food for you all the time."

"I know."

"You keepin' company with some boy, I heard. Is that why you ain't here when we eat?"

She nods. "I guess so. His name is Adrien. But don't worry. I'm gonna quit keepin' company with him, 'cause he wants to go live in New Orleans, and I ain't sure I want t' go there."

"Who is he?"

"He lives at Saint Vigilius. He's French."

"That don't tell me much. There's lots of French people here."

"Well, he ain't completely French. He comes from France, but before that he came from Martinique. He's a Creole."

"And why would y'all want to go down to New Orleans, exactly?"

"He wants to find some work down there. Excuse me. I'm gonna throw up now."

Esther grabs the bucket by the door and hands it to her. Jenny bends over, retching loudly. "You havin' a baby, ain't ya?" Esther says in a low voice after Jenny wipes her mouth on a towel.

Jenny looks up. "What?"

"That's why you throwin'up."

"It is?"

"Yes, ma'am. I seen it too many times, and been through it myself. Ain't you noticed anything about yourself? When's the last time you had your bleedin'?"

Jenny looks around the shadowy room. "I don't remember."

"Girl, you need to start keepin' a record of that. If you been doin' what I think you been doin' with this Adrien, that's what it is. You got to think about it."

Jenny reaches for Esther's candle and lights the stub of a candle on the table beside her bed. "Well, what if I am? Adrien won't mind. He'll probably like it."

"He might or he might not." Esther sighs.

When Jenny doesn't say anything else, Esther gets up and goes out, shaking her her head. Jenny gets up and walks over to the shelf and picks up her mirror. She stares at her reflection. A baby? What would that be like, to have one? Can she take care of one?

But she could learn how to do it. She saw how Hattie learned it with Thomas. If Hattie could learn it, she could too.

When Adrien comes back from New Orleans late on a Friday evening, Jenny, who's come to the alley every day for the past five days in case he returns, is waiting for him. When she sees him striding down the alley in the twilight, she stands up, holding her arms out to him.

He kisses her. "I found us a place in New Orleans," he says. "One of the women who cleans the cathedral had it. She said I could rent it for a year, so I gave her forty dollars for the whole year. It cleaned me out. How much money do you have?"

"A lot. I counted it this morning. Two hundred and eighty one dollars. "

"That'll be enough for us to live on. I wrote down the address." He unfolds a piece of paper. "Corner of Rue Ste. Anne and Burgundy, one door down."

She steps away from him. "I don't think I want to go," she says. "If you leave, you won't have a job here, and your uncle will get another janitor."

He scowls. "I'll be a disappointment to him, just like I am to my Papa. But Papa has a new wife, and a new baby, my half-brother Philippe. He'll be the one who inherits the estate, not me, because my mother was a slave. Maybe Philippe won't be a disappointment to Papa." The bitter look on his face changes to a wide smile. "In New Orleans we can live as man and wife, out in the open."

I need to tell him about the baby, she thinks. But she says, "We're not man and wife."

"I know. Let's get married." He pulls her toward the end of the alley.

"We can't get married, just like that."

"Yes, we can. Come with me." He leads her around to the darkened front of Saint Vigilius. As they walk up to the church the door opens and an old woman leaning on a cane comes out. She glances at them but says nothing. After she hobbles away down the street, Adrien pulls Jenny up the steps and they slip into the church. No one is inside; a few candles flicker around the walls. The altar is too far away for Jenny to see it clearly.

"I'll marry us," he says.

"You can't do that. You're not a priest."

But he takes her hand and leads her up to the darkened altar. Statues of saints look down from the walls. Holding both her hands, he begins to say some words she can't understand, but she knows when he says "Jenny" that as far as he's concerned some kind of marriage is being made.

Then he says, in English, "It's not legal exactly." He kisses her. "But we can't help that. It'll be legal for us. Now you'll be Jenny Jean-Pierre."

"Mumbo-jumbo words don't mean you're married," she says, pulling her hands away. "I don't want t' be married anyway."

Father Maercru waits in the shadows at the street corner near the church. He intended to go in and check for any candles that might have tipped out of their bases—he's always feared fire in the wooden church building—but when he sees Adrien and Jenny go into the church, he waits.

He knew his nephew was going to be trouble, and it wouldn't be long coming. He could tell from the first day he met the man. And Adrien fulfilled his expectations, sneaking out of his room most nights, headed for Natchez-Under-the-Hill, probably, and finding who-knows-what trouble down there. Adrien is full of questions, and he has a restless look which in a young man always brings trouble. He's glad he's thought to keep the church offering box locked away. And here Adrien is tonight, right in front of him, sneaking up the steps into the church with his girl, and Louis doubts they're going in to pray. He's seen the way they giggle together like schoolkids on Sunday mornings.

He waits in the shadows until Adrien and the girl come out of the church and walk down the street the other way. He's decided the best thing he can do for his nephew is to make the young man's departure quick and painless. He's been a priest for so many years, and he knows there's a rhythm to these things. After a while the parishioners won't remember the young man who came from France and was here for a few weeks, this spring of 1841. He likes Adrien, and what Adrien wants, Maercru wants for him. It wouldn't be the first time he's had to smooth the rails so a wayward young man can find a way out.

CHAPTER THIRTEEN

BY EARLY JULY a dry spell has settled over Natchez. The town swelters and even the birds seem to be calling for rain. Jenny walks slowly as she approaches the place where the alley turns off to the left. Of course Adrien will be waiting for her, as he is every day, but the giddy anticipation she used to feel for him has evaporated into the shimmering summer air. It started to go the night he took her into the church and said some mumbo-jumbo words, and then told her to give up her name for his. He's always had his name, she thinks; he was born with it. He doesn't know what it means to her just to have a last name. Adrien has claimed her; he thinks she's his and his alone. But she knows she'll never call herself Jenny Jean-Pierre. She's been Jenny Cornelius since she first got her freeing paper, that scribbly one, and before that, she was Jenny no-name. But now Jenny Cornelius is her name; she likes it, and she can't be Jean-Pierre just because Adrien pretended to marry her.

"Where've you been?" Adrien asks as she turns into the alley. "I bought us tickets for Tuesday on the *Arab.*" He holds the tickets out to show her.

She glances at them. "Did I say I wanted to go to New Orleans with you?"

"You didn't say you wouldn't. And I told you, I've already rented a place for us. I gave the woman my money."

"Tell her you want it back. I probably wouldn't like it."

For the first time she thinks he looks distressed. She puts her hands on her stomach, which is rumbling.

"What kind of place is it?"

"It's a house. Not far from the French market."

Adrien looks so young, she thinks. She thought he looked so manly when she first met him, but aren't his features really just a little coarse? He's seeing only the good things that will happen for them. The idea of New Orleans has grown so big for him that it erases the shack, the alley, and all of Natchez. He has it all worked out, and it's pulling him to a future he can see better than she can. She takes the tickets from him and studies them, then hands the flimsy papers back to him.

Later, as she walks back up the hill to Carefree, she thinks about New Orleans. She remembers a city of low buildings going out in all directions, a triple-spired cathedral standing at the head of a square, and boats big and small nosing in at the dock, like piglets sucking at a sow. She saw it as a child in a slave coffle. But Adrien can't see it the way she did because he's never been a slave.

And if she goes to New Orleans, Adrien will see that she has what she needs. It's been at least four months since she's had her bleeding, so there's no denying what's happening inside her body.

Right now what she needs is to lie down. Her stomach feels jumpy again. When she gets back to Carefree she's glad she doesn't run into Mal or anybody else. She lies down on her bed and sleeps.

A light knock on her door wakes her up. Esther is standing there holding a candle.

"Jenny, Master Cornelius wants to know if you'd like to take over Thomas as a nursemaid. I ain't up to a child that age, and there ain't nobody else here who can do it."

Jenny forces herself to sit up. "Tell Cornelius thank you very much, but I can't do it. I ain't sure, but I might be going to New Orleans next week. It's Adrien's idea."

"You told him about the baby?"

"Not yet."

"If you don't tell him pretty quick, he's gonna notice it." She turns to go, but then stops. "Listen, Jenny, if your man wants to go to New Orleans, you better plan to go with him. You're havin' a baby, so there's no way you should stay. If you don't go, he'll get himself another girl. I didn't go with Reynard Fanning, Helene's papa, when he wanted to head up to Tupelo, and that was the last I ever saw of him. 'Course I couldn't go unless Master Emile gave me permission, which he might not have. But you're free, so you got no excuse."

"It just don't feel right, goin' down there."

"Well, there's somethin' else you ain't thinkin' about. You got in some trouble in Vidalia. That sheriff might find out where you're at and come over here and nab you. But he wouldn't find you down in New Orleans."

"I don't have my good freein' paper yet."

"Cornelius'll see to that. You think this over." She goes out the door.

A girl has got to be pushed sometimes, Esther thinks. She remembers how Lucy Ida told her to get Stephanie married, and she did. Lucy told her she wouldn't have to work so hard if Stephanie moved away, and that was so. And right now she's worn down from watching Thomas night after night. A two-year-old's too much for a woman her age. If Jenny leaves, she won't have to concern herself with whether the girl's eaten supper, or if she's spending too much time out in town. No, Jenny has to go.

147

Jenny lies down again. Then another light tap at the door rouses her. She gets up and pulls the door open. Cornelius is standing there.

"Jenny? Tomorrow morning, let's go get you a proper freein' paper. We'll leave at nine o'clock."

"Thank you, sir!" She brushes the bleariness out of her eyes.

After a minute he says, "Esther says you're leaving us next week. Are you sure that's a good idea?"

She shrugs. "I don't know."

"You be careful," he says. He stands for another moment, then he turns away. Jenny watches his lantern bob up the brick walk and into the big house. Her stomach roils again.

I've got to go.

Walker Jackson comes up to the gallery where Cornelius is sitting with Euphonia. Thomas teeters at the top of the steps, and Walker steps wide around him, his arms out for balance. He whips off his hat and puts his other hand out to keep the boy from toppling down the steps.

"Good evening, sir, Missus." He smiles. "First off, I thank you for giving me accommodations here at your house." He looks first at Cornelius, then at Euphonia.

Euphonia stares at him, and then she slaps at a mosquito. Her mouth twists and he thinks she's about to giggle. "I hear you're the Mayor of Natchez," she says.

He steps to one side, not sure if she's making fun of him or not. You can't really figure out white ladies, he thinks. Best to steer clear of them is what he's learned.

He clears his throat. "Well, I ain't really the mayor, ma'am. I just call myself that for the free people here, the ones that used to be slaves. That's what I come here to talk to y'all about."

Cornelius, who's been watching Thomas, looks around.

"The thing is, sir, ma'am, I lost my freein' paper. It was stole from me by a man named Rufus Hall, who wanted to sell me back into slavery. I tried to show him my freein' paper; it had a seal and everything, but he just grabbed it and threw it down on the ground and stomped on it. Then he chained me up. But I got free."

Euphonia's eyes are shining and she doesn't giggle after all. "Well, Walker, getting free—that was a stroke of luck, I'd say."

"Yes, ma'am, it most certainly was. But what I need to ask you, sir and ma'am, is if you can help me get another freein' paper. My old mistress, Missus Annie Blanchard, died about three years ago. She was a good ole woman, and she let me buy myself out. But I just don't feel safe goin' around without my paper."

"Of course you don't," Euphonia says.

"I'd have to go to the county clerk," Cornelius says. "We can go tomorrow. I'm taking Jenny and Malachi and Esther to the lawyer tomorrow for their papers. Miz Blanchard must've had your papers filed at the county if she lived in Natchez."

"Yes sir, she lived right here in Adams County," Walker says.

"So the clerk should still have your record. You come with us tomorrow and I'll see about getting you a copy. We're going at nine o'clock. Where'd you live before you moved in here?"

"I had a place on the alley behind the Saint Vigilius church. It was just a shack, really. It's still there. But I'm most appreciative of havin' a solid room to live in, like I have here."

"How do you make your living?" Euphonia asks.

"Oh, I do odd jobs. There's people in town that know me. And Esther gives me handyman things to do around the place. She cooks good, Esther does. If you let me stay on, ma'am, I'd like to keep on helpin' her out. Bein' a small person, I don't eat a whole lot."

"You can stay," Cornelius says. "Malachi's moved in out there too."

"Yes sir, I've met him. The old slave house is fillin' right up. It'll be nice to have some company. It do get kind of lonesome when you all by yourself."

Euphonia walks to the door, giving up on the mosquito. She looks back at Walker. "Do you know any woman who wants to work? We're lookin' for someone to watch that boy there."

"I can think of one or two who might take it on," Walker says. "I'll ask around."

Euphonia goes into the parlor and lights the lamps. Then Cornelius comes in with Thomas and sits on the rocking chair with the boy on his lap.

From where Euphonia sits, the gilt mirror on the side wall reflects the whole room. *Look at us,* she thinks. *Cornelius and I are just an ordinary couple, not young, and we look like we've been married for a long time.* Cornelius stoops a little now when he walks. And she's a tall plain woman in a brown dress that's too warm for this summer evening. Earlier today she unlocked Sophronia's chiffarobe and took out three dresses. They don't fit her well, but at least they're well-made. Crepe, silk, and shantung were what that long-ago woman wore, while she herself, out in the Cocodrie, was wearing homemade calico dresses and shawls knitted with yarn raveled out of earlier shawls, caps, and bed throws.

She gets up and walks over to the china hutch and pulls the glass door open. "Look at all this china. I noticed it earlier today. Isn't it pretty, how each cup is painted?" She takes a cup over for Cornelius to admire, but Thomas reaches out to grab it, so she sets it on the mantel and goes back and takes out another one from the hutch. "But look, they don't all match. I think this one must be a replacement. I guess I'm a replacement, too. For Hattie and Stephanie."

"You're not a replacement," he says. "I'd better go see if Esther's ready to take Thomas upstairs. He's getting tired."

After he goes out with Thomas, she takes his place on the rocking chair and sits with her hands folded in her lap. It's plain that Cornelius will be gone much of the time. The plantation in Rapides Parish, a place she can't even picture, with its hundred slaves and its vast fields of cane—that will provide their income, and it has to be managed. And somehow he has to free the slaves there and let them work for wages.

But if she has to be alone here in Natchez, it's up to her to make her place, and she wants to do it in her own clothes, not in the dresses of some woman long dead. She brushes her hands over her rustling skirt.

She should have said more to Cornelius about the house, she thinks. He's proud that it's their home. It's beautiful, with its lofty ceilings, and Stephanie must have loved it here. She remembers Stephanie, but Cornelius's first wife hardly said a word to her during the two years she lived in the Cocodrie. Euphonia knew her as just a plump pretty woman with a worried expression. But if Stephanie were still alive, Euphonia wouldn't now be sitting in the parlor at Carefree.

Everybody always wants something, she thinks. This is her home, but she wants new furniture, so she can make it a warm and welcoming home for Cornelius, and because she'll be entertaining well-bred women married to ambitious men. And what will Cornelius want? He'll be at the top of society here. His days will be filled with business and with traveling back and forth to Rapides Parish, where a hundred slaves are waiting to be freed.

And her days will be filled with—what? They might have a child, but she thinks that's unlikely, given how seldom her monthlies appear. Some years they show up only once or twice. Thomas will be Cornelius's only son. As he's gotten a little older, he looks more and more like Hattie with his upturned nose and his hazel eyes, but his red hair comes from Cornelius. Euphonia never drew close to Hattie, knowing that rough country girl was a world away from herself. Now she'll be living in Stephanie's house, with Hattie's son. The ghosts of those earlier women will hover in the air like the motes that she sees floating in the air, little bits of horsehair yanked out from the disemboweled furniture.

In the morning Walker comes into the kitchen where Esther and Malachi are. "Today's the day," he says. "We all gonna have our papers. Ain't that somethin'?" He sits down and takes a packet of tobacco from his shirt pocket so he can roll a cigarette.

"I'm gonna need some shoes," Malachi says. "I can't go into some lawyer's office with my toes hangin' loose."

"You're right," Walker says, looking down at his own polished shoes. He got them from Mrs. Anna Crawford over on Oak Street, whose boy Michael is almost a grown man now, but back when he was twelve Michael wore these shoes. Good thing Miss Anna finally decided to clean out her closet. "Esther, I bet you can help him out with that," he says.

"I can," Esther says. "Let me see what's in Emile's old closet."

Mal sits at the table with Walker. A few minutes later Esther comes back carrying a pair of men's dress shoes and with a black jacket folded over her arm.

"Let's try these," she says. "I was just guessin' about the size."

Mal stands up and puts the jacket on over his shirt. "That fits good," Walker says. Then Mal puts the shoes on. When he picks up his foot, the shoe slips off.

"You gonna need socks, obviously," Walker says.

"I'll go find some," Esther says. In a few minutes she's back with a pair of bulky gray socks. "I knitted these myself, if I'm rememberin' right."

Mal pulls on the socks and then tries the shoes again. This time they stay on.

"I'd say they're still a little big," Walker says, "but we ain't got too many choices." Mal stands up and tries to walk across the kitchen, clumping the shoes down on the flagstone floor.

"Try to give it a little more swing," Walker says. "Your feet ain't locked in concrete."

"You'll get the hang of it," Esther says. "Those were the widest ones in the closet, and I could see you got wide feet. Do they hurt?"

"No, they don't hurt exactly," Mal says. "It's just that I ain't used to 'em."

"Keep wearin' 'em," Walker says. "It'll seem natural after awhile."

"I found me a dress that'll kind of fit," Esther says. "Between Sophronia's chiffarobe and Emile's closet, Malachi and me can look mighty presentable today."

Back in her own room a few minutes later, Esther dresses for the lawyer's office. Looking in her mirror, she notices how different she looks from the woman who's always spent her days in a housedress, her hair tied up in a tignon. When has she ever looked this fine? she thinks. Sophronia probably never thought Esther would be wearing one of her dresses.

Her eyes look tired, though. Thomas was a restless boy most of the night, wanting his daddy, and Esther spent half the night talking to him, trying to settle him. Finally he just got so tired he dropped off to sleep, but he woke up early and Esther was relieved when she heard Euphonia going down the stairs before sun-up. She took the boy down to the dining room and handed him to his stepmamma.

She goes back to the kitchen. Malachi looks dignified in Emile's jacket, Esther thinks; he gives her a shy smile, which she returns. And of course Walker's there wearing an expensive-looking green jacket and brown creased trousers, and his shoes are shined; she's not as impressed with this, since Walker's always been a sharp dresser. Then Jenny shows up wearing a brown checkedy dress that once belonged to Helene.

The four of them walk around the house to the front gallery and stand on the steps, waiting for Cornelius. Esther's never been to a lawyer's office before, and she's not sure what to expect. It's a pleasant cool morning, the birds chirping in the trees, the sun sweeping shadows through the streamers of moss on the old trees. The sky's as blue as she's ever seen it.

Cornelius opens the front door. "It's a splendid morning," he says.

"It is, sir," Walker says. "When you ready to go to the lawyer, you just let us know. Meantime, we'll just be waiting out here."

Cornelius goes back inside and Esther can picture him sitting at the table with Phony, with Thomas on his knee. But she smiles at the thought; it's obvious he won't be able to eat a proper meal knowing there's four people standing on the gallery waiting for him. She's not surprised when he comes out a few minutes later and motions them to follow him. They go out to the stable to get the carriage, and a few minutes later they're riding down Wall Street, Malachi sitting next to Cornelius and Walker in back between the two women.

People stare at the buggy as they rumble along. It's probably because Cornelius is new in town, Esther thinks; or because Jenny looks so pretty, sitting so straight and prim next to Walker. When Cornelius pulls the buggy to a stop in front of the lawyer's office, Esther takes a deep breath.

"Ain't this is a fine day," Walker says, as he reaches up to help Jenny down, and she flashes her light-up-the-world smile at him. Then they all walk up the path to the front door of the law office, Cornelius first, then Walker, who marches to keep up with Cornelius. Then Jenny. Esther and Mal are last.

The finest day I ever had, Esther thinks. *But I won't believe it 'til I have that paper in my hand.*

CHAPTER FOURTEEN

BUT NO MATTER HOW *bright the day is outside, a lawyer could probably think of a way to darken it,* Esther thinks as John Landerson comes out of his back office. *The law's never been a friend to people like us.* And for a minute she's pretty sure the way Landerson is gonna put an end to all this happiness is with the scowl on his face. He looks surprised to see them.

Master John Landerson is such a refined man, brighter than the shine on Walker's shoes. Every word he says, every gesture, tells the world this is a man born to society. His suit, his well-cut hair, the way the paneling on his office wall gleams in the morning sunlight: there isn't anything about John Landerson III that's rough, or troubled. He's as polished as the silver candlesticks that sit on the French tables at Carefree, and he's as far from herself and Walker and Malachi and Jenny as it's possible to be.

Landerson shakes hands with Cornelius and motions him into the back office. The door to the office isn't fully closed, and when Esther sits down in the straight chair next to the door, she can hear the men talking.

"And what is it I may help you with today?" John asks.

"I've decided to put my people free," Cornelius says. "Those three."

Esther hears a rustle of papers. "That's most unusual," John says.

"It is. But it's an old promise I made to my mother. And Mrs. Carson is also most insistent we not own slaves."

"Have you considered—it's hard to run a big place with no slaves?" John asks.

When Cornelius doesn't answer, he goes on, "Well, I've had a few masters free their slaves before, but usually it's to free their slave children, or their children's mother. That's not the case here?"

"No."

"You know you'll have to pay a bond for each one of them. And see to it they leave the state within a year. That's the law now."

"I know."

"Well, bring 'em on," John says, and Cornelius comes to the door and motions to them. They file into the back room and stand along the wall.

John sits at his desk and opens the desk drawer, taking out a pencil and some sheets of paper; then he sharpens the pencil with his knife, not looking at Cornelius, Esther notices.

"Who first?" he asks.

"Jenny," Cornelius says. "Her last name's Cornelius." Jenny steps forward to stand in front of the desk.

"What's her age?" John asks.

"Seventeen, I think," Cornelius says, looking at her, and she doesn't contradict him.

"And the date purchased?"

Cornelius tells him, and John jots it down. Then he continues writing, his pencil making a soft shushing sound across the paper.

He hands the paper to Cornelius, who reads it in a quiet voice, for Jenny's benefit: "I Cornelius Carson, being the legal owner of a certain slave named Jenny Cornelius, now about seventeen years of age, which slave I purchased on the seventh of June, in the year of our Lord one thousand eight hundred thirty-three, do manumit and set free and forever release the said Jenny Cornelius from all slavery, and do set her at liberty that she may go free the same as if she had been born free. Done this 15th day of June in the year of our Lord one thousand eight hundred and forty-one. Signed and delivered Cornelius Carson…"

Cornelius looks over at Jenny. "That sounds better than the paper I gave you before, doesn't it, Jenny? Proves I could never be a lawyer."

"Yes sir." She grins and steps back against the wall.

Then Malachi: John writes and then reads aloud, "I Cornelius Carson, being the legal owner of a slave named Malachi—Cornelius?"

Cornelius nods, but Malachi says, "Sir, I think I'm Carson. Same as Master Cornelius."

"All right. Malachi Carson." Mal shuffles his feet at the sound of his name.

"Age?"

"How old are you, Mal?" Cornelius asks.

"I don't know, sir. I lost count."

"He's about a hundred," Jenny pipes up. Esther motions her to be quiet.

"He ain't a hundred," Cornelius says. "Mal, let's make a guess. I'd say you might be sixty."

"Yes sir, if that's what you say," Mal says. The lawyer writes again.

Waiting for her turn, Esther smooths the fabric of her skirt over her legs. Her knees want to jiggle, but she knows that wouldn't be proper. Once her knees are steady, she folds her hands over her purse. The veins on the back of her hands criss-cross each other like ropes. When Cornelius motions to her, she stands up. The lawyer glances up at her and begins to write. After a moment he says, "Esther—Carson?"

"Yes," Cornelius says.

"Sir, I believe I'm Coqterre," Esther says.

Cornelius looks at her. *Why would you want to call yourself Coqterre, after all Emile did to you?*

"It's how I've always thought of myself," she says.

The lawyer writes. Cornelius gives her age as fifty, then turns to her with a questioning look. She nods. When he's finished writing, John reads out loud, "I Cornelius Carson, being the legal owner of a certain slave woman named Esther Coqterre"—

"—age now about—we said fifty." He looks up. When she doesn't say different, he continues. "Fifty years old, which slave I inherited as part of the estate of Emile Coqterre, Esquire, of Natchez, Adams County, Mississippi, do manumit and set free and forever release the said Esther Coqterre from all slavery, and do set her at liberty that she may go free the same as if she had been born free. This fifteenth day of June in the year of our Lord one thousand eight hundred and forty-one. Signed and delivered..."

Esther sees the room brighten, as if the sun has moved out from behind a cloud. Her freeing paper is written, and she'll carry it with her forever. If she lives to be ninety-two, like Lucy Ida was when she passed, she'll still be carrying it everywhere. And all these years in between she'll be free.

When Cornelius mentions Walker's predicament, John waves his hand as if it's of no concern. "Was it here in Adams County?" John asks Walker.

"Yes sir," Walker says. "It was Missus Alcie Blanchard."

"You can ask at the clerk's office," John says to Cornelius. "You'll have to testify to his good character. Let me get my secretary in here to make the true copies."

The secretary comes in and sits down at a small desk near the window. John hands him the penciled documents. He takes three sheets of heavy paper from the drawer, dips his pen in the inkwell, and begins to write.

Esther stands up and goes over to stand in front of the man's desk, watching every stroke he makes. Once or twice he looks up to glare at her.

"You're in the light," he says finally, waving his hand. His fingers, long and bony, flutter. "Get back."

She steps back a step but still stands close, leaning forward to follow his pen as it scrapes across the paper.

After he finishes each document, he blots it and hands it to John, who reads it over, comparing every line to the originals. John passes the documents to Cornelius, who signs them.

"So you're all free," Cornelius says as they file out of the office. "Or you will be, as soon as we get these papers to the courthouse." He hands the three former slaves their freeing papers.

Esther lets Malachi shuffle out ahead of her. He hasn't mastered the shoes, she notices. He clumps along awkwardly, but at least he's had the dignity of wearing shoes to this lawyer's office. Jenny bounces down the steps as if she doesn't have a care in the world, holding her paper by the tips of her fingers.

Cornelius says to Jenny, "Don't lose that."

Walker's looking springy too. He grins up at Esther as he goes past.

Esther stands in the sunlight on the step and looks down at her paper. It's a proper one, written by that rude man who picked up the quill pen like he's probably picked it up a thousand times before. Who's probably written all kinds of things, important and not important, right there at that desk. But she knows he's never written anything as important as this.

That afternoon when Adrien sees Jenny coming down the alley, he drops his cigarette and grinds it out with his shoe. "Where've you been?"

She dances over to him, her heels clicking together, and makes a little jig of the distance between them. She puts her arms around his neck. "I got my freein' paper." She flips open the buttons of her bodice and pulls out the paper to show him, moving it side to side in a tease.

He takes it from her and reads it over. "I thought you were free already."

"I was, but my old paper wasn't nothing but a scribble. This one's filed at the county. It says I'm free the same as if I was born free." She folds the paper and starts to button it back into her bodice, but Adrien slips his hand over hers and pulls her close.

"Are you all set to go to New Orleans?"

She pulls away from him. "I don't want to go, I said." She looks up and down the alley. "Adrien, why don't you just come live with me at Carefree? I've got a room there. Cornelius won't tell us no."

"Because I can't live with all those people around, watching me. And I already paid the rent on the house for a year. No. We're going. I can get a better job, and we can be together all the time."

Her stomach unsettles itself and she runs to the fence and throws up.

"What is wrong with you?" he asks. "Are you sick?"

She shakes her head and wipes her mouth with a handkerchief. She starts to tell him her secret, but then he says, "You better go get packed. We're goin' tomorrow."

So she turns and hurries out of the alley and up the road toward Carefree.

By the next evening she has her small satchel packed, and she almost changes her mind. She pictures herself slipping out of her room in the darkness tomorrow morning and walking down to Under-the-Hill. The *Arab* will be waiting, hooting its whistle, and Adrien will come toward her out of the crowd, and she'll tell him she's not going, and that's final. He'll board the boat and go down to New Orleans on his own.

But she knows that door has closed. She'll go.

She decides to wait until Cornelius and Euphonia finish their dinner before she goes into the big house. It's almost dark when she walks into the parlor where Cornelius is sitting alone reading a newspaper. A woman Jenny doesn't know is leading Thomas up the stairs, and the boy's toy horse and wagon are upended on the rug. Jenny picks up the toys and sets them on the side table.

"We've hired Miss Coella Taylor to watch Thomas," Cornelius says in response to Jenny's questioning expression. "And I've hired Mr. Elliott Badeau to oversee the whole place when I'm out of town. Esther'll still be the main one doing the cooking and helping Miss Phony. But Mister Elliott'll be here to oversee everything else."

Walker ain't gonna like answering to this Mister Elliott, Jenny thinks.

"I've come to tell you I'm leavin' tomorrow," she says. "I've got a steamboat ticket to go to New Orleans. And I thank you for giving me my freein' paper. If you hadn't done that, I couldn't go."

Cornelius folds his newspaper and stares at her. "You're not going by yourself, surely."

"No sir, I ain't. Adrien Jean-Pierre is going with me."

"Who's he?"

She wants to say, "My husband," but the words catch on her tongue. She knows she's not really married, no matter what Adrien says.

So she says, "I married him," thinking it's a little bit true, and not quite the same as calling Adrien her "husband." It's a way to half-tell it, and she knows if Cornelius thinks she's married he won't object to her going. "So I'll be clearing out of my room. Maybe somebody else can use it."

He looks past her through the window, where the last of the day's light shines weakly over the Natchez skyline. "I'm headed out to Bayou Boeuf soon," he says. "I wish I didn't have to go, but I've got a place there

I need to see about. Esther will miss you, Jenny. We all will. You be careful down there."

"Yes sir. You be careful, too."

"You know if you ever need to come back," he begins, but then he lets the words hang unfinished.

"Yes sir." She turns and goes out the back door, almost skipping as she goes down the steps. *That was easy*, she thinks. Going to New Orleans might be the best thing after all. She feels lighter and really free for the first time since Cornelius gave her the proper freeing paper. She's free of Carefree, free of everybody in it. The old house is changed, and it's all new people living here. And she's got her freeing paper, and she's got money. And sort of a husband, too.

Father Maercru watches his nephew walk past the window toward his room. Adrien's given up his Frenchified clothing, the vest and jacket he wore back in the spring, and now he wears jean trousers and an open cotton shirt like a frontiersman. There's no rule against it; it's summer, it's hot. But it makes him look like any roustabout from Under-The-Hill, Maercru thinks. He himself favors formal clothing even when it's not Sunday. It doesn't hurt to hint at one's status, and he hopes that's not sinful pride; it just seems to smooth things along. And besides, his parishioners expect it from a priest. But it's been clear to him from the start that Adrien wouldn't be satisfied for long with a job cleaning the church building.

And the girl. Maercru has seen her sitting in the gallery during mass, and he's seen how Adrien looks up at her whenever he thinks he can without attracting notice. She's a striking sight, that young woman, with her coal-black skin, her graceful long neck, her full lips. She's much darker than the honey-colored people who seem to be all around here. For himself, he guards against what's befallen Adrien. His vows are sacred to him, even though he broke them once. That was long ago; her name was Cecilia, and he never thinks of her. Won't let himself think. He's getting old now; he doesn't need the stress of trying to relive a wayward affair.

He finishes his wine and goes into his bedroom and kneels by the bed. But instead of praying, he thinks about Adrien. He envies his nephew, he can't deny it—envies him his youth, his beauty, his entitlements. A young man has those things, even though they're vanities, and fleeting. But a man of sixty, swelling in his legs and heavy in his belly, his joys have to be the glass of wine, the warm fire, the bed. If Adrien leaves, and Maercru is sure he will, he'll write to his brother and make excuses for the boy. It will be his final gift to Adrien, perhaps.

The thought almost satisfies him, but not quite. He hates to lose the yellow Creole, with his quick smile, his handsome features, his combed-back thick hair. And his curiosity about the world, and the way he looks to Maercru for instruction. Some young men have it in their heads to be headstrong, insubordinate, not really in need of instruction. But Adrien's willing to sit at the feet of an older, wiser man, as long as it's a short lesson and doesn't tax his restless mind too much. He's seen so much of the world for one so young, travelling from Martinique to France and now here to what used to be called New France. And if his head's been turned by a pretty girl, as a young man's head will always be, it will probably pass soon enough, and Adrien will be off on another adventure.

CHAPTER FIFTEEN

AT DAWN NATCHEZ-UNDER-THE-HILL is crawling with weary flatboatmen slouching back to their boats. A small steamboat is docked there too. Its white flag, snapping in the breeze, is painted with the image of a turbaned Bedouin, so Jenny knows this must be the *Arab*.

It's a newer-looking boat than the *John Jay*, but much smaller. And it's a side-wheeler. Barrels, trunks, and bales of cotton are stacked in the corners of the lower deck. Later in the summer, the whole deck will be packed with cotton bales, she knows. She waits for Adrien, thinking he's late; she halfway hopes he's changed his mind. But then he strides toward her out of the crowd, grinning. He takes her hand, and when the steamer whistles blows, he takes her arm and they walk up the gangplank. With the Bedouin fluttering over their heads, they climb the steps to the upper deck.

The river smells of fish and sawed lumber and cottonseed meal. And so it's goodbye to Natchez, Jenny thinks, but down here at the dock you can't see much of the city. She wonders what Esther's doing, back at Carefree. She's probably setting her big black pot over the fire, and Walker will be coming in to get his coffee. He might already be sitting in the chair she usually sits in, cupping his hand around his coffee cup like he does, and tapping his cigarette ashes into the saucer. Esther'll scold him for that. Goodbye to all of them—Cornelius and Euphonia and Malachi too.

167

Adrien paces up and down the deck; and when the whistles hoots, he leans over the rail to watch the boatmen throw the ropes off. Only a few passengers get on, so Jenny sits down in one of the chairs on the foredeck, thinking she'll be able to stay there for a while, unless she's told to move off for some white lady. The whistle hoots one last time and the engines rumble. The *Arab* pulls out into the middle of the river, gliding south under a pearly sky.

The banks of the river are green walls of trees, and the river is a gray-brown curling ribbon—just the color of Adrien's eyes, she thinks. Plantation houses begin to appear out of the quiet deep forest like white ghosts, one after the other. Avenues of trees run from the riverbank up to the houses. She's not surprised that no one hails the boat from any of these big houses. The *Arab* is just a dinky sidewheeler, a puny river runner, and anyone traveling from those splendid houses would probably wait for a better boat.

When she looks around for Adrien, she sees that he's perched himself by the engine room window, his arm resting on the sill, as he talks with the captain. He's looking straight ahead at the river, just as the captain is. *Adrien would like to have that man's job,* she thinks.

The boat doesn't stop until they reach Bayou Sara, where more passengers get on. Jenny stands up, knowing she won't be able to keep her chair. When the boat pulls out again into the river, the woods on both sides grow jungly. Vines hang down from the trees and palmettos are thick around the trunks of the trees. Herons glide over the river and then drop down to stand unmoving near the shore.

The *Arab* isn't alone on the river; flatboats are going down the river with them, but the steamer is faster than they are, with its powerful engines. Most of the flatboatmen are lolling atop the floating barges, since it only takes one man to handle the rudder. The boatmen look like backwoodsmen from the north, she thinks. Adrien would like that life too. But he's not free like those boatmen are; he has a child coming. And he's married, sort of.

The boat rumbles on to Baton Rouge, where the *Arab* takes on more passengers, more cargo. As they head back out into the river, a white cri-nollated castle stares across the river from the east bank. It looks strange to see a castle sitting there, and it reminds her that the *Arab* is spiriting her toward a fate she has no control over. Her life's changing today, and she didn't stop it from changing when she had a chance to, because she halfway wanted it to change. And now there's nothing she can do to stop it.

It's late afternoon when the *Arab* gets to New Orleans. Jenny knows they're getting close when the boat passes a shanty town built along the riverbank; that town will be gone in the next flood, she thinks. And then all at once, there they are, at a place she saw long ago with a child's eyes. All these years later, she's never been sure if her memory was of a real place, or if it was just something her mind made up. But here it is, the gray three-spired cathedral looking across an open square to the river, just as she remembered. And there are more boats here than she's ever seen—flat-boats, steamers, and a couple of high-masted ocean-going vessels.

As the *Arab* pulls to the dock, she hears a low rumble of sound coming from the riverbank. At first it's just a hum, then louder. It's the sound of a big city: people jabbering in who knows what language, whistles hooting, dogs barking. She remembers that sound. Yes, this is *la Nouvelle Orleans*, a slave-built place if ever there was one.

Adrien takes her arm and they go down the gangplank. Right next to the *Arab,* a seagoing vessel is disgorging its pale passengers. Men in stovepipe hats and women in headscarves spill down the gangplank and stumble onto the dock, hanging on to their ragged children. When they reach the bank they put their feet down gingerly, testing whether the ground is solid beneath their feet. Then they disappear into the riot of color and sounds on the dock. Women with baskets on their heads sashay past, their hips swinging, and black men, glistening in the sunlight, hoist crates and barrels onto pallets to be loaded onto the boats. Yapping dogs and slinking cats are everywhere.

She wonders if Kofi could be here. This is close to the place where he was yanked away from her. He'd be a big boy by now, nearly grown.

"Let's go find our house," Adrien says, taking her arm. He leads her through the crowd and they go across a street. At the corner he pulls out a paper and studies it. "This way."

They walk toward the cathedral and then turn down a side street. Here the houses are built one next to the other, right on the sidewalk. Some of the doors are open, and Jenny tries to look in as she passes, but the interiors are dark. And Adrien is walking too fast for her. A man drives past them in a donkey-cart, shouting "Rags!" A woman comes out of a doorway up ahead and hails him to stop. She picks some rags from the pile and then hands him a coin and waves him off. Farther down the street, two women are laughing together in the doorway of a corner grocery as they pick through baskets of tomatoes and corn set out on the sidewalk. Jenny hears a banjo playing somewhere down the block.

They walk down another block and the houses become shabbier; here each house sits in its own narrow yard. Adrien points to a mustard-colored house on the far corner. "There it is. That's our house. The key's supposed to be under a pot."

It's a cottage with a bright blue door opening onto the unpaved street. *It looks so old*, Jenny thinks. The roof is so tall and heavy, it looks as if it could crush the house. The sunlight throws stabs of shadows across the street, and sure enough, when Jenny looks closer she sees a concrete pot sitting as an ornament beside the step. Adrien tips the pot back and takes the key.

As he struggles to turn the balky lock, she stands back, looking at the house. The yellow paint is peeling, revealing whorls of an earlier color, a smudged gray, underneath. When they go inside, the air in the closed-up house smells dank and mossy. There are two rooms, one behind the other. One rickety wooden chair and a sagging settee are in the main room, and in the other room is a sloping bed. Jenny follows Adrien through the back door to the yard where a black-walled cistern stands. At the far back corner of the yard is a privy leaning to one side. Water stands in low places around the yard.

Adrien points at the cistern. "That's our water." He turns the rusty tap and water dribbles out onto the hard-packed ground.

"Don't we have a well?" Jenny asks.

"They don't use wells here," he says. "Well water tastes nasty in New Orleans."

They go back inside. "I leased the house for a whole year," he says. "It's paid up. Forty dollars. That cleaned out most of my money. What have you got?"

She opens her purse and takes out her wallet and hands it to him. "Two hundred and seventy-two dollars. I counted it this morning to make sure."

"You're rich." He glances through it and takes out most of the bills, folding them into his wallet. "There's five dollars still in there," he says, handing her flattened packet back to her. "Put it in a safe place, maybe under that mattress. This'll tide us over 'til I get some work. There's stores here with everything we'll need, and the French Market down by the dock has all sorts of foodstuffs. So—here we are."

She feels the lightness of her purse now that he's taken her money. "Give me my money back."

"You'd better let me keep it. If you need any, you can ask me."

She starts to say *no*, but he's gone into the front room. She follows him. "I like this room better than the other one," he says, as the low sun casts a yellow glow through the window. "You'll have to wash that bedspread."

"I'll get to it. Are you tired?"

"Of course I'm tired. You can't ride a steamboat all the way to New Orleans and not be tired." He bends over to pick up a newspaper that's lying on the floor. "It's the *Picayune*," he says. "And only a week old." He sits down on the settee and opens it.

She walks to the front door and looks out. "Is that where the city ends?" she asks, pointing down the street to the left.

He looks up. "There's nothing out that way but a marsh."

"What's past the marsh?"

"Lake Pontchartrain. It's a big blue lake. You can't see across it. I went out there and saw it once when I was here last month. There's a train that runs out to it. "

"I'd like to see it," she says, but he's already turned back to the newspaper.

Just before sunset they walk to the French Market, a colonnade of white columns with awnings propped out to make the stalls bigger. Adrien walks with a bounce in his step, and he wants to walk faster than she does, so she strides to keep up. The French Market is the biggest market she's ever seen, and the most crowded, but the merchants are starting to close up their stalls for the night. She quickly puts some eggs and a tin of coffee in her basket, and at the last minute she grabs a couple of baguettes. Adrien pays and as they head out he walks alongside her, his arms folded behind his back. She moves through the stalls as quickly as she can. The whole place smells of vegetables tossed aside in the sun, and apples gone bad, and molasses, and fish. The odors make her gag, so she thrusts her basket at him and runs out, ducking under the awning into the nearly-dark street to retch into the gutter. When she straightens up, she looks around for Adrien. She sees him a few yards away, sauntering past every stall, studying every display that's still open.

"Let's go back," she says when he comes out, and he hands her the basket.

"This is Decatur Street," Adrien says, pointing at a sign on the corner. Some men are sitting around a table on the sidewalk, where they've set up a card game. They lean back in their chairs in a cloud of cigar smoke, and Jenny and Adrien have to walk around them. The odor causes Jenny's stomach to clench and a little farther down the street she throws up again into the gutter. She waits for Adrien to catch up with her; he hands her his handkerchief and takes her basket. Then he looks back over his shoulder at the men with the card game. She can see the house with the blue door up ahead.

Night rises from the ground like a purple shroud. They sit together on the settee in the front room with the door open to catch the breeze, and Adrien lights the stub of a candle and sets it on the floor. Then he leans over and kisses her.

A moment later Jenny looks around as a shadow flits past the doorway. "What was that?" she asks. "Did you see it?"

He shakes his head.

"Something ran by the door," she says. "I hope it wasn't a rat. I saw a rat catcher down the street when we were coming back from the market. I don't think you saw him."

He breaks off a piece of the French bread, ignoring the shower of crumbs that rain down on the floor. "How'd you know it was a rat catcher?"

"I've never seen one before, but he had a cage with a cat in it, and I saw a dead rat hanging down from his cart. I hope we don't have rats."

"Was it really a rat catcher? Like in Hamelin?"

"Where?"

"It's a story. I learned it in France when I was little. A rat catcher came to a town called Hamelin, and he promised the mayor he'd get rid of the rats. But after he killed all the rats, the mayor wouldn't pay him. So one night the rat catcher came back with his magic pipe, and when he played it, all the children in town left their beds and followed him away."

"Away to where?"

He shrugs. "Into a big cave, I think. I didn't hear that part. But the children were never seen again."

Jenny sits up. Drums are thrumming, a low undertone to the quieting racket of the city. "Listen. What's that sound?"

"Sounds like drums," he says, cocking his head to one side.

She looks at him, watching the candlelight wash shadows against his face. *Can Adrien be a father?* she wonders. He's trying to be a man, and he's learning how, little by little. And he knows things she doesn't know.

But she feels older than he is. He doesn't know the things she knows, what it's like to be a slave working in a cotton field, or how it feels to be moved around from place to place when you don't want to go. He's never been bashed on the face, or robbed of his money. Well, now he's taken her money. Maybe that's how it is, when you're married. Or even half-married. Adrien is sailing on a different river than the one she's on. If he comes to a snagger on his river, he'll float like a heron over it. But her river will always be the Mississippi, or Bayou Cocodrie. Sawyers and snaggers will always clot her course.

Later, as they lie in bed looking out the one window, Adrien murmurs, "Tomorrow, *a demain*, I'll go find a job."

174

Jenny feels a touch in her belly, like the brush of a fingertip. Then it goes away. She reaches for his hand so he can feel it if it happens again, but it doesn't. He's already asleep.

Tomorrow I'll tell him about the baby, she thinks. She lies awake for a long time, listening to the drums. The room has the dank close smell of plaster. It's sticky hot; one window doesn't bring a cross-breeze, and she doesn't want to leave the door open, in case there are rats. And then there's another touch, easy as a butterfly's wings.

CHAPTER SIXTEEN

IN THE MORNING Adrien dresses quickly, slicking his hair back from his forehead and brushing down his trouser legs. He pulls on his black suit jacket and ties a cravat around his neck. Jenny sits on the side of the bed and watches him dress.

"It'll be hot today," she says. "You won't need that necktie."

"I need to look proper if I want a good job."

She watches him take his brown wallet, thick with her money, and slip it into his inside coat pocket. Then he fumbles in his satchel and brings out a small calendar. He sets it on the table and folds it open.

"Today is July fourteenth," he says. "Bastille Day." He takes out his pencil and marks an "X" on one of the squares. "Our rent started a week ago. This will be a record of it." She gets up to look at the mark he made, and then reaches up to straighten his cravat. She wants to say, "I need to tell you something," but he turns quickly and says, "I'd better get going. Au revoir." He bends down and kisses her quickly, then goes out the door, his quiet shoes whispering down the sidewalk.

Emptiness settles over the house, with him gone. *This is where we diverge*, she thinks. *You go one way, and I another.* When she looks out the door, he's already gone around the corner. She goes back to the bedroom and pulls her dresses from the satchel, dresses that Helene and Theresa wore before they were sold away, and the one yellow dress that was Miss Stephanie's. The dresses are wrinkled from being stuffed in the satchel, and she doesn't have an iron. That will have to be one of the first things she buys. She frowns. An iron is so heavy, and so quick to burn your hands; even in the heat of summer you'd have to have the fire going, just so you could iron clothes that will be wrinkled again before the day is out. It's the closest thing to drudgery in a woman's life.

There are nails in the walls at odd places, from whatever generations of people lived in this house before she did. She hangs the dresses on the nails, smoothing down the skirts as best she can so the humid air will take out some of the wrinkles. For today, she'll wear the biscuit-colored dress she had on yesterday. She sets her hairbrush and hairpins on the table next to the bed and looks around for a mirror, but there isn't one. She should have brought that little shard of a mirror she had at Carefree, but she thought it would get broken.

This house, these two rooms, will be her home for at least the next year. Cobwebs dance in the corners by the ceiling, but she can sweep them down. And mud is tracked across the floor, but she can get a mop. The odors of New Orleans, the sounds of the city, this is all new to her now, but it will seem ordinary in a few days or weeks. And Adrien will find the job he wants, and the money will flow in. Meanwhile, she has the food they bought yesterday at the French Market. And she can make herself some coffee.

This is a different life, though, from what she's had before; at Carefree, Esther would have already made the coffee and fixed her breakfast. And Walker would be coming in to the kitchen with that smile he has, just for her.

Two hours later, Adrien is only a few blocks away, walking toward the dock, under a blazing sun. His face is set in consternation, but he tells himself that he looks like any businessman in his black suit, heading out on some important business. He strides toward the ticket booth at the dock where a chalkboard sign is propped up. The *Eclipse of Memphis* will leave in an hour, with stops in Baton Rouge, Bayou Sara, Natchez, Vicksburg, Memphis, St. Louis. So he can be back in Natchez by dark, if he chooses to go. He gets out his wallet and flips through the few bills left in it. He has twelve dollars, enough for a steamer ticket, but that's all.

He paces back and forth, trying to think. Other travelers come to the booth to buy tickets, and then they drift away to stand where the *Eclipse of Memphis* is waiting.

He pulls off his jacket. His cravat is untied and the tails hang down in two wings on his shirt front. The heat is rising; it will be unbearable by noon.

He hardly gives himself leave to think about the morning. Even before he left the house he was thinking about the poker game, hoping he could join it today. And sure enough the same three men were sitting at the card table in the same spot, chomping their cigars and laughing. He watched them from across the street. Two were swarthy old men, broad-chested and sun-bronzed; the third was a wiry imp, completely bald. *Saint Vitus Dance*, Adrien guessed. He knew a man in France who'd lost his hair that way.

"Hey, Creole!" one of the older men called, waving him over. And in an instant Adrien stepped out to cross the street. He felt happy as he pulled out a chair and sat down with the men. He was known as a pretty good player, back in Lormont.

But the cards didn't go his way; there must be cheating going on that he couldn't see. In less than an hour the game took most of his money, and he knew he'd been swindled. The faces of the men who looked so cordial an hour ago now looked menacing. So he opened his wallet and took out the last of his two hundred and sixty dollars and handed it to the imp, whose wrinkled white palm was open on the table.

He scraped his chair back and stumbled away down the sidewalk, black spots dancing before his eyes. *This cannot be real. Cannot be right.* That he let that money slip away in an hour's time. He was a fool. One poker game, a few minutes of comraderie with these encouraging mates, and he had to hand his money over. All it took was a stacked deck, some sleight of hand, a too-fast shuffling of cards.

Now, on the dock, he thinks, *I can't go back and tell Jenny.* He could head back to Natchez, but why? Someone there would ask about Jenny, and what could he say? And all he would have to go back to there is a janitor's job.

Or he could get a job that would take him far away, on a sea-going vessel, perhaps. Maybe on the ship that's docked here now.

But before he sets his course, since he can't think straight, he decides to give it one more try. He'll go back to the place where the card game was, and if the men are still there he'll tell them he has to have his money back, for his wife, who's sick, throwing up. He'll let them keep a little for their trouble—twenty dollars, say.

The day can still be set right. Of course he must go back. He feels in his pocket for his knife, and then turns around and walks back toward the place where the alley opens onto the sidewalk under the lace-filigree balcony. He claps his hands together as he strides along the sidewalk.

The vegetable seller, the rag-picker, and the women at the corner grocery notice the small black woman who walks along Burgundy Street in the early afternoon. A new face in a neighborhood is always noticed quickly, especially on a street like Burgundy, where free people live. A house long sitting empty suddenly has a lamp in the window and smoke coming from the fireplace. How could the neighbors not notice? Faces appear behind windows, curtains rustle open; people are watching. The merchants, more public, will give a tentative wave, a nod, and memorize the new face, especially when it's a pretty woman, full-breasted, small-waisted.

She walks with no particular destination in mind; she wants to learn her new neighborhood, that's all. One thing she's learned already is that New Orleans is honeycombed with courtyards. The gates to most of the patios are closed, but she stops at one gate that's open and peers in. The fronds of some palm trees dip and rise beside a black cistern with an onion-shaped top. She turns away and walks to the end of the block, where she can see the three spires of the cathedral towering over the rooftops.

When she turns back to her new home, the late afternoon light is soft and the sidewalks are steaming. A misty rain begins. She hurries back, thinking Adrien is certainly home by now. But when she opens the door and calls his name, there's no answer. On the shelf beside the fireplace are a couple of cups without handles and a dented, blue speckled coffeepot. When Adrien comes back he'll be tired; he'll want a cup of coffee. She draws some water from the cistern and makes a fire so she can boil the coffee. Then she carries the chair from the front room and sets it on the sidewalk in front of the door so she can watch for him. Directly across the street, a woman is sweeping her steps. She looks over at Jenny and waves, and Jenny waves back.

The woman calls, "Hi! You new here, ain't ya?" Then she sets her broom down and walks over, picking her way around the puddles. "I'm Rosie," she says. "You just moved in yesterday, didn't ya?" A smile dimples her broad face, which is shiny from the heat.

"I'm Jenny. I'm waitin' for my husband. He went to go find a job, but he's not back yet." She feels lighter, having someone to talk to.

"Who's your master?"

"We're free people."

"Oh, that's good. Y'all come to the right street to live on. Most everybody that lives along this little street is free. Me and my husband are free too. His name's Antoine. You got any kids?"

"Not yet."

"You got one comin'?"

Jenny nods.

"Oh, I thought I could tell you did," Rosie says. "You ain't too far along, though."

"About four months," Jenny says, thinking that now someone in New Orleans knows a secret even Adrien doesn't know yet.

"It'll be a li'l Christmas angel. Ain't that nice." Rosie looks back across the street. "I just got the one child, my boy Charlie. He's two. I guess I better get back on over there. Antoine's watchin' him and you never know, he's probably feedin' him that cake I made for tonight." Her broad face dimples again. "What's your husband's name?"

"Adrien Jean-Pierre."

"I seen him goin' out this mornin'. Well, you need anything, Miss Jenny, you know where I'm at. Pleased to meet you."

Jenny watches Rosie pick her way back across the street, dodging a donkey cart. When it gets dark she lights the candle in the front room and then curls up on the settee. When Adrien comes in she'll want to hear what job he's found, out in the city. Maybe he's started work today and won't get off until late. She hears the drums again, a deep muffled throb; and then she sleeps.

"He didn't come back all night?" Rosie's face creases into a frown. Jenny, standing on Rosie's top step, shakes her head. She looks up and down the street as if Adrien might suddenly appear at the corner. She'd recognize his jaunty walk as he turned onto Saint Ann Street. But all she sees are two brown dogs loping past the corner. The sun is rising above a bank of clouds in the east.

"Do you think he might've been working all night?" Jenny asks.

"Girl, I don't know." Charlie toddles over and Rosie hoists him to her hip. "You could ask Miss Hedro. She's that old auntie who sits out on the sidewalk all the time, just around the corner. She watches everything that goes on around here."

Walking toward the corner, Jenny thinks she's in some kind of frozen cocoon, even though it's going to be another hot day. She slept hard last night, the settee soft in spite of its decrepit state. She thought Adrien would surely be in the bed beside her when she woke this morning. When he wasn't, she felt her future seemed less like a territory she could understand. It occurs to her that maybe Adrien found work on a fishing boat that headed out in the Gulf, and he'd be back in a few days. But wouldn't he have told her before he went?

When she turns the corner she sees the woman who must be Miss Hedro, an ancient woman with her hair tied up in a bandanna, her small face shrunken into deep creases. Miss Hedro's wooden chair is missing braces from the legs, but as skinny as the woman is, the chair's not likely to give way. The woman's eyes are bright and curious as she turns to look at Jenny.

"I'm lookin' for my husband," Jenny says. "He went away to find work and didn't come back. Did you see him anywhere?"

"Was he that Creole I saw goin' out of here yesterday mornin'? That fine-dressed man? I ain't seen him since then," Miss Hedro says. "You the ones just moved onto the street, ain't ya? Into that yella house?" She pulls out a once-white handkerchief from her bodice and wipes her face with it. "Honey, I ain't seen him."

Jenny starts to turn away, but then Miss Hedro opens her toothless mouth to say something else.

"There was a man got murdered down St. Ann Street yesterday," Miss Hedro says.

"Murdered?"

"That's what I heerd. The police come yesterday mornin' and took a body out of that alley over there. It was a Creole man, I heerd."

Jenny begins to walk, run, down the street. The sidewalk is a blur in front of her eyes, and when she dashes across the street a man driving a wagon has to pull his mule back to keep from trampling her. When she gets to the mouth of the alley, she stops, not sure what she should be looking for. Whatever happened there, what the old lady saw, is over and done with. There's no sign of any murder. Miss Hedro must be mistaken.

Jenny steps into the alley, and she sees Adrien's red cravat lying in some weeds beside the wall. She picks it up, thinking *No!* The necktie is sticky with dried blood, and there's a black spray of blood on the wall, on the dirt, on the trash that's strewn along the wall. Jenny sinks to the ground, ignoring the blood and dirt and filth, and she picks up the cravat. It's clear to her now; Adrien will never get the chance to really become a man. His life has stopped. He'll never know about his child that's coming. He's gone to a pauper's grave, here in an alien city, and this scrap of silk is the last thing the world will ever see of Adrien Jean-Pierre, Frenchman, Creole, beloved child of Martinique.

The world has turned on its axis in a way it's never turned before. She folds the blood-stiffened necktie into the palm of her hand and stumbles back to her house.

The next morning Jenny is barely awake, her eyes swollen nearly shut, when she hears a rapping at her door, timid at first, and then more insistent. She goes to the door and opens it a crack to see who's there. A tall woman wearing a bright red dress, with her hair wrapped in a white tignon, stares back at her. She says something in French that Jenny doesn't understand. Jenny shakes her head, *"Non, Madame."*

The woman smiles. *"Anglais, petite maman?"* she says. "That's good. I speak better English anyway. I've come to see about you. I'm Margot, your *sagefemme*. Your midwife. Rosie who lives across the street told me to come see about you." She steps past Jenny into the house.

Jenny rubs the bleariness from her eyes. Her sleep was so broken last night; she woke up every hour thinking maybe she was wrong, that Adrien isn't dead, and he might open the door and come in with some logical explanation. But as the hours went by, he seemed more and more like a ghost. Now it's a new day, the sun streaming onto the fronts of the houses across the street.

"Rosie told me you were havin' your first *bebe*, but she said you wasn't ready to have it yet, so I know I don't need to be in any big hurry. Just yesterday I helped two others get born in Faubourg Marigny, two li'l boys, fine as anything. You shoulda seen 'em squallin' when they came out. They were big babies, too. But I'm wanting' to meet you." She steps into the room and looks around. "You getting' ready for him?"

"For who?"

"Your *bebe!*" She holds her hands up. "You must start thinking about that babe. You can't wait til the last minute. Rosie tol' me you don't have anybody here to see about you. No *famille*, she said. That can't be right, I said. So I thought I'd just come over and see for myself. But you know, in

New Orleans, there's lots of people come here without nobody else. They come in on the boats, all the time. You come in on a boat, didn't you?" She reaches out and puts her hand on Jenny's stomach. "Oui, *petite maman*, I can feel you are coming along. And you got no husband?"

Jenny stares at the tall, sharp-featured woman. This woman is used to being in charge, she senses. Margot walks fast, talks fast. Her honey-colored skin shines in the summer heat.

"He was killed, the day before yesterday."

"Well –." Margot hesitates. Jenny sees that the woman is thinking, what kind of trouble is this girl in, with a babe coming and a husband who's dead?

Margot walks into the other room, looking at the bed and the chest. "Your husband—what was his name?"

"Adrien Jean-Pierre. He was a Creole."

"What did he look like?"

"He was light-skinned, not dark like me. Gray eyes. Straight hair."

"I am sorry. That sounds like a Creole. Rosie said he didn't seem like the kind to just pick up and go. She watched y'all move in. Plenty of men do that, just pick up and go. You cannot tell." She pokes at the bed. "This bed'll do all right. We'll have to get some more sheets, though. Childbirth'll mess 'em up good. And you got to have help. You don't know anybody in New Orleans?"

"Just Rosie. And Miss Hedro, who lives down the street."

Margot shakes her head. "Hedro's too old. She can't help, with her back bent over and all. Have you got money to pay a midwife?"

Jenny pulls the packet from her bodice; it lies flat. "I had some money, but I gave it to Adrien. He took it when he left."

Margot opens the packet and looks in. "This is *all*? Five dollars? Not enough. Well, don't spend it, 'cause I must be paid when I deliver you.

And you have to eat." She looks around the room. "Is that his satchel?" she asks, pointing to the scuffed bag on the floor where Adrien had set it. Jenny nods. Margot picks it up and snaps it open. She flips through the garments inside. "I'll take this satchel," she says. "I can sell his clothes. That's a start." Jenny starts to protest, but Margot brushes past her and goes into the front room. She sits down on the chair. "So your husband died, and here you are without much money to get by on. And not enough to pay me either, for deliverin' you." She looks around the room. "But let's see. I don't have much of a place to stay, just a stall in the patio by Madame Devrot. And now the roof there has started to leak."

"Is Madame Devrot your mistress?"

"Child, I don't have a mistress. I'm from Jamaica, and I'm *liberee*. I have been free for ten years. My master sent me here when I was nineteen years old. 'That's it,' he said, 'you go on, you free now.' So I been in New Orleans ever since. Why don't I just move in here with you? I can buy food for us. You will need help, this bein' your first baby. I could stay here in your house, and then when your time comes, I'll be here to deliver it. I'll have everything ready." Margot's features seem to melt a little. "You won't make it by yourself. Why did you come to *la Nouvelle Orleans*?"

"Well, Adrien—" Jenny hesitates. It suddenly seems complicated to say that Adrien didn't want to be a janitor anymore. She gets up and goes to the door, looking out, her hand resting on her stomach. Maybe it wasn't Adrien who was killed. There must be many Creoles here. Any one of them could find themselves knifed in an alley. But when she turns around and sees his cravat lying folded on the hearth, black with blood, all she can think is—what led him into that alley?

The scene across the street blurs before her eyes. Antoine and Charlie are sitting on the step, and Rosie is sitting in a chair peeling a bowl of shrimp. Antoine raises his hand to wave at her.

She has to face death again, just as she had to face it when Miss Stephanie died, and then Miss Hattie. Dead, all of them. There's just open spaces in the world now where those living people used to be.

Margo puts her arm around Jenny's shoulder. "Well, anyway, Madame Jenny, you'll have trouble if you don't have money. I can help you with that. We can make sure it lasts, and I can figure out some way to get more. You can help me, and I can help you. I make good money as a *sagefemme*. I've birthed over a hundred babies."

"A hundred babies?"

"*Oui, Madame Zhe-nee*. So don't worry about having your *bebe*. There's nothing about birthing I've not seen. I seen men so happy to hold they big babies, they jus' go dancin' 'round the room, and I seen a few go out cursin' a blue streak, whether it was a boy or girl, no difference. But I never seen a woman anything but happy when that babe comes out squallin'. It's just gettin' to that point that's the hard part. That's where a good midwife comes in. I learned midwifin' in Jamaica from my mammy, and she learned it from her mammy. It goes *way* back, all the way to Africa."

Jenny brushes her hands over her cheeks to dry them. She turns to Margot. "I'm scared of how much it's gonna hurt."

"Oh, it'll hurt, there's no helpin' that, but I know the Jamaican ways to make it better. And if you're lucky, it might come quick. Sometimes they do. But the first one ain't likely to. They take longer. Why don't I move in here with you now, and I can help you. And then I'll be here when the little one comes."

Jenny thinks this over. She decides that this sharp-featured woman, masterly though she is, really is a kind person in spite of her fox-quick ways.

"*Merci*," Jenny says. "All right, then. You can sleep on the settee."

CHAPTER SEVENTEEN

MISS DOLORES'S DRESS SHOPPE is usually quiet most weekdays, but today Miss Dolores has a new customer, one she's glad to have: Mrs. Cornelius Carson, the new proprietess of Carefree. She knew the first Mrs. Carson, who was Stephanie Coqterre before her marriage, when she sewed her some schoolgirl frocks and then created a splendid dress for her wedding reception. Not that Dolores likes thinking about Carefree; she remembers happy days when Emile Coqterre lived there with his wife Josephine and Josephine's daughter Stephanie, and now they're all three dead. It's dreary to think about.

But the house might be coming back to life, which would be good news for Dolores. With the tornado that roared through three months ago, the clean-up's been on everyone's mind, and most of the ladies of Natchez haven't been in to get new dresses this summer. They're all busy with the rescue and repair mission, having organized themselves into guilds to help the displaced. With the streets littered with bricks and roofs gaping open to the heavens, pretty dresses aren't on too many ladies' minds.

Dolores pats her gray hair back into place and sits down on the sofa next to the new customer, studying her out of the corner of her eyes. Mrs. Carson isn't pretty, but her face has a plain integrity. She has a broad jaw, a high forehead, and a long nose. Certainly she doesn't have the soft prettiness that Miss Josephine and Miss Stephanie had. And when she speaks, the new Mrs. Carson has a country accent but a deep cultured voice. This is a woman whose intelligence commands attention, Dolores thinks.

"I need some city dresses," the woman says, cradling her bag in her lap. *Drayses* is the way she says it. "I'd like the finest fabrics." This is familiar; Stephanie Coqterre said almost the same thing when she ordered her dress for that big wedding reception her father put on. *The finest.*

So Dolores brings forth some of the bolts of silks and woven taffetas that are leaning up along the back wall of the shop. Mrs. Carson fingers each fabric thoughtfully, and then chooses two, both in subdued hues: a claret-colored silk and a deep teal taffeta. And when Dolores shows her sketches of how the dresses will look, she nods. These will be suitable; they're planning a soiree.

Why Carefree would host a soiree Dolores doesn't know. A thought flits across her mind like a bird across the sun: maybe that's the pattern for that house: a big soiree, then silence and ruin. But maybe this time Carefree will come back to life and stay that way.

"I'll need some clothes for everyday, too," Euphonia says, and Dolores sees that this customer will keep her busy throughout the season of repair while Natchez is putting its roofs back on. The two hundred dead from the March storm are buried. The tornado came so suddenly; and after it passed through, everyone talked about how quickly life can turn, how you can be alive one minute and then the sky darkens and death roars through. And who can forget the steamer *Hinds*, caught out in the river and overturned by the tornado, and how it floated downriver with a cargo of corpses. Lord have mercy.

So fabrics are selected, lightweight and lustrous, and patterns discussed. This woman isn't for the ruffly frills most Natchez matrons favor,

Dolores can tell. Instead, her dresses will have a few discreet tucks across the bodice. And pockets. The woman wants pockets, which are unheard of in city dresses but which she insists on. Well, a woman of means can have a dress made any way she wants. Dolores guesses Mrs. Carson wants to look attractive for her husband, so she'll be sure the dresses show off the woman's waist and her generous bosom. Mrs. Carson can be the customer who gets her through the season. Dolores's fingers will be calloused with plying her needle. If Mrs. Carson came to Natchez without any decent city clothes, which seems to be the case, she'll have to order a whole new wardrobe. Dolores can see there'll be good profit in this tall, gangly woman.

Walker sips his coffee and watches a cardinal at the window peck along the sill as if it's looking for a way in. Esther is leaning over her big iron pot and stirring something that smells good. Then she straightens up, puts her hand to her back, and walks over to sit opposite him.

"That smells good," Walker says. "You want me to stir it awhile for you?"

"It's stirred for now."

"You should take it easier," Walker says.

"You like to eat, don't you?"

"I sure do." He pours her a cup of coffee. "When you think Jenny might be coming back?"

"Never," Esther says. She stirs her own coffee. "Why would you think she's comin' back?"

"I guess I'm just hopin' she will. I miss seein' her around here."

"You know, Walker, when you see a girl you like, you gotta tell her," Esther says. "But once Jenny went off with that Adrien, I think that was it for her here. She's gotta make her own way, even though I thought he wasn't the right one for her. That Frenchman or whatever he was."

"Sometimes Jenny ain't got a brain in her head," Walker says. "And then other times, she's smart as anything. Where'd she come from, anyway? She ain't a Creole herself, is she?"

"No, she can't be. I think Master Cornelius bought her off some trader here in Natchez. Maybe she come straight from Africa."

He whistles. "That must'a been hard on a little kid."

"She's got a brother somewhere in slavery," Esther says. "She said she wants to find him. Kofi's his name." She presses her hand to her back. "My back's killin' me these days. I got to start restin' more."

Walker lights a cigarette. The aroma of whatever Esther's cooking distracts him. After a minute he says, "Coffee? That's her brother?"

"Kofi," Esther says.

"Coffee? Shoot. I know him." Walker stretches out his legs under the table. "I know right where he is."

Esther's spoon clatters against her saucer.

"Yep, that'd be him, now that I think about it," Walker says. "He's real dark, just like Jenny. Looks like her too, some."

"Well, where is he?"

"Oh, he belong to old Missus Aikens, who's got a place on the river down by St. Francisville. Yep, that's gotta be him. Everybody knows Coffee."

"It ain't likely it's the same one. How old is he, this boy you know?"

"Oh, he's 'bout fifteen, sixteen. He's kinda tall, and of course Jenny herself ain't tall, but yep, he's got that same big smile she's got."

Esther lays her hands flat on the table. Now here's another thing to consider. Why couldn't he have said this before, when Jenny was still here? Funny how an ordinary day can bring up all sorts of information, when you weren't expecting any.

"Well, if she ever comes back we oughta let her know about this boy named Coffee," Esther says.

"Okay," Walker says, blowing a smoke ring. "I still got a feelin' she'll be back one day. I hope so."

Then Esther thinks, that's another strange thing Walker says now, "Okay." Where does he pick up these funny words? He says "Okay" all the time, even though it's a word that makes no sense.

Since we been freed, we act different, she thinks. *We act like we're in charge of things, and don't give it a second thought. We just go about our business and don't wonder whether some master's gonna like what we're doin' or not. We act different with each other too. Just always thinking, what should this person do, or that person? And we tell 'em.*

Well, for now she has to bring the noontime meal in to the big house. Euphonia and Thomas have to eat three times a day, and so does Miss Coclla, the lady that's taking care of Thomas. As for herself, she gets paid every Friday, a dollar and a quarter. It's nice to have some money coming in every week, regular as a clock, even though it's not enough. And Miss Euphonia said she can have Sophronia's old clothes. It didn't seem to bother Miss Phony that those dresses are way too fine for a slave woman. Except Esther Coqterre's not a slave woman any more. And every day she puts on a well-made frock, always black or brown or dark red, knowing there's something not quite right about her wearing it. But even when she ties her apron over it, it's nice to feel the crisp fabric.

"I can't tell Jenny about her brother if she ain't here," Walker says. "And I can't just go sailing up to Missus Aikins and say I want to see your boy Coffee, check him out to see if he's related to this other person I know. I could buy him out, though, if I had the money. Maybe he could come live here when Jenny comes back. Wouldn't that be grand for her?"

"If she ever comes back, which I don't think she is, Cornelius might buy him out if she asks him to. He hates slavery," Esther says.

"Think I oughtta ask him?" Walker asks, stamping out his half-smoked cigarette and pinching the tip cold. He drops it into his shirt pocket.

"Maybe I better be the one who asks him. He knows me better," Esther says.

"If Coffee just showed up here, you think Jenny would know him? She ain't seen him for a long time," Walker says.

"Blood knows blood." Esther looks out the window. "I wonder if Cornelius would help me find my girls. They was sold off in Louisiana somewhere. You don't know where *they* is, do you? You know just about everybody."

"I do know lots of people. It's my speciality, just like yours is match-making. But I ain't heard a thing about your girls. We could ask Cornelius, but if we fount 'em, he'd have to see if their owner would sell 'em. We don't even know if they're in the same place together."

Esther's face falls. "Don't say they ain't," she says in a low voice.

When Euphonia comes back to have her new dresses fitted at Miss Dolores' shop, the garments are even more elegant than she dreamed they'd be. Especially the dark red one with its ribboned v-neck; in the Cocodrie she never wore anything but round-necked calico dresses, and this dress with its leg-of-mutton sleeves makes her skin look whiter than buttermilk. And it makes her shape more womanly than it's ever looked before.

She knows just what jewelry she'll wear with the dress: a string of pearls she found in Stephanie's old dresser. When she opened the drawer, the pearls rolled forward, skittering with a sound like teeth chattering. She's never had pearls before, but now she'll wear them with her new low-cut dresses, and her neck will show to advantage. The dresses are expensive, and the pearls seem like an unexpected gift.

She's seen to it that Cornelius ordered some suits from the tailor; when they ride about Natchez in their new barouche, passersby notice them. They bought the new carriage only a week ago, and Cornelius parked the old black buggy behind the Dependency. The new barouche has two seats facing each other, and when they drive about town Euphonia feels as if they're floating above the Natchez streets. The barouche requires two horses, so Cornelius bought two stallions, Eagle and Chico. Mister Badeau is the driver.

Euphonia carries a parasol over her shoulder now, and Cornelius wears a new hat and a string tie. They nod and smile when people seem to know them, even though those are people whose names they can barely place. They're in a new city, and the rebuilding going on downtown seems like a symbol of their own situation. Cornelius spends his days bent over his desk, and when she needs money he takes out his wallet and hands her a stack of bills. It seems a cornucopia of plenty has engulfed them.

At night they lie together in the yellow bedroom with the windows open to catch a breeze, and they listen to the bugs hitting the window screen. Cornelius puts his arm under her, and she likes lying like that with her head on his shoulder. Then he caresses her long body and she never refuses him, even when she's tired or thinking of something else altogether. He can melt it out of her. She likes his power over her, and when it's over she lies breathing hard and listening to him breathing hard too. We're like a symphony together, she thinks. It seems like the most natural thing in the world. It surprises her, the way she reaches for him night after night, eagerly, and not embarrassed at all.

An invitation comes in August for a garden party at the Elenora House, the home of John Landerson and his family. The invitation is written in careful script on a beige card, and the slave boy who brings it in grins as if he knows the answer before Euphonia does. She takes the invitation into Cornelius's study at the back of the house, where he sits at his desk with papers spread out in front of him.

"We're invited to a party," she says, laying the card on the desk in front of him. He picks it up and reads it quickly. "We can certainly attend, can't we?" she asks.

"I don't see why not," Cornelius says. "But then right after that I really do have to get out to Rapides Parish. I've been writing to Bernard Ratout, but I get no answer. I've got to go see what the devil's going on."

Smiling, Euphonia walks into the parlor and takes a sheet of her stationary from the end table drawer. She writes her response quickly and folds the paper and hands it to the child. "Go on out to the kitchen," she says. "Esther'll give you a sweet."

"Thank'ee, ma'am." He takes the note and whirls around and skips down the hall to the back door.

"Don't you drop that," Euphonia says as he disappears down the back steps.

She goes up to the bedroom and opens the chiffarobe doors. Yes, here they are, her new dresses, and she'll wear the garnet-colored one. The women of Natchez are bound to be fashionable, and she has to show that she can be just as smart as they are. They won't know much about her, and first impressions are so important.

As the guests begin to arrive at the Elenora House, John Landerson stands by the front door to welcome them. This is their first soiree of the season. Many of the fashionable sort have gone north for the summer, but what with the storm this spring that distracted everyone, and with his law practice to attend to and a wife who's spent her whole life here, summers as well as winters, John feels no great pull to head north. Natchez is their home more than any summer cottage in New York could ever be. Fortunately, this summer there are still enough society people around that a decent party can be held.

His glass tinkles with ice. As the guests come up the walkway, he shakes hands with the men and chats for a moment with the women. From time to time Elenora appears and stands behind him. She wears a simple white frock this summer evening, and her skin glistens in the heat. But she's tied a ribbon around her waist, and she's wearing her mother's pearl earrings. It's more jewelry and frill than she usually wears, and he's happy to see it. Maybe she's coming out of her cold ways, he thinks, although remembering how she usually sleeps with her back to him, and how she turns the children over to the slave women, it's not likely. Even little Cyrus, his favorite, practically thinks Delphine's his mother.

As the sun sinks lower, a last buggy pulls up the drive and Cornelius Carson and his wife climb down. John stares. The last time he saw Mrs. Carson she was a regular country wife wearing a calico dress and a sunbonnet. His impression then was of a woman with a long face and a sober expression. And yet here she is, descending the carriage like an aristocrat, with her hand on Carson's outstretched arm, and she's transformed. What a change three months can bring. She no longer has a sun-bronzed face. Now her face is soft and white, softened by the creams and lotions the local pharmacist stirs up, no doubt. And her hair is coiffed and curled up on top of her head, except for tendrils which cascade across her shoulders. She carries a fan and a beaded bag, and she wears an expensive-looking gown of some deep red color. It's not exactly what the other women are wearing, but it's becoming.

John shakes Carson's hand and speaks smoothly of the weather, but something about the man rankles him. He remembers the day Carson came into the law office to claim an inheritance he had no right to, but which was his anyway, courtesy of crazy old Emile Coqterre. And then Carson returned a few days after that with three slaves he wanted to free, and a pint-sized man who needed papers. That in itself is enough to set his teeth on edge. Freed slaves shouldn't be wandering around. If they're to be freed, fine, but they ought to be made to leave on the next steamboat headed north. Get them out of here. What would the slaves think when they see a free man or woman with skin as dark as their own? They'll get ideas. It's just not right.

And Carson with his courtly manners; John remembers the wedding reception after Stephanie eloped with him. He'd mingled with the other guests that day, smooth and gentlemanly, a farmer from the backcountry who'd won the prize. And now he has Coqterre's money, his fine city house, and his plantation.

Having Carson here makes the evening seems off, somehow. It's all John can do to be courteous to him. As the guests move out into the garden behind the house, where daisies bloom in well-tended rows along the sides of the yard, and the roses Elenora no longer cares about nod in a gentle breeze, John stands at one side of the garden. He looks over at his wife, who's talking with old Josiah Hargraves at the far corner of the garden. She's paying little attention to the other guests.

So he walks toward Euphonia Carson, who is standing next to a rose-bush, and who looks just a little alone. Which she certainly is, a woman who's new to Natchez and who can't yet mingle well. And who looks rather pretty this afternoon in her scarlet dress, with her Paris hat tied to one side under her chin. And whose husband is talking with some other men, far away down at the other end of the garden.

After the guests leave, Elenora goes upstairs to her bedroom with her candle. John has gone in to the nursery to see about Cyrus, who's teething. Elenora hears Delphine talking to John, and then the shadow of a candle moves across the wall and tells Elenora that Delphine's headed out to the ice house. Cyrus screams until she returns; then he abruptly quiets. She pictures it: John sitting in the rocking chair, holding the ice wrapped in a towel to the baby's tender gums.

She goes to her chiffarobe and takes down a box from the upper shelf. It's an old box, the cardboard speckled with age. When she takes off the lid, a musty aroma rises. She holds her candle close to study the stack of papers inside. Why she'd kept the letters written by her school friend Stephanie all these years, she can't remember. Stephanie sent her a flurry of letters in the weeks after her wedding, even though a buggy ride across Natchez would have brought the two friends face to face. But Stephanie wrote in such panic, such fear, tormenting herself about her marriage, about her angry papa, her coming reception and her move to Louisiana. Anguish is what Elenora read in those letters; a cry of the heart. But Stephanie was already married; the damage was done. When the letters came, Elenora had no ready answers, so she didn't reply to any of them. Instead, she put them in this stationary box and set it high on the shelf in her chiffarobe .

Tonight, Euphonia Carson showed up dressed like the belle of the ball, and John spent the evening standing close to her. Elenora tried as best she could to make conversation with the other women, but really, she thought, how must it look, John ignoring her while he fell all over himself with Euphonia.

She takes out the letters and lays them on the bed. Then she picks them up one by one and holds her candle up so she can read them. The letters are so poignant, so fresh, it's almost as if Stephanie were still alive, penning them this very night. But she's gone.

After she reads them over, Elenora opens the drawer of her side table and takes out her sewing scissors. She begins to cut, carving the letters apart sentence by sentence, and within a few moments the letters look like schoolgirls' hair-ribbons, lying on the silk counterpane.

CHAPTER EIGHTEEN

THE POLICE COMMISSIONER of New Orleans, Placide Gervrais, marked the police report *"Fini"* the day after the body of the young man was brought in, along with another man's body found later the same day. He'd given the case to Alain Pitot, one of the free blacks the department hired. Standing at his office window on Carondolet Street, he wondered about the crime-ridden city. The department couldn't keep up. So much was handled by vigilante justice, anyway, and while he couldn't approve of vigilantism, he realized there was no other way to clear the dockets. But no vigilantes would go after whoever killed this young Creole. He wouldn't find justice; that was almost a certainty.

He looks at the evidence bag Pitot handed him a moment ago, and then he takes out the items and lays them on his desk. There's precious few things in the bag, as he knew there would be: a soft slipper which would have left few footprints, now splattered with blood. A lock of the man's black hair, tied with a string. A whalebone button from his coat. And a pocket comb and a scrap of paper, the only things left in the man's pockets. Pitot is always thorough about going through the contents of pockets, Gervrais thinks; he's one of the best free officers on the force.

Gervrais picks up the scrap of paper and opens it on his desk. The tan paper has a hastily scribbled note: "Saint Vigilius, Natchez." Now what is the meaning of that? This young man did not look like a priest, or a brother. But he had some connection to that church in Natchez, obviously.

Gervrais folds the paper and smooths it out and slips it back into the evidence bag. Someday he'll write to the priest at that church, and ask if the man has any knowledge of a young man who might have been a parishioner there, perhaps. This man needs to be identified. Even if the body's long gone to the paupers' grave outside of town, the records need to show his name. And perhaps his family is connected to that church, and they will need to know about his unfortunate end. He copies down the name of the church on his note paper. He'll write the letter when he gets time. But first he needs to look at the evidence from the other man found dead the same day. More dead will come in before the day is out. It's an endless parade. Gervrais has plenty to keep him busy, and it seems there's really not much to tell here.

In October Cornelius rides Eagle out to Bayou Boeuf. When he gets to Rapides Settlement, he discovers it's hardly a town at all, just a jumble of run-down buildings half-hidden behind some moss-draped oak trees that look older than the town itself. When Cornelius rides up to what he thinks must be the post office, the place seems abandoned. He dismounts and walks a few feet down a wooden sidewalk to "Fortenberry's Mercantile Establishment," a false-front store that is surely ambitious for what the population will support, he thinks. He pushes the door open and sees a scant supply of wares for sale: a couple of bolts of calico fabric, potatoes in a bin, crocks of sugar and flour, all of it dignified by a pressed tin ceiling. The floor creaks as he walks in.

The woman who comes out from the back room looks at him curiously. "I don't really know where that place is," she says when Cornelius inquires after the plantation belonging to Emile Coqterre. "I've never heard of anyone by that name."

"Would you know Bernard Ratout?"

"No sir. I might ask my husband, though."

She opens a door that leads into another room and calls "Robert!" A man in rough coveralls comes out wiping his mouth. Cornelius knows he must have interrupted the man's dinner, but it can't be helped; he needs a guide. He's relieved when Robert says, "I know the place. I'll take you out there."

They ride north of the town and turn west on a road that leads along Bayou Boeuf. Wide unplanted fields stretch in every direction, butting up against low stands of willows and black-gum trees and taller stands of pines in marshy woods. Cornelius tries to memorize the road, which after a few minutes becomes nothing more than tracks that almost disappear in the jungly undergrowth.

Finally the guide pulls his horse to a stop and points. "If you look way over there you can see the owner's house," he says, and Cornelius squints. Yes, he sees the slope of a roof; the house, buried in green, is as small as a matchbox from this distance. Why the fields are all unplanted is puzzling.

"There's some other buildings over there, too, but you cain't see 'em from here," Robert says.

Cornelius takes a coin from his pocket and pays the man, who nods and rides away.

He looks around to orient himself. There's Bayou Boeuf, a shiny stream that gleams between the willow trees growing along the banks. He rides along the bayou path to the house, a plain log building with a porch across the front. Two rooms, Cornelius thinks, by the dimensions. It appears deserted. When no one answers his knock, he pushes the door open and goes inside. The furnishings are simple; in the main room, two wooden chairs, a stool, and a square pine table, all probably crafted right here on the plantation. In the bedroom a buckskin jacket hangs on an antler rack, and the bed is neatly made, covered with a quilt. Opening the top drawer of the chest, he sees Emile's folded shirts; his pants hang on a hook inside the door. Cornelius always thought of Emile as a grandee, but here in this place he can see that for much of the time the man lived a simple life. Perhaps Carefree with all its elegance really did mean little to him. He built that grand house in Natchez to win a pretty wife, and he did win Josephine, but the birth of their deformed son and the murder of Josephine and the child on the Natchez Trace must have made it all seem hollow and empty. If it weren't for the plantation, Emile couldn't live the rich life he lived in Natchez; but after Josephine died, he chose to live at his plantation much of the time. And cane was such a profitable business.

But this simple house tells him something else. Emile wasn't in Natchez much because he saw no reason to be there. But what about his stepdaughter? Stephanie was left with no father at a time when she'd already lost her mother. The loss of her mother was always a void in Stephanie's life. Why didn't Emile consider that?

Cornelius goes onto the back porch and looks around. He sees another building some distance away; he mounts Eagle and rides toward it, thinking it must be Ratout's house.

"Hello?" Cornelius calls as he rides up, but there's no answer. Birds chirp in the trees. Another deserted house. He dismounts and knocks on the door, then rattles the handle. The door doesn't open.

A quarter-mile to the west is a line of cabins facing the bayou. He rides over to them. Some chickens are pecking in the grass by the bayou, and a hog snorts in a pen. A horse and a mule graze in a field behind a barn. But the cabin doors are all closed, and the place seems deserted.

Then he hears a baby's cry. A young woman comes out of the nearest cabin.

"Sir?" she asks. She has a baby tied to her chest, and she walks with a shuffle. Looking at her feet, he sees that she's wearing a man's over-sized shoes.

He swings down from the saddle, staring. Her dress hangs loosely on her gaunt form, and the hem of her skirt is dragging on the ground. Her hair is tied up in a rag ripped from some other garment. This woman must be one of his slaves, but where are the others?

"I'm looking for Mister Bernard Ratout," he says. "Is he here?"

She half-turns away from him and looks at the ground. "No sir. Master Bernard's gone away. He's been gone since the wintertime."

Which is why I got no answers to my letters, Cornelius thinks. "What's your name?" he asks.

"I'm Traysa, sir."

"Where is everybody? All the people who live here." When she doesn't answer, he says, "I'm the owner now."

She looks up at him in surprise, and then looks down at the ground again. "There's just a few of us livin' here now. Just us women and babies, and some old aunties."

"Where are the field hands?"

"They're all gone. Master Bernard sold 'em off. He said Master Emile weren't never comin' down here no more, so he just sold off all the men and the strong women. The ones still livin' here, we didn't have nowhere else to live."

Cornelius looks off into the distance. How could Ratout sell slaves that didn't belong to him? But then he considers. Ratout figured Emile was dead, and selling slaves would be no harder than selling unbranded cattle, if he sold a few here and there, and for a bargain price. Few records would be kept. Many a trader would wink at the legal niceties for a lower price. A few slaves sold on one day, a few on another day, in a different town—a hundred slaves could be disposed of pretty quick.

After another long pause, she says, "Us that's left are just ones that couldn't work 'cause they was about to have babies, or them that was too old. Master Bernard just went away and left us here. We got up one mornin' and he was gone."

"Gone where?"

Traysa shrugs. "I don't know, sir. He said he was goin' back to the north."

Cornelius ponders this. The horse steps forward and Cornelius pulls the reins to steady him.

So Ratout has cheated him, sold his hundred slaves and left the land unploughed, and abandoned these few poor souls to their fates. They haven't starved, although Traysa looks like she's near enough to it. *I hate slavery*, he thinks. Her baby is fat, though.

"Gather up the others. Bring 'em out here in the lane."

"Yes sir." She turns around and shuffles back toward the cabins.

Cornelius watches her go. She goes from cabin to cabin, opening every door and going inside for just a moment. One by one the women emerge. Two have babies, and three are old. One woman leans on a walking stick.

They stand unmoving in the road, except for the two with babies, who jostle their fretting infants. Cornelius dismounts and goes over to stand on the rickety step of the first cabin. He waits until the babies quiet down before he starts to speak.

"Y'all gather 'round over here." When they come closer, he says, "My name is Cornelius Carson. I own this plantation now. I inherited it from Mister Emile Coqterre, who died last year. My wife was Master Emile's daughter, so the plantation came to me."

Their faces show no reaction. *All slaves wear masks*, he thinks.

"So I've got to understand—how are y'all living here without an overseer?"

Traysa steps forward. "We been livin' all right, sir, 'cause we have some food left over. But it's gettin' mighty low. Master Bernard, he sold off the husbands of all the women, and then he sold most of the women too."

Cornelius wipes perspiration from his neck with his bandanna. These women, left here with their children, have survived for months alone. They haven't touched the main house or the overseer's house, but they lived here with their clothes falling into rags, watching their foodstuffs dwindle.

"We didn't know what to do, sir," Traysa said. "We didn't know if Master Bernard was ever comin' back, or Master Emile either. So we just stayed put."

"I count ten of y'all, countin' the babies," Cornelius says. "Is this everybody? Nobody left in the cabins?"

Traysa shakes her head. "This is all of us."

"I won't leave y'all here by yourself," he says. "I live in Natchez, Mississippi. But I've come here so I can figure out what to do. I need to know everybody's name."

Traysa says, "I can name 'em for you." She points at each one. "That's Filisa, and Cassie, and Bo; and Dancy with her baby Henry. The old aunties are Virginia and Jane and Margaret. My baby is George."

The women stand unmoving. They're afraid, he knows; a new master means danger, often as not. But he'll have to plot his course. He doesn't know what else to say to say to them.

"Well, for now I'm staying at the main house back over there," he says, pointing. "Y'all need anything, let me know. I have to figure out what to do." He swings up on Eagle and turns away, kneeing the horse to a trot. He rides past the overseer's house, then out along the edge of a field that obviously had once been planted. When did Ratout decide the place had no living owner? Maybe in the first year when Emile didn't show up as he usually did. Would a man like Ratout wonder what his responsibilities were, to keep a place going without reporting to an owner? And where was he now? He probably went north like Traysa said, but that didn't mean he'd stay in the north. Overseers don't stay in one place for long. If he asks at the settlement, he might learn something.

Because this is a theft. The slaves were his property just as surely as Malachi and Jenny once were. He freed them to get back to that place where he'd promised his mother he'd never stray from. And he thought he'd accomplished it. Esther, Malachi and Jenny are all free people now. But he hadn't figured on inheriting a hundred slaves, only to have them stolen out from under him before he ever laid eyes on them. Because as much as he wants to honor the memory of his mother, and stay in the good graces of his wife, a man can't just overlook a thievery. He stares out across the wide field.

So he has ten slaves left here, all women and babies. He can't set them free in Rapides Parish; he'll have to make some kind of provision for them. They wouldn't have made it out here by themselves much longer. He sees how big their eyes are in their faces. And who knows what the thinking in Rapides Parish is, for freeing slaves? There might be no other freed slaves in the entire parish. That wouldn't surprise him, given that there aren't any big towns out here. Everyone here works the soil, one way or another. No, he can't just turn his people out on their own. They'd be kidnapped back into slavery before nightfall, and money would be jingling in some trader's pocket.

I should've brought Mal with me, he thinks. *Having him around usually gives me the answers to a lot of questions.* Mal even came up with the name for this new black horse he's riding. Eagle. Who'd think to name a horse after a bird? But Mal suggested it, and now the name fits the horse pretty well. He leans forward to pat the stallion's neck.

When he gets back to the main house he sits on the porch and opens his knapsack. The last of his hardtack is in there. There's no food in the house, but he won't ask the women to share their little dinner. He'll just wait until tomorrow, and in the meantime he'll ignore his rumbling stomach. He'll sleep on the situation. Sometimes that helps.

He wonders what Phony's doing. Right about now Miss Coella will be bringing Thomas in for his supper, and later Phony'll drink her evening glass of white wine in the parlor. In the months since they married he's gotten used to Phony's ways; she's a more complex person than he realized when he married her. But of course, back then he only knew her as a neighbor and a willing dancer at the frolics. She's taken to city ways now. Watching a scorpion run across the porch, its forked tail in the air, he thinks, who could blame her?

He goes into the bedroom, but seeing the dusty bedspread he thinks better of sleeping under it. He folds the spread back and pushes it and the sheet onto the floor. Then he lies down on the bare mattress, his hands under his head. Eight women and two babies. What will he do with them? That's the question that nags at him as the stars come out outside the window.

Over at the cabins the women will have gathered themselves together, and they'll be talking over what it means that this new master has showed up. He'd been able to read so little in their faces. He can't even remember all their names: Bo, Dancy, Traysa, Jane, Virginia, Margaret...the babies Henry and George...

He's still rich. He knows how much money Emile left in the Planters' Bank of Natchez, and it's enough to keep him and his family in style. Maybe he could invest in some business. He won't have to be a cane planter, which is just as well since he knows little about cane. And he'd rather stay in Natchez anyway. Emile made this four-days' ride from Natchez time and again, but Cornelius would rather stay home. And a man's better off if he sticks with what he knows.

CHAPTER NINETEEN

WHEN HE WAKES in the morning he's bleary-eyed and achy. He goes out to the privy, swinging the door wide in case any snakes or scorpions are inside. When he goes back to the house a woman—Bo?—is waiting in front of the porch. She hands him some eggs and sliced bread and walks away without a word. He watches her go. Like Traysa, she's stick-thin, but barefoot. He eats on the porch step with his plate on his knees. A white column of smoke rises from a cooking fire over at the cabins.

After he eats he rides over to the cabins. A young woman - Dancy? - is sitting on a patch of trampled grass with a fat baby -Henry? - on her lap.

"I need to talk to all of you," he says to the woman. "Are you Dancy?"

"Yes sir."

"Get everyone gathered together out here, will you?"

She gets up and hefts the baby to her hip, and then walks away with a limping gait. A deformity from birth, he thinks; or an infected thorn. No, there's no question of leaving these women here alone.

They come out of the cabins in twos and threes, Traysa and Dancy holding their babies on their hips, the other women hesitant as they creep toward him. The old women Virginia and Margaret walk more slowly than the others; Jane leans on a cane. Cornelius dismounts and walks over to the nearest cabin where a chair is leaned up against the wall. He sets it in the middle of the road for Jane. The other women stand around, staring at the ground, their eyes flashing up at him now and then.

He counts them. "Is this everybody?"

Dancy nods.

"The first thing is, I need to find out as much as I can about the men."

Dancy speaks up. "All we know is, Master Bernard rounded all of 'em up and took them to an auction in Pineville. We was doin' all right before that. We had our families together, and we all got along. It was hard work getting' the cane in, and Master Ratout wasn't kind about it. But after the men left we didn't know how long we could hold on. But now you've come, and we know we're saved."

Saved, Cornelius thinks. *Don't give me more power than I've got.* "All right. Since I live in Natchez, I'll have to take y'all back there. I've got a place there where y'all can live. I need to get a wagon. Is there one around here?"

Dancy points to the barn. "There's a cane wagon behind that shed."

"Are there any horses?"

"There's one horse, Old Dun. And we got a mule too, Woody. They're both out in that field. Master Bernard used to hitch Old Dun up when he wanted to go somewhere. He carried all the men away in that wagon, load after load. It took both the horse and the mule to pull it."

Cornelius pictures the sight, Ratout shackling the men to haul them off while the women wailed. He can envision the pistol gleaming in Ratout's belt.

"All right. We'll use that wagon. Can y'all get ready to go? It won't be easy traveling that far. Pack up whatever food you got that'll keep, and I'll stop in the settlement and buy some more food to get us through the trip. We need water jugs too. We'll stop as often as we can, and at night

SYLVIA ANN MCLAIN

we'll find shelter along the road. Bring all your clothes and whatever the babies need. We can head out as soon as you get everything in that wagon."

But the women stand together, not moving. Then two women step forward and walk toward him.

"Sir, my name's Filisa," one of the women says in a low voice. She twists a rag in her hands so tight it would squeeze water out, except it's dry. "I want to find my husband. He was sold off."

"What was his name?"

"Hawthorne. I just need to know where he's at."

"All right. I'll try to find him. But I can't promise anything."

"He might be right around here somewhere, sir. There was plenty of people that knowed him, and I think they'd want to use him on their place. He was took away with all the other men."

Then the other woman steps out from behind her. "I'm Bo, sir. I can't leave 'til I find my son Daniel. Master Ratout sold him off."

"You know where he's at?"

"No sir. But he ain't but twelve years old. He's too little to be out on his own. Can you help me?"

"I'll see what I can do. I'll ask in Pineville. There might be records there." It's clear he won't be heading back to Natchez just yet. "Is there anyone else I need to see about?" he asks, addressing the group. But the women stand silent, dignified in their rags, and every face wears a mask.

Filisa walks back to stand beside the other women, still twisting her rag. Bo says, "We think the men are gone for good."

"Y'all, everybody, give me their names. I'll write them down. All your men."

He takes a pencil and a piece of old ledger paper from his saddlebag and sits down on a tree stump. He props the paper against his leg and

213

writes. One by one the women step forward and he writes the names they give him: Daniel, Hawthorne, James, Likely, Whitman, Jacob, Frank.

"Is that all?" he asks when no more women approach him.

Bo nods. The women didn't all have husbands, he guesses.

"Well, this is going to take some time," he says.

He spends the rest of the day riding about his land, trying to understand the place as it would have been worked when Ratout was here. The flat fields are wide, and some of the land is too marshy for planting, he thinks. From time to time he dismounts and lets Eagle rest, thinking about the tasks he must do before he heads back to Natchez. When he gets back to the house, Bo brings him a bowl of chicken with a few dumplings stirred in. The women consider this an ordinary day, he thinks; they've had months to consider their abandonment. They probably aren't sure they can trust him. But he's said all he can think to say to them.

The next day, under a slate-gray sky, he rides to Pineville.

A small building on the edge of town has the name "Gordy" and the word "Slaves" painted over the door, but no auction is going on when Cornelius rides up under growling black clouds. He ties Eagle to the post outside and goes inside, a few steps ahead of a downpour.

"Beat that rain, didn't you?" says a man standing inside at the window, watching big drops pound the earth.

"Just barely," Cornelius mutters, not much wanting to talk to this man.

The building is empty, but looking around, he recognizes the familiar setup; the raised dais at one end of the sorry room, hay scattered about the floor. The place reminds him of the auction house at Franklin and Armfield's in Natchez, where the prices were so high. He was there on the day he bought Jenny. Being at a slave auction troubled him then, and it troubles him to be here now, even though there's no auction going on. Slave-mongering is a muck he used to dip his foot in, but he's sanctified of it now. Then he thinks, *Well, because I can be. When I couldn't be, I wasn't.* As his mother said, don't be sanctimonious.

"Can I he'p you?" the man mouths the question around the stub of a cigar. He looks at Cornelius with narrowed eyes.

"You Gordy?" Cornelius asks. The man nods.

"My name's Carson. I'm looking for some of my slaves who were sold through this place," he says. "It was probably about a year ago now. My overseer Bernard Ratout brought some field hands here and sold 'em off without my knowledge. You know where Ratout is?"

"Last time I seen Mister Bernard, he brought in some field hands to be auctioned, and after they was sold, he left and that was it. That was a big lot of slaves. We put up flyers all over to advertise it."

Cornelius takes his list out of his pocket. "There were a lot more than this, but right now these are the ones I'm particularly looking for. James, Likely, Whitman, Frank, and Jacob are field hands. And there's two more: Hawthorne, who's also a field hand, and Daniel, a boy about twelve."

Gordy's cigar moves from one side of his mouth to the other as he looks at the list. "Well, Hawthorne woulda went with the others. All them field hands was bought as a group, and they were took to Texas is all I know."

Texas. That's discouraging. "What about Daniel?"

"Oh, I 'member that boy. He was bought by old Sam Williams, who lives here in Pineville. Sam needed some help in the house. He's a old man, lives with his sister."

"You got written records of the sales?"

"Yes, I do. But my records ain't open to just anybody's eyes."

Cornelius floats a five-dollar bill out of his pocket. Gordy takes it and leads him into a back room, where he slides into a chair and unlocks his desk. He brings out a ledger and pages through it, folding the pages back. Then he points to the date at the top of the green-lined page, and gets up. Cornelius sits down and looks at the crabbed signature at the bottom of the page, verifying the sales: Bernard Ratout. This signature tells Cornelius that Ratout was unpracticed at holding a pen, but he held it well enough to sign his name to a wholesale theft. Cornelius runs his finger down the column of names: age; complexion; health; skill. Here are his slaves, rightfully owned, a lot of over a hundred men and women, scattered to some unknown fate in Texas. *How is it that we've come to have that right, to scatter people about like leaves to whatever fate awaits them?* he wonders. He lifts his finger from the page as if it burns.

The boy's name is on the third line down from the top of the second page: Daniel, age about 12. Small built. Dark complection.

Hawthorne's name he finds halfway down the third page: Hawthorne, 41, Big built, dark. Strong worker, field hand.

He runs his finger past the other names: John, Whitman, Michael, Ezekiel, Lucy, Carla ... They were all his, and now they're gone

Cornelius taps his finger on the sheet. When Gordy steps into the other room for a moment, Cornelius quietly rips the sheet from the ledger book and folds it into his pocket. Then he closes the book. When Gordy returns, Cornelius hands the book to him and strides to the door. The cloudburst has moved past.

He wipes off the saddle with a rag and swings up on the horse, thinking, *I should've given a false name, in case he comes after me for his missing ledger page. I'll do that next time, maybe using my mammy's maiden name. Cornelius Day. When you're touching slime, you may as well not leave fingerprints.*

He finds Daniel late in the afternoon the same day. Pineville is bigger than it looks, a down-at-the-heels kind of place, but an inquiry at the post office tells him where Sam Williams lives. He finds the big white house with peeling paint; it looms over a street of plain cottages. When no one answers his knock on the front door, he walks around to the back yard, where he sees a half-grown boy stooped over a washtub scrubbing some gray-white shirts.

"Daniel?"

The boy straightens and looks around at him.

Cornelius motions him back to work and then goes up the steps to the back door. This time a gray-haired woman in an apron answers his knock.

"I need to see Mister Sam Williams on some business," Cornelius says after introducing himself.

"All right, sir. Come on in." She ushers him into a musty-smelling parlor where he sits beside a smudged lamp, looking up the staircase.

A few minutes later a door creaks open upstairs and a white-haired man creeps down the steps. Cornelius stands up and introduces himself, and the man flops into a chair, his cane between his knees. A negotiation begins; twenty minutes later it ends with Cornelius paying $1000, far above a fair price, for the boy.

Daniel rides behind him on Eagle as they head back to the plantation. When they reach the cabins, the boy slides off the horse and shouts "Mama!" as he runs toward his home. Bo opens the door and falls to her knees in front of her boy.

But as for Hawthorne and the other men, the only thing Cornelius can tell the women is "Texas."

Early the next morning they have the cane wagon packed, and Cornelius hitches up Old Dun and Woody to it. The women bring out their clothes stuffed into cotton sacks which they pile along the sides of the wagon. Cornelius checks to see that they have the water jugs filled and corked. Wooden boxes of pots and pans are set in the center of the wagon.

When they've packed everything worth taking, Cornelius walks over to the hog pen and props the gate open with a log. Then he gathers the women together.

"Can any of y'all drive a wagon?" Cornelius asks them.

"I can," Daniel pipes up, stepping forward.

"No, you can't, boy," his mother says, yanking him back. "You stay right here by me. Don't you go botherin' Master Cornelius."

"Filisa can drive," Dancy says.

He looks at Felisa. Of all the women, she alone has broad shoulders. "Can you?" he asks her.

"Yes sir," she says. "I was a field hand before. The only reason Master Bernard didn't sell me was I come down with the Yella Jack. But I'm over it now."

He motions for her to climb up on the buckboard, and the other women climb in the wagon and sit with their backs against their clothes sacks, their legs straight out in front of them. Daniel sits himself right up front behind Filisa, crouching down so he can watch the road. Cornelius rides Eagle up ahead. They stop at the settlement and the women wait outside in the shade of a tree while Cornelius goes into the store to buy what they'll need for the trip.

CHAPTER TWENTY

IN HER UPSTAIRS bedroom, Euphonia twirls before her mirror, looking over her shoulder to study herself from the back. Her new silk frock is the color of bronze, and the ecru lace at the dropped neckline is just in from Paris, Miss Dolores said. The woman's wrinkled hands had danced over the lace as if she'd handled finery like this a hundred times before, and Phony is sure she has. After all, Miss Dolores has spent her whole life sewing up dresses for Natchez belles, and she's not young. Her face is a network of lines and her hair's gone mostly white. And she has such skill; her hands are so quick with the pins and her fingers crumpled the fabric so expertly to show Phony how it would look made up into a frock, gathered and pintucked. This is sewing such as Phony's never seen. When she and her mother stitched up their plain dresses out in the Cocodrie, their stitches would hold, but they weren't tiny and even like these.

A tap at the door interrupts her thoughts. Esther stands at the door.

"Excuse me, ma'am, but I thought I should tell you, Mister Cornelius is comin' up the road. I seen him when I was sweepin' off the gallery."

"He's coming back? Now? Oh, I'd better hurry." She slips out of the taffeta dress and tosses it across the bed. Then she puts on one of her new summer dresses, a bright green checked calico that might have passed even in the Cocodrie, except the fabric is from France and Miss Dolores has put in a row of covered buttons down the front. She ties a white ribbon around her waist for a belt and then runs down the stairs and out to the front gallery.

"Cornelius?" she says, although he's too far away to hear her.

Yes, it's him, driving a dray wagon with a load of women swaying back and forth in the back. The wagon lumbers up the drive. Eagle walks behind the wagon with a boy she doesn't recognize riding him.

Cornelius stops the wagon at the foot of the drive that leads to the slave house. He gets down and walks over to her.

"What on earth?" she asks. "Who are those people? Did you come all the way from Rapides Parish with that wagonload?"

"I did. And camped out at night with them. We were lucky it didn't rain on us."

She stares. Thomas comes out onto the gallery and Cornelius hoists the boy to his shoulder. "Hi, pal," he says. While Thomas prattles, Cornelius explains to Euphonia what he found in Rapides Parish.

"You can't just bring a bunch of women here like that," she says.

"I can and I did," he says. "For now they can live in the slave house. There're still some empty rooms out there. I'll free them as soon as I can."

She looks at the women. They sit hunched over in the wagon, looking up at the big columned house.

Esther comes out onto the gallery. She stares at the wagon for a moment, and then she turns to Cornelius and says, "What do you want to do with them, sir?"

I wish I knew the answer to that, he thinks. "For now, just get them settled in the Dependency," he says. "There's eight women and two babies. And that boy, Daniel. Eleven in all, counting the babies. Daniel goes with Bo. Give the old women ground floor rooms; don't make them go up the steps. They'll have to double up. It'll be crowded, but we have to make it work."

"They look like they'll need some decent clothes," Esther says in a low voice.

"They will. You take care of that."

Esther walks over to the wagon and puts her hand on the side rail. "Y'all gonna come with me," she says to the women.

They stand up slowly, pulling their shawls around their shoulders. Traysa and Dancy tie their babies to themselves. The women's tignons have come loose, and their clothes are in shreds. The older women go first, slowly; Jane's cane wobbles in the air as she lowers herself to the ground. Esther points toward the slave house, and they all move up the slope of the hill.

"I can't imagine what people thought, to see you driving through the streets with a such a rough looking wagonload," Euphonia says to Cornelius.

"I don't give a fig what they think." His eyes skim her figure. He's noticing her new dress, she thinks. Miss Dolores knows how to fit a dress, something she and her mother never mastered.

He puts Thomas down. The boy reaches up to Euphonia, but she says to him, "You're gonna wrinkle me." Coella comes out and takes the boy's hand and leads him back inside.

Euphonia watches the women as they straggle up to the Dependency.

"Cornelius," Phony says, "There's only five rooms out there they can use. Esther has a room and so does Malachi, and Walker Jackson. How will we fit these people in? "

"They have names," Cornelius snaps, and then thinks he's spoken too harshly. "They'll have to pair up, that's all." He points to the women and names them for her. Euphonia shakes her head.

Cornelius watches as the women climb up the slope. These are the worse looking slaves he's ever seen, even in the deepest parts of slavery. He can't see their faces from here, but he knows their haggard looks well, from the four days of traveling. With their humped shoulders and their grimy shifts and shawls, everything about them looks desperate and defeated.

"I wish I'd taken Mal with me," Cornelius says. "He would have been a help."

"Can any of them work in a kitchen?" Euphonia asks. "Esther's gonna need some help if she has to cook for so many."

"They cooked for me when I was out there, so some of them know how to. The problem was they didn't have much to cook."

Euphonia goes into the house and stands at the foot of the stairs, fidgeting with the puffed sleeves of her dress. Cornelius follows her inside.

"Phony, it'll all work out, one way or another," Cornelius says. He pulls her close to him and kisses the back of her neck. "Let's go upstairs. I need to worry about something else for a while."

In the hallway he catches a whiff of Euphonia's perfume, and it excites him. She's taken to wearing fragrance since she moved into Carefree, and he likes it. In Rapides Parish, the smells were not pleasant at all, just stink, and desperation, and the realization that the hundred or more slaves he expected to find were dwindled down to these abandoned few. His burden was heavy during the four days it took them to get back. Now they're all here, and everyone's safe, and he wants to lay that burden down.

Phony stands beside the bed. She unpins her hair and shakes it to hang down her back. "Look at that tree out there," she says, nodding toward the window. "The leaves are falling today. I always think that's a pretty sight."

They stand together watching the yellow leaves waft downward. "We'll get them raked up," he says. He nuzzles her neck, pushing his face into her damp hair.

"Maybe I should get Esther to draw you a bath," she says.

"Oh, you think I need one? Don't you like my man smell?"

"No." She giggles. "I like you better without it."

"I even bathed in a stream last night, 'cause I knew you'd like me clean." He takes her hand and dances her around in a little circle, snuggling against her.

"Quit," she says, pulling back, laughing. But he knows she doesn't mean it.

On a mild evening in early November, John Landerson walks into the parlor of his house as his children, playing on the rug, begin to squabble over the blocks that are scattered there. The nursemaid Emma has stepped out for a moment. Elenora is sitting in the wing-back chair near the cold fireplace, and as usual, she's buried her face in some distraction; this evening it's her needlework. Cross-stitched pillows nestle in the corners of every chair in the room and crocheted antimacassars lie flat on the arms of the sofa.

I have everything I ever wanted, he thinks; a perfectly appointed house filled with imported furniture, Persian rugs, tall frondy plants in front of every window, and five handsome children. But they have a distant mother. He wonders how Elenora's attitude toward the family changed so imperceptibly, over these years of their marriage. If it weren't for Delphine, and Emma, and the other nursemaids—

But he can't really complete the thought. Little Cyrus in his bassinet starts to fret, and Elenora glances up again to see if John will pick him up. He's taken on a lot of the care of Cyrus when he's home, and the baby has come to depend on him. When Cyrus gets big enough to talk, and he cries out in the night, John thinks it'll be "Da-da!" he calls, not "Ma-ma!"

But as he walks across the room to pick up the baby, Delphine comes in and swoops Cyrus up and takes him out to the kitchen. In a moment Emma comes back; the teenage girl tries to shush the squabbling children, but the boys continue to pick and push at each other.

"Enough of that," John says, and motions to Emma to take them out. "Get them their baths."

"Yes sir." Emma takes Lissy by the hand and shoos the kids to the back gallery like a gaggle of geese. Silence descends.

This should be a peaceful evening, John thinks. Delphine will be nursing Cyrus in the kitchen, and the weather is mild, so Emma will take the older children out to the back gallery to peel off their clothes and scrub them in the washtub. He pictures their skinny bodies, three boys and a girl, splashing and slippery in the big tub.

He turns up the lamp, pushing it closer to where Elenora is squinting at her cross-stitch.

He sits down on the sofa and opens the *Natchez Gazette*. "Do you want to hire some more help?" he asks Elenora.

"Hire help?" She looks up in surprise. "Why?"

"Well, when Cyrus gets bigger, can Emma handle them all? She's only what—fourteen?"

"Why would we want to hire anyone? If we need more help, we'll just buy another slave."

"Well, I was thinking, Cornelius Carson has some women he's brought from the other plantation he owns, and you know Euphonia can't stand to have slaves around her, so he's freed them. They're living over there in the slave house. But I imagine they'll be looking to work for wages, since they're free."

"Why can't he hire them himself?"

"I doubt if he has use for all of them. How many can it take to run a house? And he's got Esther, and a couple of others. I just thought I'd mention it."

"Euphonia Carson needs to get her head on straight," Elenora says, studying her needlework.

John looks at the newspaper, but the stories don't hold his interest. His wife's comment rankles him. Elenora and Euphonia are two women as different from each other as can be, opposites like north and south poles. Elenora, tired to death of the rich life she leads, and not knowing where else to find a life she'd like better—not with five children anyway—and half a mile away sits Euphonia Carson, who undoubtedly loves the new life she's fallen into. He likes to hear Euphonia talk; her country accent is charming and she has bold unapologetic opinions. But he knows Elenora dislikes the strange new woman who's joined the circle of wives.

As he dislikes Cornelius. He thought he could put Stephanie Coqterre out of his mind, but he finds that her face darts at him at odd moments. Pretty Stephanie, with her porcelain skin, her chestnut hair.

He sets the newspaper aside. "I might run for the legislature one of these years."

"Hmpf," Elenora says. It's not even a word of acknowledgement. She bends down to her needlepoint again. "If you think you'd like that."

He shakes the paper again and thinks, *Maybe I'll see Euphonia at the next soiree.* Elenora doesn't like her, but women are expected to make a society all around their men's living, to visit, and gossip, and keep up. That's just how the world works. He has a hunch that pretty Mrs. Carson might be the subject of some sharp barbs. He knows how women can be. He hopes Euphonia won't be a cast-out from the women's groups. She's a newcomer; she'll need the other wives more than they need her. But the other women might grow green eyes of envy. She's a striking woman, in her way, and when he sees her around town she's always dressed to the nines. She must have bought herself a whole new wardrobe, spending Carson's money at Miss Dolores's Shoppe of Finery. Well, Carson has lots of money. Euphonia won't come to the bottom of it.

CHAPTER TWENTY-ONE

ON THE FIRST COLD MORNING of December, and on a day, as it happens, when Margot is away delivering some other woman, Jenny, lying in bed under her quilt, feels the first pull in her stomach. It's a sensation she's never felt before, an iron band encircling her belly and slowly tightening its grip. The tightening isn't hard at first; it's amazing how her belly pulls and then softens, but she knows what it means. When it passes she gets up and goes to the window to look out, to see if Margot's anywhere in sight. But she knows it's not likely that Margot would be coming down the sidewalk just at this moment. It's just an ordinary day; the vegetable hawker drives past in his donkey cart and turns toward the river; a couple of nuns walk past, their wimples bobbing. Miss Hedro is probably sitting in her chair at the corner, wrapped in a shawl. The sounds are the ordinary sounds of the neighborhood; she's gotten used to them.

As she turns to walk back toward the bed, a warm liquid gushes down her legs, out of her control.

Once the torrent stops, she pulls off her gown, which clams coldly to her legs. Naked in the room, she wonders what she should do next. She needs to put something on, but what did a woman having a baby wear? No one's told her.

She grabs a cloth from the kitchen nail and sops up the liquid as best she can. Then she gets her loosest shift out of the chest and drops it over her head. She lies down again and pulls the quilt up to her chin. Every few minutes the tightening comes, squeezing harder each time. She has no help. She tries to get up between the pains, but then another tightening comes, so she can't stand up. Then she hears the door open.

"Margot? Help me!"

But it's a man's voice that answers. "Miss Jenny?" The broad dark face of Rosie's husband appears in her doorway.

"Antoine, help me," she breathes as another tightening seizes her. "I'm havin' my baby."

He stares at her. Then he says, "Oh, I just come over to see if you want me to move that garbage barrel off the sidewalk. Somebody pushed it out there again. You havin' your *bebe* right now? Ain't you got nobody to help you?"

"Where's Margot?" Jenny pants. "She's supposed to be helpin' me. But my babe's comin' now and she ain't here. What do I do?"

"Just lie still, and don't fret," Antoine says, holding his palms up. He backs away. "I don't know about havin' a *bebe*. Lemme go get Rosie."

"Oh, get her. Hurry!" Jenny says through gritted teeth. "Can she help me?"

"I don't know, but she'd be better than me," he says and then disappears, leaving her alone.

Between pains she looks out the window where she can see the slate roofs of the houses at the corner. It's a gray day. *This is my baby's birthday,* she thinks. *Today.*

Rosie comes through the door a few minutes later. She's a big woman and she fills the door, smiling her gap-toothed smile. Her hair is tied up in a bandanna, and she wears a stained apron.

"Miss Jenny, it's Rosie. Antoine says you havin' your baby." She walks to the bed and puts her hand on Jenny's stomach. Jenny smells the aroma of shrimp and sweat mingling in the air. "I reckon you are. Well, I ain't never been no *sagefemme*, but if Margot's not here, I'll stay and help 'til she gets here. Antoine took Charlie to my mammy's house. I can't leave you all alone in your labor, can I?"

Jenny gasps between tightenings. The pain's become a white sheet that she thinks will pull her apart.

"My mammy come and helped me when Charlie was born," Rosie says. "Where's your mammy?"

"Not in New Orleans," Jenny says, but the pain makes it harder to talk. She doesn't want to talk anyway. She wants to hoot like an owl in a tree. And she does.

"A baby's gotta hurt if it's gonna get born," Rosie says, folding back the skirt of Jenny's shift. "Lemme take a look. You just go ahead and yell if you got to."

Jenny looks at her through a fog of pain. What is this woman talking about? And where is Margot?

"I don't see no baby coming out yet," Rosie says. "I guess there ain't nothing to do but wait. I think I'm gonna stir up that fire and put some water on to heat up, in case we need it. It's gettin' cold outside."

She goes into the other room and Jenny hears her scraping the logs around. Then the fire crackles. She comes back into the bedroom and drags the chair up beside the bed. Time passes, but Jenny has no sense of how long Rosie's been here.

Finally, late in the day, Jenny says, "I can't do it," and then a sound comes out of her like no sound she's ever made. She thinks it must be an animal howling in some nearby bayou.

"It's gonna be all right, Jenny," Rosie says.

"Help me up," Jenny says when she can speak again.

"You can't get up. That baby might fall right on out of you." Rosie folds Jenny's skirt back again and looks. "Now, there is somethin' comin' out, some blood or somethin'. Lemme get a towel. But I don't see no baby yet."

"I'm gettin' up," Jenny says, lunging forward and standing unsteadily beside the bed. She crouches on the floor and bends as far as she can over her swollen belly, grimacing as her belly tightens again. All at once she knows she has to push down; it feels as if the pressure of the world is suddenly sitting on her belly, pushing her to the floor, to the earth. She grits her teeth and pushes hard, and then something wet forces itself out of her and slides onto the floor. It lies limp and still.

"Oh, it ain't movin'," Rosie says. "Oh."

Rosie reaches down and raises the baby's arm, which falls back to the floor. "I don't know, I don't know. Lemme see about cuttin' the cord. That's somethin' I know has got to be done." She goes to the sideboard and picks up the big knife Jenny uses to chop onions. After she severs the flattened cord, she picks the baby up from the floor and looks into its face.

Jenny feels the need to push again, and says "Oh," as the afterbirth emerges from her. A moment later it lies in a pile on the floor.

Rosie rubs the baby's back. Its arms and legs hang down. "Let me go get my mammy. She might know how to get her started." She grabs Jenny's wet dress and wraps the baby in it and hurries toward the door. When she opens the door Jenny hears the wind blowing outside, but she doesn't hear the door bang shut. There's a shift in the air in the house, as if someone has beat a drum hard. And then she hears a scratchy startled cry, like a catch in a cat's throat.

Rosie comes back in with the baby. "It was the cold that did it," she says. "It gave her a start. Now she's gonna cry real good, and be livin'."

"Wrap her in something dry," Jenny says. "She's got to warm up."

Rosie lays a folded towel on the bed and wipes the baby off. Then she smiles. "Well, ain't this somethin'?" Rosie says. "I ain't never seen nobody actually have a *bebe* before. Look, Miss Jenny, you got yourself a pretty little girl. Look at her."

Jenny lies back on the floor and says, "I can't look."

"Sure you can. Look at that black hair all pressed tight to her head." The baby makes a soft clucking sound. "I better wash her off real good," Rosie says. "I remember they did that with my boy. That water's probably still warm."

Rosie gets another towel and lays the infant on it. She takes the basin to the other room to fill it. When she comes back she washes the squirming baby off, dipping a cloth in the water while the infant frets. "You give me a big scare, little one," she says. "I'm glad you started to cry. Jenny, you got somethin' to dress this baby in?"

Jenny motions toward the chest in the corner. "In the top drawer there's some baby gowns I sewed."

Rosie takes a gown and slips it over the baby's head. "You got any diapers?"

"In that second drawer."

Rosie opens the drawer. "It's good you planned ahead," she says, looking at the stack of brightly colored diapers made from old fabrics. She diapers the baby and ties the strings. Then she tucks the baby under the blanket on the bed.

Then she helps Jenny to her feet. "Let's clean you up too," Rosie says. Jenny peels off her blood-smeared dress. Rosie takes the basin of water outside to the street and Jenny hears her slosh it into the gutter; then she comes back in and pours a pitcher of clean water into the basin. She wets a towel in it and washes Jenny and helps her put on a dress. Then she gives

Jenny a dry towel to put between her legs and helps her lie down on the bed next to the baby.

"What do I do?" Jenny asks. The baby's hands reach out as if grasping the air.

"You don't need to do nothin' just yet," Rosie says. "Just rest a li'l bit. You and her both need to rest. She's new to the world, and that's a lot to get used to. You been through a lot yourself, this bein' your first one and all."

Rosie bends over the bed and reaches for the baby's tightly curled finger. "It's a shame this baby's pappy ain't gonna get to see this li'l one. She's a lot prettier than my Charlie was. Charlie is a fine boy, but he weren't too pretty, I will say that. What you gonna name her?"

Jenny lies on the bed with her arm across her eyes. "I don't know." She starts to say something else, but then she realizes her whole body is shaking from head to toe, a warm shudder.

"Well, you need to come up with a name. I seen some people, they just call the baby 'Baby' for the longest, or somethin' silly like 'Puddin', but that don't seem right to me. I think even somebody as little as this 'un ought t' have a real name."

A gust of cold air causes them both to look at the door. Antoine comes in, holding Charlie. "I come over to see how things was," he says. "But I see that little one's already here." He leans over to show Charles the baby. "Oh, ain't that real pretty," he says. "Is it a girl?"

Jenny nods. Charles cries and turns his face away. Antoine jiggles him and says, "Don't worry, she ain't comin' home with us."

"Y'all go on back home," Rosie says. "I'll get there soon as I can. Get Mamma to come over to watch Charlie. I got to stay with Miss Jenny here."

After Antoine goes out the door, Jenny asks, "What's your real name? Rosalee?"

"You mean, besides Rosie? It's Rosabel. My mammy liked fancy names for her chilrun, but everybody just calls me Rosie."

"I was thinkin' of callin' her Esi," Jenny murmurs. She reaches for Rosie's hand. "That was my mammy's name. But I think I'll call her Rosabel, after you. That's so pretty." She closes her eyes and sleeps.

Spring comes early, soft New Orleans breezes coaxing blossoms from blackberry bushes and pear trees all over town. Jenny feels restless; in spring you want to get moving, she thinks. Her whole body wants to get out, to walk, to experience what's happening up and down every street. So one day she leaves Rosabel with Margot, who sleepily agrees to watch over her, and she walks to the French Market.

It's the first time she's been away from Rosabel since the baby's birth, and it's an odd feeling. Since the baby was born two days before Christmas, the infant's small face has become the globe of her world. Her days are a cycle of nursing, diapering, and listening for Rosabel's light breaths, her little sighs. Margot helps her with Rosabel now and then, when Jenny asks her to, and Jenny's glad to have the help.

"But remember, I only deliver 'em," Margot's said more than once. "After that, it's up to their *maman*." The woman's eyes sparkled when she said it. "And I get *paid* to deliver 'em." Margot has a black beaded purse but the bottom was ragged, so Jenny sewed it up so whatever Margot carries won't spill out. Sometimes Jenny hears the clank of coins when Margot walks past her carrying her purse. Margot tucks the purse underneath herself when she curls up to sleep on the settee.

Jenny passes beneath narrow balconies with pots of flowers almost ready to bloom, and along the gray side wall of the cathedral. Mass is ending and in front of the church a crowd of well-dressed people spills out of the church doors. She steps away to walk around them. Adrien would have liked working at that cathedral, she thinks; he'd have liked everything about it, its plaster saints, its high altar, its massive walls. She can picture him sweeping the aisle, brushing stray leaves from the marble floors, his shoes whispering. She doesn't really think about Adrien much anymore; but when she does, it's the cathedral that brings those memories up. But he's a ghost to her now, as transparent as a reflection in the rain puddles that line these flagstone walks.

Over at the river a seagoing ship is just docking. Jenny walks over to watch the spectacle. The ship's tall rigging dwarfs the steamers and flatboats already docked there. It noses up to the dock, a hulking giant. Sailors scurry around the deck, throwing the mooring ropes off. Passengers line the railing, gaping and pointing as they look out at New Orleans.

Once the passengers start to come down the gangplank, Jenny turns away. The French Market is just two blocks away; she'll go there and fill her basket, and then get back home.

But the passengers cross in front of her as they make their way to the square, and they're a spectacle in themselves. She stops to let them pass. The women have a furious haunted look, and the men look odd, formal in tattered topcoats and old-fashioned stovetop hats. As they pass in front of her they pick their feet up in an exaggerated manner. Their legs are unsteady, Jenny knows. Their heads are still out in the waves, even though their feet are now on dry land.

A man rolling barrels up to the dock stops beside her and mops his face with his bandanna. She recognizes him as a dock worker she used to see here before Rosabel was born, and sometimes he'd wave at her.

"Where's this big ship come from?" she asks him.

"I think they got on at Liverpool," he says. "These are Irish."

"How come they look so poor?"

"'Cause they *are* pore, sure enough. I hear they ain't got much to eat in Irish-land. That's why they come to New Orleans. We ain't rich here, but we sure ain't starvin'." He pats his round belly.

"I ain't starvin'," Jenny says. "But some people are rich here."

"Yeah, they sure is."

Sailors in dirty white uniforms come straggling down the gangplank. "I expect them boys want a drink," he says. "It's a month or more to Liverpool. Sometimes a lot more, dependin' on how the wind blows. It's a rough trip, too, is what I've heard. I'd keep away from those people if I was you. They all got lice. And that ship's bound to be pretty nasty. It's probably crawlin' with lice. It'll have to be washed down and scrubbed good before the captain takes it back for more."

"There's more comin'?"

"There's always more. I been workin' down here at the docks for a whole year, and I seen those ships come in one behind the other. My name's Jubal, by the way. What's yo' name?"

"Jenny Cornelius."

"Who's your master?"

"Ain't got one."

"I ain't seen you out here for a while. Where you been hidin'?"

"I had a baby."

"Oh yeah, I remember you was gonna do that. What was it?"

"Girl."

"That's mighty nice." He has a broad, friendly face. "My master's Mister Jack LaBranche," he says. "So I guess I'm Jubal LaBranche. He treats me pretty good. He don't mind me workin' down here. He says I can make money where I can, long as he knows where to find me if he needs me. Which ain't hard 'cause he lives right over there on Bourbon Street."

Jenny isn't really listening to him, because over his shoulder she sees a child who's come off the boat alone and now stands at the foot of the gangplank. No one has come to fetch her, and her face is about to crumple. Jenny knows that look. The girl's mouth twists to one side and she looks around, circling slowly.

"What's wrong with that girl over there?" Jenny asks.

Jubal looks over to where she's pointing. "Oh, we see that sometimes, with the kids," he says. "Sometime where they come from, they put the chilrun on the boat to come over, and then they write to their kinfolk here to let 'em know when the child's comin' so they can pick 'em up. But the ship gets here before the letter does, and there ain't nobody here to meet the child."

"What do they do?"

"The chilrun, or the kinfolk?"

"The chilrun."

"I don't rightly know. The ones I seen, just like that young 'un, they're gone the next day. So I guess somebody shows up to take 'em. Or maybe the nuns take 'em. There's an orphanage here somewhere. Ain't they a mess, those people?"

"Why do they come to New Orleans?"

"You tell me. What I heard is, it's cheaper to get tickets to New Orleans than goin' to a lot of other places. Who'd want to come to a place where we got yellow jack and malaria? I mean if they had a choice? They're takin' a chance, seems to me."

Jenny turns around to see where the other passengers have straggled off to. Most of them have dropped onto the grass in the square in front of the Cathedral. They're waiting to get their land legs back, she knows. They're all white people, gray-white, but brown is how she sees them, brown clothes hardly covering their legs, the women with their hair tied up in brown kerchiefs.

"What'll those people do now that they're here?"

"Oh, they'll get work," Jubal says. "Sometimes people like to hire these Irish instead of usin' slaves. The women can scrub and clean good as anybody, and the men are handy with a hammer. I've worked with 'em. You should've seen us building Master Jack's new house last year. Us black folk and them Irish, we was like a bunch of bees knockin' that place together."

Jenny looks back at the girl and then she can't look away from her. The child is lying down curled up on the dock.

Jenny walks over to the lump that is the girl. She bends over. "Little girl," she says.

Red-rimmed blue eyes look up at her. The girl's birdlike chest heaves, and then she says something Jenny can't understand.

"What's your name?"

The girl's eyes are locked on Jenny's.

"Who're you waitin' for?" she asks.

When the girl doesn't answer, Jenny moves away. She has to get back home; Rosabel needs to be fed.

"That girl ain't your business," Jubal says when she walks past him. "Let the white folks worry about their own."

She stops. "How old do you think she is?"

"I don't know. These Irish so skinny you can't tell nothing 'bout how old they is. She's 'bout six."

Jenny looks back at the girl. She shouldn't have come over to the dock. Now she's got something to worry about that's not her business at all. Jubal is right.

Over in the square, the ship's other passengers are starting to mill around. The men stamp around impatiently, and the women try to hang on to their children. Some white men come over to talk to them. To cheat them out of their money, Jenny thinks. If they have any money. These people don't look like they'd have but one red cent in those satchels, and if they're not careful thieves'll get that last penny before nightfall. And if what Jubal says is true, wherever these Irish end up they're gonna scratch themselves raw.

She looks down at the ground. Dark red circles are appearing on the bricks. Rain is sprinkling its way up the street, and the street steams. When it rains New Orleans smells like a praline, she thinks. And like piss and stink and vegetables that should've been thrown away yesterday. She glances back. The hump on the dock is still there.

She feels her breasts filling. She crosses Decatur Street and walks up St. Peter Street. It's an easy walk for her; the city's familiar to her now. She's been here a long time, most of a year. Maybe that was a good thing Cornelius did, to move her around. It got her used to different places. She wasn't like some people who stay in one place their whole life. Today she didn't get her bread, but she didn't want to walk home in the rain anyway. She hates a drippy basket with soggy bread, and she didn't bring a cloth to cover it.

The rain begins to spit down harder. When she gets to the corner of St. Ann Street, she looks back; all she can see is the ship looking like a skeleton, its high rigging all rolled up. When she crosses the street she looks back again. The girl hasn't moved.

I guess I'm gonna be wet no matter what, she thinks as the sidewalk steams. She turns and watches two nuns walking near the dock. They'll go right past the hump, and surely they'll stop for the girl.

But they turn at the corner and don't look toward the dock. They stride away from the river, deep in conversation, like purposeful women; they open their umbrellas, their white wimples bobbing. Men who work at the docks walk past, laughing and pushing at each other good-naturedly, and a couple of fast women in feathered hats mince down the street, their mouths red.

Jenny walks down the next block and can see the yellow house up ahead. Then she stops and turns around and runs back to the corner. In the drizzle, the crowds have thinned out, and she can see all the way to the river. The lump is gone.

"Good," she says out loud, and she turns back around and dashes toward her house as thunder rumbles. Her breasts are leaking and two sticky rings have formed on her bodice. When she opens the blue door, she sees Rosabel lying on Margot's lap, chewing on her fists.

At noon the next day Jenny decides to take Rosabel with her when she goes to French Market. She still wants some baguettes, and yesterday she never even got as far as the market. And she wants to get out of the house again. Margot is humming and rocking by the window, waiting for someone to summon her for a delivery, no doubt; she goes often, and at all hours. In the night sometimes Jenny will hear a knock at the front door, and then the scratch of a match to light a candle and some shuffling around as Margot takes her packet of things and slips out.

She thinks Rosabel will like a walk. The air is fresh today after yesterday's rain, so she wraps the baby to her chest with a shawl and strides down the sidewalk, nodding to the rag man and stopping to show the baby to Miss Hedro at the corner.

She walks toward the river. The usual racket of people and flatboats are at the dock. Rosabel frets and Jenny pulls the shawl back from the baby's downy head and talks to her. In spite of herself, and in spite of what Jubal said yesterday, she can't help but scan the length of the dock. But she's sure now; the lump is gone.

She crosses Front Street. The ship is still there where it was the day before, but no new tall ships have come in. She doesn't see Jubal. Off to the left is a pile of discarded wooden boxes thrown against a fence; a dog noses among the boxes. Putting her hand under Rosabel's bottom, which is slowly dampening, Jenny walks over to the boxes. The dog backs away, barking. Jenny bends down to look inside. A small dirty face peers out at her.

"Little girl," she says.

The girl's watery eyes lock on hers.

Jenny says, "You come with me." She puts out her hand and when the girl slowly extends her own hand, Jenny grabs it and won't turn it loose.

CHAPTER TWENTY-TWO

NOW WHAT YOU GONNA DO with that white child?" Margot asks. "And what's her name, anyway?"

"I don't know." Rosabel's finishing nursing and Margot took her and burped her and now has the baby lying on her lap, lulled by the rhythmic motion of her knees. The girl sits at the table with a bowl of grits in front of her. She picks up the spoon and lets the grits dribble back into the bowl.

Margot's sharp features crease into a frown. "You don't know one thing about that young'un."

"She don't like grits," Jenny says.

"Maybe she never had 'em before, where she come from," Margot says. "I wish you'd 'a let that girl stay where she was. Somebody would'a fount her. And you got your other one to take care of. How you gonna manage with two?"

"I'll manage."

"You can't save every lost child in this world. There wouldn't be no end to it. We can't hardly even save ourselves."

Rosabel begins to cry, a sudden rend in the air. Jenny takes the baby and puts her to her shoulder.

"Two's too much work," Margot says, handing Jenny a folded diaper. "And there's bound to be white folks here that want that child. She might have kin."

"She might not, too."

Margot glares at her. She takes the baby from Jenny again and goes into the bedroom with her. Jenny hears her talking softly to Rosabel, settling her on the bed.

Jenny goes over and sits down in the chair next to the girl. "My name is Jenny," she says, patting her chest. "Jeh-nee."

The girl's eyes are too big for her narrow face, and she wears a stained gray shift. She says nothing. Jenny reaches over to put her arm around the girl's shoulder.

"You'll be all right," she says. The girl sucks on her fingers. "I can see we got to find somethin' you like to eat. Would you like a biscuit?"

The girl doesn't answer, but Jenny gets up and takes a biscuit from the tin and butters it. She hands it to the girl. The child tastes it cautiously, then begins to nibble it. And she drinks some of the milk Jenny pours into a cup.

"Where's she gonna sleep?" Margot asks when she comes back in.

"She can sleep on the floor by me," Jenny says.

"You better wash her up good," Margot says. "Them Irish have lice."

The next morning Margot comes into the bedroom. "I won't be here much longer," she says. "I only said I'd be here for the birthin', remember? Now that Rosabel's bigger, I'm gonna have to go back."

"Go back to where? Your roof's still leakin', ain't it?"

"I'll set a bucket to catch the drips. I can get more business if I'm there, anyway. Madame Devrot knows I'm a midwife for all the gals around here, and she recommends me. Once in a while I even midwife for one of her white lady friends if they can't get nobody else. She likes me to do that, and they pay good."

"The place in her patio won't be near as nice as this house."

"No, it won't, but it's mine." She stands in the doorway. "I was afraid when you had this baby you wouldn't know one thing about takin' care of it, and that's why I stayed. That, and your man's died on you. But now you pretty good with this babe, so I'm just gonna move on out. I'm tellin' you, you don't need to take on a half-grown white girl. I don't know what you're thinkin'. Where's she gonna live? This place is pretty crowded."

"It'll be all right, her livin' here."

Margot turns and goes into the bedroom, and when she comes back to the front room, her face is like thunder. "That girl can't live with you when she gets bigger, and you know it. How's she's gonna live here with us colored people? Even if we free, we can't just take in a white child. It ain't right."

"I ain't gonna put her back on the dock. Who knows what'd happen to her then?"

"Somebody would take her in."

"Somebody might, but it might not be the nuns. It might be a lot worse. And why would she be better off goin' to an orphanage than stayin' here with me?"

"Orphanage might not be so bad. She wouldn't starve. She'd get fed."

Jenny looks over at the girl. "I gotta figure out what she'll eat. Skinny as she is, she won't last long if she don't eat." She sighs. "Somethin' bad must'a happened back where she come from, for them to just put her on a ship and forget about her."

"You don't know they forgot about her. Somebody was probably supposed to meet her when the boat came in, and they just didn't get there in time. They might be lookin' for her right now."

"Or they might not be, 'cause there ain't nobody. I didn't see anybody lookin' for her. I bet her mammy put her on that ship 'cause they were starvin', and she didn't have nobody to take her in. The mammy might've had money for only one ticket. And maybe the mammy was sick, and she put the child on the ship and then she went away."

Margot shakes her head. "Well, you can make up stories all you want, but if you keep her here, you might be stealin' this child from her own family."

"Or she might've been on the boat with her mammy, and then the mammy took sick and died, and they buried her at sea. And there weren't no other kinfolk on the boat who knew the child."

"You're makin up stories. Well, I'm gonna go back to Madame Devrot's patio. There's two or three gals I think's gonna spring before long, and I better be around to help 'em before they sign up with some other *sage-femme*. I reckon you can do what you want."

Margot starts repacking the little satchel she takes when she goes to do her midwifing work. It seems to Jenny she's making more noise than necessary. Jenny knows she'll miss Margot's helping hand with the baby, and she'll miss noticing how pretty Margot looks sometimes, in her red dress. Jenny thinks, *when Rosabel gets bigger I'm gonna make me a red dress just like Margot's, with a rose made out of the same cloth to pin on the front.*

The girl goes into the bedroom and Jenny follows her. The girl sits on the side of the bed. Jenny decides again to try to learn the girl's name. She sits down beside the child.

"Listen," she says. "I got to give you a name. I know you got one already, but I don't know what it is. If you won't tell me, I'll have to make up one for you." She pats her own chest. "Jeh-nee," she says. "Jeh-nee." She points at the girl. "Who are you?"

After a minute, the girl says, "Maeve." Her voice is hoarse and barely above a whisper.

"Oh, you're May?" Jenny reaches over to hug the girl. "Glad to know you, May."

"Maeve."

"That's good." Jenny gets up and goes into the front room, where Margot is half-lying down on the settee, cradling Rosabel. "Her name's May."

By noon, Margot has packed her things and gone.

May sleeps on a pallet on the floor next to Jenny's bed, and she's taken to following Jenny around everywhere, even to the outhouse, until Jenny started wedging her toes in the space under the door to keep it closed.

Margot's gone, but other people come and go; they all coo and make baby sounds over Rosabel, who smiles and gurgles to encourage them; and they have curious stares for the white girl who's living with Jenny. Lucinda, the ragpicker's wife, came in one day with a couple of dresses for the girl, not that they fit her well, but they're good dresses, not ripped. Jenny was surprised the next morning when she woke up and found May had put on one of the dresses, the blue one, and she was putting on Jenny's apron and trying to tie it behind her back. Jenny sat on the side of the bed, watching, and then the girl walked over and stood with her back to Jenny to get the apron tied.

"You look pretty," Jenny said.

Every day she takes May and the baby down to the docks to look at the boats. It's interesting to watch the boats coming and going, she tells May, but really it's to see if anybody looks like they're watching for a child to come off a ship alone. Jenny's decided if someone's looking for a girl of May's age she'll talk to them, find out if they really know who she is, and if they want her. Otherwise, May would stay with her. From what Jubal said, whoever was supposed to meet the girl when she got off the ship might never have laid eyes on her.

She wonders where Jubal is. He used to be here regular as anything when she came to the docks, but she hasn't seen him in a few days. A lanky Creole who looks no more than sixteen seems to have taken over the spot where Jubal used to work, rolling barrels onto the boats.

She walks over to him. "What's happened to Jubal?" she asks.

"He the fella that used t' work here?"

She nods. "I used t' see him here all the time."

The young man shakes his head. "He got sold off, is what I heard. He's off in the cane fields somewhere."

Jubal got sold. Jenny knows not to be surprised, but it's still a punch in her stomach to hear the words out loud. So Master LaBranche wasn't such a kind master after all. Jenny looks at the ground. It's hard to lose a friend, even one she didn't know any better than she knew Jubal. He was so happy when he found out she'd had a baby girl.

There's no one on the dock looking for a stray kid. There never has been. The news about Jubal darkens the day, and Jenny leads May back home. She goes into her house and lays Rosabel on the bed, careful to prop pillows around her. The baby's getting big, and she can roll over by herself.

Jenny knows she'll have to leave New Orleans soon. With Margot gone, it's hard for her to keep up with both the baby and May. And her money's almost gone. There's ten dollars left in her purse, money she earned from sewing some shirts for Charlie. And with the five dollars she'd stashed under her mattress. Ten dollars should be just enough—barely—to buy deck-passenger tickets for herself and May, and they won't charge the baby for a ticket; and she might even still have the five dollars left when she gets to Carefree.

Cornelius will let her and Rosabel stay in the slave house, she's sure of that. She'll take her old room back. She'll need a baby bed for Rosabel, big as she's getting, but there used to be a crib in the attic at Carefree, and Esther told her it was the one Miss Stephanie slept in when she was little. Jenny remembers its iron slats. And on mild days she could hang a basket for Rosabel on the back gallery, and the baby could nap out there with a mosquito net. While Rosabel naps, Jenny can sew herself that red dress.

It would be good to see Esther and Malachi again, and Walker Jackson. The free people in New Orleans are good to her, they help her, bringing her food and clothes for May and Rosabel, and they talk to her with friendly eyes and hug her when she isn't even expecting a hug. And they share what they've got, but they don't have much.

So on a mild morning a week later she wraps the baby to her chest and takes May across the street to stay for a while with Rosie, who likes to have May play with Charlie and who doesn't mind watching Rosabel too. Then Jenny goes back for her purse. She decides to leave the five dollars under the mattress for now. She'll need it for the trip.

She walks down to the dock and goes to the ticket window. "It's the *Big Hatchie*," the ticket-seller says, handing her two purple tickets. "Leaves at eight on Friday morning."

Jenny nods and takes the tickets. She studies the writing. Two words, one short, one long, and with two dots. She'll have to find the boat by looking for the name with two dots. She tucks the tickets into her purse.

Walking back to her house, she knows she'll miss New Orleans; but she's not going back to Natchez the same girl she was when she left. She's a grown woman now; she's had a baby and lived for a long time in her own house. She's cooked and cleaned and fed her baby, and when May came she fed her too and slept with her every night. She's met the people on her street, and they've helped her out when they could, and she's helped them out. But now since her money's running out, it's time to go. Esther will help her.

When she gets back to the house she collects May and Rosabel from Rosie's house, and then puts the baby down to sleep on the settee, setting a chair beside it so Rosabel won't roll off. May sits on the floor humming some unknown tune and fiddling with a rag doll Rosie gave her. Jenny goes into the bedroom and pushes her heavy mattress off to one side and reaches far under it to retrieve the envelope. But when she opens the crackling paper, expecting to find her five dollars, the packet is empty. She sits down hard on the side of the bed, the flat envelope crumpled in her hand. Margot has cleaned her out.

The next afternoon Jenny folds her clothes and May's dress in her satchel, and puts Rosabel's baby gowns and diapers in a potato sack. Rosabel frets and kicks her legs, knowing there's some change coming. May leans over the baby and starts to sing a song Jenny's never heard and in words she doesn't understand. The girl's voice is high and tinny.

Adhraim mo leanbh beag tagth' ar an saol
Codail, a linbh, go samh
Adraim a laige, a loime nocht faon
Codail, a linbh, go samh

"Well, I wish I knew what you're singin'," Jenny says.
The singing stops.
"What happened to your mamma?"
Just the pale-eyed stare.

Jenny sits on the side of the bed and reaches out to take May's hands in her own. "Now May, I know you don't understand much, but I been thinkin'. Margot was right, you can't live with black people. Black like me." She holds her hands out so May can see. "See? I ain't got no right to keep you, but I ain't puttin' you back out on the dock. I took you, and nobody else was there to get you, so I don't think you had kinfolk. So, here's what we're gonna do. I got a little money left, and we're gonna go on a boat ride up to Natchez. My old master there has a big house, and I know he'll let us stay."

May stares at her.

"I don't know if you ever gonna learn to talk, though. Well, first I got to get you cleaned up. If we're goin' on a steamboat, they might not let us on the boat if we look too ragged, us three. If anybody wants to know why I got a white girl travellin' with me, I'll just tell 'em I'm takin' you to your grandma up at Natchez. They'll believe that. But you got to look presentable. Let me see if I can find you a better dress somewhere. When we get to Natchez, I won't have a penny to my name. But I can probably get work in Natchez, sewing. I'm good at that."

When May goes back to playing with her doll, Jenny walks back across the street to tell Rosie she'll be leaving the yellow house in the morning. And she needs a better dress for May for the trip. And sure enough, before nightfall Rosie walks across the street holding a nice blue dress for May, not new but certainly respectable if a person doesn't look so close that they see the threads fraying at the hem and sleeves. And there's even a ruffled white pinafore to wear over it. Jenny didn't ask Rosie where she got the dress, but with a clothesline behind every big house in the city, Rosie would've kept looking 'til she found a dress just the right size.

When Rosie is ready to leave, having hugged May and kissed Rosabel on the forehead, Jenny steps out to the sidewalk with her while May stays inside trying on the dress.

"Rosie, do you know any women who're gonna need deliverin' pretty soon?" she asks.

"There's two I know of," Rosie says. "They're a couple months off yet. And one or two more who might be comin' in the fall."

"The thing is," Jenny says, "don't let 'em call for Margot. That *sage-femme* ain't the one for 'em. You helped me so good with Rosabel, you could do it yourself and make money. But Margot, no. She only knows the old Jamaica way of deliverin',' and it ain't good. She don't know how to make the pain less. Tell your friends they need a *sagefemme* from right here in New Orleans, who knows the New Orleans way, not the old Jamaica way." She looks down the street in the direction Margot went when she left; Jenny remembers how the skirt of Margot's red dress swung back and forth and how fast her heels clicked on the cobblestones.

"And besides," she says, "Margot charges way too much."

The next morning they're in line for the *Big Hatchie* an hour before it leaves; Jenny wants to be sure to get a spot by the cabin house so they're not stuck out at the railing all day. The *Big Hatchie* is a bigger steamer than the *Arab*, and newer too. She had no trouble matching the letters on the ticket to the name painted in big letters on the side of the upper deck. She stakes out a spot along the cabin wall and sits down beside May, the baby on her lap. As the *Big Hatchie* glides out into the milky gray river, Jenny can't help watching the city recede and then disappear as they move north. It's been almost a year since she came to New Orleans, and in that time she heard nothing about her brother Kofi. But here in New Orleans she became a widow, birthed a baby, and found May. She laughed with Rosie and Antoine, and negotiated with Margot for her keep. She saw the place where Adrien died. The city is as familiar to her now as the Cocodrie once was, or Natchez itself.

The hours pass. In the late morning she hands Rosabel to May so she can find the privy, and then she sends May to it, watching until the girl comes back around the side of the engine house. The baby sleeps, and May looks out at the passing riverbanks. They eat the sandwiches she packed. May plays with her rag doll, talking to the doll in words Jenny can't understand. When Rosabel naps, Jenny lays the baby on the blanket and sits forward to shade her with her body. May hums her song. The girl doesn't whine or complain, but she does rub her eyes and finally curls up against the cabin wall to sleep.

Going back to Natchez is like rewinding a spool of thread you already unravelled, Jenny thinks; she sees the same sights she saw when she came down on the *Arab*, but backward: the same shacks and shanties, the same white plantation houses, the same wooding places. No one has asked her about May, but she has her story ready, just in case.

The sun is setting over the Louisiana flatlands by the time the *Big Hatchie* pulls alongside the dock at Natchez-Under-the-Hill. Jenny tries to brush the wrinkles out of May's dress and she reties the ribbon which has almost pulled loose from the girl's hair. She looks at her own reflection in the cabin house windows and does her best to press her hair back into place.

When the gangplank is lowered Jenny ties Rosabel to her chest; she holds May's hand as they go down the gangplank. They walk quickly through Natchez-Under-the-Hill and begin the long hike up Silver Street. She hopes the fretting baby will stay quiet until they get to Carefree.

At the top of the hill, a man with a shock of white hair pulls his wagon to a stop. "Y'all need a lift somewhere?"

"Are you headed up past Carefree?"

"I kin go up that way. Climb aboard."

May climbs up onto the back of the wagon and sits with her legs dangling. She smooths her wrinkled pinafore down over her legs. Jenny unwinds Rosabel and hands the fussing baby up to May. Then she climbs up beside May and reaches for the baby.

"We're on, sir," Jenny calls to the driver.

He shakes the reins and they jostle along. Jenny unbuttons her bodice and nurses the baby, who opens and closes her tiny fists, staring into Jenny's eyes.

"Y'all related to them folks at Carefree?" the driver calls over his shoulder.

"Yes sir. I'm taking this girl to her grandma. She's been poorly, and her mamma thinks the air is better up here than in New Orleans."

"Well, we do get the river breezes," he says.

After Rosabel finishes nursing, Jenny buttons her dress and hoists the baby to her shoulder.

"That's a mighty fine baby you got," the driver calls over his shoulder.

"Thank you, sir. And thank you for the lift. It was a long trip from New Orleans."

"I'd say it is," he says. "I ain't never been there myself."

Jenny thinks about this. This old man's never been to New Orleans? Has he been nowhere but Natchez in his whole life? Even when she was a slave girl, she'd been to New Orleans. And right here on this wagon are two people, her and May, who've crossed a wide ocean and sailed halfway around the world on ships so big they make the *Big Hatchie* look like a toy.

How is it that some people never go anywhere, by their own choice, and some people go everywhere, whether they want to or not?

When they get to Carefree he stops the wagon at the bottom of the drive. "Here y'are," he says. "You take care of that li'l lady," he says, meaning May.

"Yes sir. Thank you for the lift," Jenny says. She hands the baby to May and hops down. Then she takes the baby and May jumps off. The girl gapes at the red brick house with white columns, but Jenny doesn't have time to explain Carefree to May. There's too much to tell, and it would use up the rest of her strength to try to explain everything, after such a long and tiring day.

In the evenings Esther likes to go out to a place behind the kitchen where she can rest on an old bench and no one can see her. She looks down the hill to the pond and sometimes some big cranes circle the pond, languid on the breeze, and then they drop their stick-like legs and land. *These birds, they see so much*, she thinks. Lucy Ida always enjoyed seeing the birds, because they were free to fly wherever they wanted. Esther thinks, *Now I'm as free as those birds are, but I don't know how to be a free woman. What do I do? Am I missing something?*

Her freedom is something she's never settled her mind on, even though it's been most of a year since Cornelius gave her the freeing paper. She carries that paper in a flat kidskin pouch she took from Sophronia's dresser, and every morning without fail she slips the packet inside her chemise. It rests there all day, and then at night she pulls it out, smooths it, and places it on the table by her bed. That piece of paper represents the one solid thing in her life, her freedom.

So much has changed at Carefree: the Dependency is full of people, every room taken. The big house looks better since Miss Phony had the sofa and chairs re-covered ; and she had new curtains hung.

And there's life in the house now. Thomas has livened it up, running back and forth with his toy horses and wagons, and Coella chasing after him, good-natured in spite of his antics. And when he squeals and giggles, Esther remembers how long it's been since she heard a happy kid make that giggling sound, like silver bells. When Thomas laughs, the sound makes Esther smile, reminding of her own two little boys who are ghosts now.

And Miss Phony in her fine dresses. What a change the woman's made from the day Esther first laid eyes on her. Now she wears satins and lace and she goes with the other women to soirees and teas at all the big houses of Natchez. Miss Phony doesn't invite the other women here too often, which suits Esther just fine; otherwise Esther and Dancy would be making petit-fours and arranging delicacies on silver platters all the time. It's not that Miss Phony's become a snooty woman like some of the others; she's just eased herself into their circle, and she wears clothes like theirs and pins her hair the way they pin theirs. And when they lower their heads together to whisper gossip, she whispers too. It's usually the same ladies: Mrs. Wilson, Mrs. Jensen, Mrs. Fornway, and Mrs. Landerson, who's with child. While Miss Phony joins in their little gabfests, Mrs. Landerson seems to pull away, Esther has noticed. That woman has a restless far-away look. Esther knows the Landersons have a passel of kids. Well, the Elenora House is big enough to hold them; all Natchez knows the house with the fine cupola. And Esther knows Delphine, who nurse-maided the Landersons' last baby.

Miss Phony's not a bad employer, and Esther's glad of that. She doesn't criticize much, and she seems to understand that Esther knows more about running Carefree than anybody else. So she just tells Esther when she has people coming for dinner or for tea, and Esther takes it from there. And certainly Mister Cornelius doesn't interfere at all, but he knew her so long ago, and he knows the house is her domain. So except for missing her girls, which is the biggest thing in her life, her situation's not too bad. And she's free.

But she still feels stopped, frozen in her tracks. She misses her girls. Helene and Theresa, so different from each other: Helene, short and wide-built, her face as round as an apple, who married Israel, Landerson's slave who got his foot chopped off; and Theresa, wild when she was young but tall and sober-minded later on. But now Helene and Theresa are sold off to somebody in Louisiana, and Israel's sold down the river; and old Master Landerson is dead, and so is Master Emile. Everything's changed. But she's still here at Carefree.

She closes her eyes. Right about now Mister Cornelius and Miss Phony will be in the parlor, and Thomas is probably sitting on his papa's lap. Miss Phony is working at her embroidery.

Mister Cornelius and Miss Phony seem peaceful together. They talk like people who've been married for a long time, but Esther has a hunch they haven't been married too many months. She makes the tangled bed every morning, and if she's not mistaken you only see that tangle in people who haven't been married long. And other signs are left on those sheets too.

But Miss Phony's got no babe coming, and if Esther's not mistaken, there probably won't be one. She's seen the little fretwork of lines at the corner of Miss Phony's eyes, and she knows she's a woman of some years. Older than Mister Cornelius, certainly.

She hears a voice and goes back into the kitchen, but no one is there. She steps out onto the brick walk, shading her eyes from the sunset. A long shadow falls across the grass, and when she follows it to where it starts she sees Jenny trudging across the lawn with a baby tied to her chest, and with a white girl trailing behind her.

"Oh my lands," she says.

CHAPTER TWENTY-THREE

JENNY SQUINTS AT THE BRIGHT BEAM of sunlight on the Dependency. Most of the doors are open, including the door to her room, and two women she doesn't know are talking together in front of the building with babies on their laps. They turn around and look around at her as she walks toward the kitchen. Another woman comes out of the big house with a basket of laundry and disappears around the back of the building.

Then Esther comes out of the kitchen and runs toward her. "I can hardly believe it's you," Esther says, panting. "You been gone so long, you look like a ghost. Are you back for good?"

"I'm back for good," Jenny says. "I've been gone so long I got this *bebe* and this girl, too. So now there's three of me."

They hug, and then Esther reaches to take the fretting baby from her. "Oh, this is a sweet one," she says, looking into Rosabel's face. "Who's this other child?"

"This is May. She's been with me for a while now."

Esther is still fussing over Rosabel. "Look how pretty, the way her eyes are so bright, and her hair so curly." She fingers the baby's tight black curls. "What's her name?"

"Rosabel."

"Did her daddy come back with you?"

Jenny shakes her head. "No, Adrien died." The baby reaches for her and she takes her back from Esther and hoists her to her shoulder. "He was murdered." She pats the baby's back. "Now that I'm back, I'll have to go tell Father Maercru what happened to him."

Esther says, "Oh, you not gonna be able to tell him, 'cause he ain't here any more. Last Christmas they had a fire at that church and it burnt to the ground. The postmaster said the priest got a letter from the police in New Orleans, and that very night there wasn't nothin' left but ashes. The priest left town and nobody knows where he went. Everybody that used to go to church there goes to Saint Mary's now. But who's this other child?"

"This is May."

"Who's child is she? What's her last name?"

"Cornelius, I guess. Same as me. I got her off the dock at New Orleans."

"Now, Jenny, you and me both know you don't just pick up a child off a boat dock," Esther says in a low voice.

"It wasn't like that. She came to New Orleans with nobody to meet her. They have street urchins in New Orleans, but I didn't think she'd make it with those rough boys. And she don't know English. I kept goin' to the dock to see if somebody was lookin' for a child like her, but there wasn't." Jenny hands Rosabel back to Esther, who's holding her hands out for the baby.

"What're you gonna do with her?"

"Just keep her, I guess. She's been eatin' good since she's been with me. As long as it ain't grits, she'll eat it. She was even skinnier when I got her."

Esther stares at the child as if she wants to say something else, but Rosabel frets, taking her attention.

When they get to the kitchen May wriggles herself onto a chair at the table. Jenny sits down with Rosabel on her lap.

Esther says, "May can't live in the Dependency, you know that. We got no room out here anyway, for her or you. Every room's taken up. I don't even know where you gonna stay."

"Who are all these people? I saw them when we were comin' up here."

"They come from Bayou Boeuf. Cornelius has put 'em free, and now they're helpin' out around here. Well, some are helpin'. Some's just in the way." She smiles down at Rosabel, who smiles back. "Maybe you better go inside the big house and show Cornelius you're here. And take May, too. I'll take Rosabel to my room."

Jenny watches Esther carry the baby out. Then she sits down opposite May and tries to smooth the girl's hair down. She takes her hand and they climb the back steps into the big house.

The house looks different, Jenny thinks, and it smells different too. There's new wallpaper in the hallway, blue pineapples printed on gold wallpaper; it used to be striped. And the dining room is painted a soft gold color now, not the pale green she remembers.

They walk down the central hall and Jenny looks into the parlor. Euphonia is sitting in a side chair Jenny doesn't recognize, and Cornelius is sitting on the sofa with the newspaper open. Jenny whispers to May, "Wait here." The girl stands against the wall, her finger in her mouth. Jenny takes the girl's hand away from her mouth and taps lightly on the door frame to announce herself.

Cornelius pours himself a brandy and clears his throat. "You been gone for how long now?" he asks. "A year?"

"Almost."

"And in that time, you had a baby."

"Yes sir. Her name's Rosabel. Esther's watchin' her for me right now. And I have somebody else, too. May. She's waitin' in the hall."

Phony looks away, her lips pressed tight.

"Who's that?" Euphonia asks.

"I'll bring her in," Jenny says.

She goes out into the hallway, wondering, will all this work out? Will they let me and May and Rosabel stay here? Miss Phony looks different now, with her hair swept up on top of her head, and she's wearing a silky dress and Miss Stephanie's pearls. A year can change a person's looks.

She brings May into the parlor.

"So here you are," Cornelius says. "Look at you."

"You're planning to stay this time?" Euphonia asks, frowning.

"Yes ma'am," Jenny says. "I've got the baby to take care of, and May's got no place to live."

"And where'd you snatch May from?" Euphonia asks sharply. "Who is she? Can't she talk? Cat got her tongue?"

"No ma'am, cat ain't got her tongue. She can talk, but not like we do," Jenny says. "She has other words. She can sing too. I've heard her." She thinks, Miss Phony doesn't want us here, not me, or Rosabel, or May. She looks at the floor, at the deep colors of a new rug there. "She was livin' on the dock by herself in New Orleans. I couldn't just leave her there."

Euphonia looks at Cornelius as if she expects him to say something. Then she says to Jenny, "You should've taken her to an orphanage. They have those in New Orleans."

"Yes ma'am, they have 'em. But—it didn't seem right. I don't know what those orphanages are like. And I had room in my house for just one more little kid. It was just me and Rosabel after Margot left. So I took her in. But you're right, ma'am. May don't talk hardly at all."

"She must've learned that from you," Cornelius says.

"Sir?"

"Well, May—that's her name?—she can't stay out in the Dependency," Cornelius says. "She'll have to stay here in the big house. Maybe Coella can handle both her and Thomas. We have so many staying here now, with the ones I brought from Bayou Boeuf. There's no empty rooms out there, and everybody's kind of doubled up. But you and Rosabel can live in Sophronia's old bedroom. Would you go upstairs and get Miss Coella? Tell her I need to talk to her. You can leave May here."

When Jenny comes back a few minutes later, May hasn't moved; but Miss Phony's gone somewhere else, probably out to the gallery, Jenny thinks. Cornelius is standing at the window looking out across the lawn. He looks around when Jenny comes back in.

"Thomas is nearly asleep. Miss Coella says she'll come down as soon as she can get him to drop on off," Jenny says. "He's so big!"

"He's growing up," Cornelius says. "Y'all wait in here for Miss Coella." He walks out into the hallway and then Jenny hears the quiet click of the front door closing as he goes out to the gallery.

Euphonia, staring straight ahead, doesn't look at Cornelius when he comes out to the gallery. He leans against a column, his arms folded.

"Cornelius, we are already housing an entire African village," she says.

When he says nothing, she goes on, "And we're the talk of Natchez, and not in a good way."

"I don't care about that."

"Well, I do. We come here, complete strangers, and then we let all these people move in. And then this white child shows up. People. Will. Talk."

"Let them."

Cornelius looks at Euphonia out of the corner of his eyes, studying her. The plain girl of the Cododrie has changed; now she worries about her dresses, and the impression they'll make when they go to parties, and how they look when they drive around town in their new carriage. And what he fears is, that when Euphonia gets over worrying about her clothes and her fine hats, and the creams she smooths into her face at night, there'll come a day when she realizes that all that is empty. That vanity is a false value. And that what's real, and important, is Carefree, and the home it provides for Esther and Malachi and Walker and the freed people from Bayou Boeuf. And now three more people have come, Jenny and Rosabel and May. They're real, too.

It's a lesson he's known since he was a boy. His mammy was a good teacher, and he's learned her lessons all over again these past few months, looking at Emile's ledgers, trying to decipher the man's notations. The oldest accounts, dating back to the time when Josephine was alive, are neat and proper and legible. But then as the years went by, the entries became erratic, sloppy. Cornelius can hardly make out the man's chicken-enscratch writing. He still doesn't have a full understanding of all Emile's assets. The man's debts, thankfully, were minimal. But one thing that's clear is the money remaining in the Planters' Bank. That will keep them going for as long as Cornelius can see into the future. And before long he's got to make yet another trip to Bayou Boeuf to see about selling the acreage there.

The door opens and Jenny comes out onto the gallery with May. "One more thing, sir," she says. "As soon as Rosabel gets bigger, I need to go find my brother."

Cornelius nods. Euphonia rolls her eyes.

"I need to find my brother," Jenny repeats to Esther as she sits at the table nursing Rosabel, a few weeks later. Rosabel's taken to arching her back and looking around upside-down as she nurses, but she doesn't relinquish the nipple. She's getting to be a big baby now.

"If that girl gets any stronger you'll need to move her to a cup," Esther says as Rosabel twists herself still farther from Jenny's grip.

"I think you're right."

May sits at the end of the table eating a piece of cornbread; her face is a scatter of yellow crumbs. And she's wearing a dress that was Miss Stephanie's when she was little. Esther must've kept the plain grass-green dress all these years; Jenny remembers it hanging in a chiffarobe in the back bedroom before Stephanie and Cornelius were married.

The girl doesn't look much like the straggly kid she found on the dock. She's still skinny, just not skin and bones like she was. She almost has a round little belly now. Since they've been at Carefree Miss Phony's seen to it that May has decent clothes, or Coella has. They aren't fancy clothes, but respectable. Today May is wearing a white pinafore that Jenny doesn't recognize, and she has proper lace-up shoes. And praise be stars, the girl can talk, and some of it's not even Irish. They can all understand a word here and there, and more words almost every day.

May's begun spending a lot of time out in the kitchen, and Esther's taken to her, mother-henning her like she once did Miss Stephanie. Which is probably a relief to Coella, Jenny thinks, and Euphonia won't care since she never pays the kids much mind anyway.

Walker Jackson comes in with an armload of firewood.

"You been busy," Jenny says, buttoning her bodice with one hand. She sits Rosabel up and pats her back.

"Yes, I have, and just between you and me I think it's a shame the Mayor of Natchez has gotta work this hard." He gives her a mock stern look and grins. Jenny laughs. He drops the wood beside the fireplace and sits down at the table.

"How's your li'l Rosybelle today?" he asks, reaching for Rosabel's plump foot. He gives it a gentle shake. "Esther, ain't this the prettiest baby you ever saw, and livin' right here at Carefree? Good thing we got li'l Henry and li'l George, living here too. Them three chaps'll have a right good time growin' up together."

"I ain't sure Henry and George gonna be here that long," Esther says.

"Why's that?"

"'Cause Dancy and Traysa told me they want to go find their husbands," Esther says, wiping her hands on the towel. "They was sold off after Master Emile died. They might be somewhere out in Rapides Parish, and Dancy and Traysa want to go back out there to look for 'em. It's hard for a woman to lose her man like that."

"Well, it'd be good if they could find 'em." Walker pours himself a cup of coffee. "But how they gonna get 'em out of slavery? Traysa and Dancy ain't gonna want to go back into slavery, just so they can be with their husbands."

"I've heard of it happenin'."

"That'd be a big mistake. I might have to talk to those gals. It ain't good, a man in slavery and his wife free. I think that'd be a hard thing."

"It might not be as hard as not havin' a husband," Esther says.

Walker shakes his head. "Yes, it would. You think you could stand t' have a husband in slavery?"

Esther shrugs.

"Well, I'm here to tell you, you couldn't. And neither could Jenny." He looks at Jenny, who mouths, "No."

Walker stretches out his legs. "Jenny, maybe someday you can tell us what happened to this baby's pappy."

"There ain't much to tell," Jenny says, wiping drool from the corner of Rosabel's mouth. "You mind your own business."

"Gal, I spend my whole life *not* mindin' my own business. How you think I got to be the mayor of Natchez?"

"I think Natchez got enough busybodies without you addin' to it." But she smiles at him so he'll know she's jesting. She likes Walker.

He says to Esther, "So how's Traysa and Dancy plannin' to go find their men?"

Esther hands Jenny a towel. "They think Cornelius'll help 'em."

"Maybe Phony'll help 'em. She hates slavery," Jenny says.

"I ain't so sure 'bout that," Walker says. "I've 'bout decided she just hates slaves. Some people are like that. They might hate slavery, but when it comes down to the real slaves, they have different ideas. But Cornelius is a man with high principles."

"He is. He gave us all our free papers," Jenny says. "Me first."

"That's because you was in jail, which luckily none of the rest of us ever has been. If I ever have a son," Walker says, "which I probably ain't, I think I'll name him Cornelius."

Jenny gets up and takes the sleepy baby over to a wicker basket padded with a blanket and settles her there. Jenny wonders about George and Henry, if they wouldn't be too rough for Rosabel. Two little boys could gang up on one little girl. And Thomas would be here too—maybe he'd be the only one here—and he'd probably be the roughest of all. Well, she'll worry about that when they're older. George and Henry are just learning to walk and Rosabel's still a lap baby.

May leans her head against Esther's arm. "You finished with your spellin' book?" Esther asks.

May nods.

"You want some coffee?"

May's eyes light up, and Esther pats her on the head. "I never seen any little girl who didn't like coffee. And you ain't too young, I don't care what Mister Cornelius says. Any child likes coffee with cream and a lot of sugar." She gets a half-size cup and pours coffee into it, then adds a heap of thick cream and three big scrapes of sugar. May raises the cup with both hands and sips it.

"How you like sleepin' in the room with Thomas?" Jenny asks May.

May wrinkles up her nose. "I don't. Actin' bad when goin' to sleep. Miss Coella say Thomas is fightin' it." *Ahctin bod* is what they hear her say.

"That's Thomas all right," Esther says.

"Miss Coella say I can have (*hahf* is what they hear) mine room when I bigger. I can *hahf* the other room."

"Ain't May learnin' how to talk good?" Esther says, hugging the girl. "It won't be long she'll be talkin' up a storm like any other kid." After all these weeks at Carefree, with Coella leading her through her spelling lessons and Esther letting her spend part of every day in the kitchen, May's begun to talk English more than Irish.

And her face is filling out. It's no longer the triangle face going down to a chin that wasn't hardly there. And Coella has tamed her stringy hair better than Jenny could, and she's pulled it back with a ribbon up on top to keep it out of her face. It's still thin hair, still looks dull, but Jenny thinks Coella's gonna have the girl shaped up before long. Coella favors her over Thomas, Jenny thinks, because she's a lot easier to look after than he is. And Coella's probably glad to have a little girl to take care of.

"Well, I hope Traysa and Dancy find their husbands," Jenny says after May finishes her coffee and runs out the door. "I wonder if Mister Cornelius would help me find my brother."

"You talkin' about Coffee?" Walker asks. "Me and Esther talked about him when you was in New Orleans. He'd be easy to find. I know right where he's at."

Jenny stares at him. "You know where Kofi is?"

"I sure do. There ain't but one Coffee, so that's gotta be him."

"How you so sure it's him? There might be lots of boys named Coffee. And it ain't Coffee. It's Kofi."

"Well, I know a boy named Coffee. I don't know no Kow-fee. I'm guessin' if his name was Kofi they thought it was Coffee. And there ain't no other Coffees around that I know of. Most people ain't gonna name their slave boys Coffee. Can't you just imagine? Some missus sayin' 'Bring me a cup o' coffee, Coffee.' You can see that don't make sense. Nope, I bet that's him. He'd be what—sixteen, seventeen by now. Yep, that's him all right. He's a dark person, too, like you."

Rosabel starts to whimper. Jenny says, "Where is he?"

"Well, last I knew of, he was at a place called Windrush Plantation. It's down by Bayou Sara." He pulls a packet of tobacco out of his pocket and taps the tobacco onto a cigarette paper. He rolls it and then looks at Jenny. "You don't need to worry about him, Jenny. This Coffee I know is a house boy, not a field hand, so he ain't got it bad. I think the old lady there might've even made him her pet."

"If he's her pet, she ain't gonna want him to go away," Esther says.

"That's true, she might not," Walker says, nodding.

"Walker, would you take me to where he is?" Jenny asks in a low voice. "I really want to see him."

"I'll go if Cornelius'll go," Walker says. "I ain't walkin' down no country roads by myself anymore, especially down by Bayou Sara. Sure, I'll take you. We could even take a steamer. We know how to ride on a steamboat, don't we, Miss Jenny? We done it before." He chuckles, but Jenny ignores him. He stands up. "Well, I gotta go. There's some things I gotta check on."

"What things you gotta check on?" Esther asks.

"Things in Vidalia," he says. "I like to keep up with what's happenin' over there."

"I'd stay away from there if I was you," Esther says. "You just gonna pick up trouble." But he's already gone out the door.

CHAPTER TWENTY-FOUR

ON MILD FALL EVENINGS Malachi comes up to the gallery to visit with Mister Cornelius and Miss Phony too, if she's sitting out with him. Cornelius always hands Mal a glass of whiskey and the two men discuss the day, with Mal sharing the latest news from the Dependency. Moss hanging from the big oak trees sweeps shadows back and forth. The mosquitoes are gone this late in the year, and it's a good way to finish the day, Mal thinks.

Mal doesn't know much about the work Cornelius does these days, just that he spends most of his time bent over that big desk in his office. Papers are spread out on the desk, and Cornelius pores over them all day long. He looks stern when he's doing that, Mal thinks, and that's because Cornelius has business matters on his mind. It's a far cry from the days when the work was all cotton planting, cotton chopping, and keeping li'l Jenny out of trouble. Those days on the Cocodrie seem so far in the past now. And so do the days in Texas, when Cornelius wrangled cattle in Pine City, which wasn't much of a town, much less a city. And Cornelius wasn't much of a wrangler.

Here Malachi takes it easy mostly, enjoying Esther's cooking and listening to Dancy and Traysa and the other gals talk about what they're goin' to do, now they're free. They don't pay him much mind, but he likes sitting with those gals and their baby boys. Not that he ever wants to hold the little chaps or help out with 'em. He had enough of young'uns with Thomas, when he and Cornelius made that run for Texas. Restless children aren't for him. He's too old. Sometimes he does a few chores around the place, and he figures that's fair, for his room and board. Esther likes to be bossy anyway.

But in quiet moments like tonight, Mal always thinks of the same place, Virginny. He's looking out over the lawn tonight, but it's not Natchez he's seeing. Just this morning, right when he got out of bed, his heart acted up. He didn't mention it to anybody, didn't see any reason to. But his heart just made a big flip-flop, right in the middle of his chest, and then for a minute he couldn't breathe. He didn't fall down; he just stood by his bed wondering if this was the day he was going to die. But he didn't die; his heart straightened out again, and then he laid back down. But it made him think: if he's ever going to Virginny, he'd best go before long.

Tonight Cornelius looks like he's thinking hard about something. Miss Phony comes out for a minute, but then she says, "It's too cold out here for me." And she goes back inside.

"Sir, there's one thing I need to talk to you about," Mal says to Cornelius as the door closes.

"Mal wants to go to Virginia to find his brother," Cornelius says to Euphonia an hour later as they get into bed.

"How on earth would he do that?" Phony asks. "He can't make a trip like that, old as he is. He can't even read."

"No, he can't," Cornelius says. "He was a field hand his whole life. I had a hard time getting him to even wear shoes, but he's finally learning how. He wore 'em to the lawyer's office last year. I knew if he got the right fit he'd learn to wear 'em. He didn't like 'em at first, but now he's got some thick socks so he don't get calluses."

"Where'd he get the shoes?"

"Esther found him an old pair of Emile's, but they really weren't a good fit. I got tired of seeing him hobble around in them, so I took him to the cobbler on Main Street. He had some in his window, used shoes, so I took him there and he tried 'em on and they fit. Esther's been knitting him some socks."

"I think anybody living in Natchez ought to be wearing shoes."

Especially here at Carefree, Cornelius thinks. Phony wants to maintain the pretense that the people living in the dependency are really just a troupe of house servants. It must look odd to the Natchez ladies, Cornelius knows, to have so many free people here; so the only way Phony can turn it to her advantage is to make it look as though they have many servants working in the house. But he knows the word must've gotten out in town, that the so-called servants here are all free people. That alone would make them pariahs in some parts of society.

"I can't go with Mal right now," Cornelius says. "I've got to get back out to the Boeuf, to see what to do about the land there. I told him I'd take him in a couple of months."

His arms are folded under this head as he stares at the ceiling. She puts her hand on his chest.

"Couldn't someone else go with him?"

"No, I'll go. He'll need somebody with him who can read. We could take the steamer up to Ohio, or down to New Orleans, then get ourselves to Virginia. Albemarle County is where he's from. But I looked at the map, and it's deep in Virginia. We could take a ship to Norfolk and ride the rest of the way. That's the only way I can think to do it. Any way we do it, it's a complicated trip and I don't think he's up to it by himself."

"How old is Malachi, do you think?" Phony asks, turning on her side.

"I don't know. We said sixty when I got him his freeing paper, but I don't think he's quite that. Maybe fifty-five? Anyway, his brother would be older than him, so I'm hoping he's still living. His mother might've passed on." *As my mother has,* he thinks, with a flash of sadness. The little farm on a hillside in Georgia seems as remote to him as the stars. "Anyway, I won't be in Rapides Parish long. I've got to get the place surveyed so I know what's what. I don't really like going there. The place seems haunted to me."

"Haunted by Emile?"

"Emile or those slaves he sold off. A hundred ghosts." He reaches for her hand and squeezes it. "When I get back, I'll go with Mal. The trip'll take a month or more. You won't mind if I'm gone that long?"

"No. Go," she says.

Euphonia listens to Cornelius's regular breathing, and thinks about the place in Rapides Parish. He wants to stay away from the place there because he thinks it's haunted. But she'd never fear a haunted house. Stephanie haunts this very house where they're sleeping right now. She sends messages that seem real enough, that come through the regular mail. Would a ghost send messages that way?

The messages starting coming last summer, and since then they've shown up sporadically, first one message, then two more. The cryptic notes are always signed "Stephanie C."

"Oh, help me, dear friend. I am bewildered," said the first message.

"Can you help me? I beseech you," said the second.

"I am so afraid. I reach out to you in desperation," said the third.

Well, Euphonia Carson will not be frightened out of her own home. She knew the ghost of Stephanie Coqterre was hovering here at Carefree from the moment she set foot in this house. But she wasn't afraid then, and she isn't now. She knows enough about ghosts to know you can't let them get the upper hand.

The next day Cornelius is working at his desk when he hears a familiar voice at the front door. A moment later Dancy shows John Landerson in. Cornelius stands up and shakes John's hand, and John sits in one of the leather chairs in front of the desk.

"Care for a drink?" Cornelius asks.

"I never drink during business hours," John says. "But I could make an exception. I'm here on money matters."

"Oh? Well, that's important then." Cornelius pours the drinks.

"Matter of fact, it is important," John says. "By the way, how's your business going? I heard you found all your slaves in Rapides Parish gone but a handful, and you brought them back. I only hear the gossip that Elenora brings home, of course. What happened to your overseer?"

"It's true, what you heard. Dancy, who just showed you in, is one of them. As for the overseer, he flew the coop, along with most of the slaves. And without any hands I couldn't even start a crop, so it's just an empty place out there. I need to sell it. It's got two substantial houses and some cabins, and since the ground's lying fallow it'll be fertile for a new planting."

"Well." John clears his throat. "I'll handle the sale for you, if you'd like. And the paperwork. I can advertise it in New Orleans."

Cornelius nods. "I've been thinking that's the way to go. I'm not a cane planter anyway. Emile was, but I'm not. Some planter could start over, make a go of it. Of course, cane prices 've been falling. But a buyer could put in cotton. That'll usually go."

"I'll draw up the papers. But meanwhile, I've really come here on another business." He gets up and eases the door closed. "I've heard of some business opportunities I thought you might be interested in. Business ventures are always looking for investors."

Cornelius nods.

"Some men are partnering up to form a bank in town, The Atakapas Bank of Natchez. There'd be good profit in that, I'd say."

Cornelius stares out the window at the oak tree; a breeze rustles the tired leaves. "I'm not much for working in finance," he says. "I've been studying Emile's accounts 'til my head's spinning."

John sets his whiskey down on the desk and reaches for his briefcase. "I understand. And then there's another thing. Some men here in Natchez want to form a consortium to build a steamboat. Would that interest you? I'm personally involved in both of these things."

Cornelius looks at him. "A steamboat? That's something I'd have a feel for, seeing how I used to be a boilerman, years ago, when I first came down here to Louisiana."

"Well, I always think it's helpful if a man has a basic interest in what he's investing in," John says. "Not just because it's profitable, which it would be, but because he'll take an interest in the thing and pay attention to the details. I've brought some basic information." He hands some papers to Cornelius. "The plan as it's being discussed is to build a steamboat different from most that are on the river. It'll be a floating palace, really, so the passengers can enjoy the trip and not spend their time picking cotton seeds out of their clothes. It might have to carry some cargo, but most of the focus would be on passengers. It could be made profitable if the ticket prices are right. It would be something the river hasn't seen before. This gives you the basics, but I'll get you the drawings and plans and such."

Cornelius looks through the papers, nodding. "I can see myself invest-ing in something like this, sure enough."

"All right. Glad you're on board." Then John speaks in a lower voice. "By the way, I had a visit from our sheriff last afternoon," he says, closing his briefcase. "It seems a warrant's out for your arrest over in Vidalia."

Cornelius feels a chill settle over the room. "Does the sheriff over there always alert you when there's a warrant?"

"Not always," John says, "but he did this time. Because it's you. We don't normally get warrants on a man of means. But then on the other hand, sometimes it's more likely if it's a man of means. Depends on the sheriff."

"A man of means can be as criminal as anyone else."

John shrugs, a silent acknowledgement. "You still have a slave girl living here named Jenny?"

Cornelius doesn't answer for a moment. Then he says, "I used to. As you recall, I freed her in your office."

"I'll take care of it," John says. "You study those papers and get back to me. As far as the sheriff, I don't think you have anything to worry about. I'll head it off. I'll send you my bill later." He stands up and pulls the door open.

"How are Elenora and the children?" Cornelius asks.

"They're well." John stands up. He wants to get out of here. There's a *frisson* in the air. *This man lives differently than I would live,* he thinks, thinking of his own twenty slaves. And he doesn't really like Carson; the man has radical ideas. But the need for a wealthy investor in his own pet projects has overcome his personal feelings.

"Do I need to be concerned for Jenny?" Cornelius asks.

"Oh—" John waves his hand in the air—"just have her lay low for a while. I think Sheriff Haynes over there won't take this too far. He's get-ting old and he has plenty of other things to take care of across the river."

Cornelius nods. The men shake hands. Euphonia appears in the doorway, and for John the room has brightened. He nods, "Mrs. Carson."

"Why, hello, John. I didn't know you were here." She steps to one side in the hallway as the men walk past her toward the front door, and then she follows. John's glad she's following them. He likes the fragrance of her perfume. And he's glad too when she leaves Cornelius standing in the doorway and walks across the gallery with him, to see him off.

That evening Cornelius sits alone on the gallery and considers what John said. To build a fine steamer—that holds promise. John proposes a vessel far more splendid than what's on the river now, a boat that passengers would take pride in booking passage on. Cornelius pictures a large sidewheeler, painted white, with filigreed railings. She'd come down the river like a haughty queen, her carved fan-stacks smoking, and in the main salon there'd be hovering servants to meet the passengers' every need. Little boys watching from the riverbanks would shout at the vessel when it appeared around the bend, hoping it would pull to shore at their dock. In small towns it would even be a point of pride and talk, that the finest boat on the river docked right here at Hannibal, or New Madrid, or Caruthersville. And instead of bales of cotton and hay, it would be leather trunks that the stevedores hoist up the gang plank. They could even call it the *Euphonia Carson*. He smiles at that thought.

But then he remembers the other thing John mentioned, which he's been trying not to think about.

The world's not a safe place, as his meeting with John today reminded him. There are things he doesn't know about, things he can't foresee, so he can't head them off. John will protect him from the sheriff in Vidalia, but what about the next danger? He feels a chill of uncertainty. Who knows what tomorrow will bring, or the next day?

He goes back into the house. Before he goes upstairs, he takes his pistol from the locked drawer in his office desk and slips it into his pocket. He's never carried a weapon routinely, never saw the need. But it doesn't hurt to have some protection. He goes up to the bedroom where Phony is lying in bed, half-asleep. He sits on the side of the bed.

"What's that you've got?" she mumbles.

"Nothing," he says. He slides the gun under his pillow. From now on, he thinks, he'll carry it everywhere.

CHAPTER TWENTY-FIVE

TWO WEEKS LATER, Cornelius, riding a long stretch of road as he leaves Bayou Boeuf for what he hopes will be the last time, thinks again about the situation with the sheriff of Concordia Parish. John assured him he could head off the danger, but the sheriff obviously got wind of where he and Jenny are. With John in his corner he'll be safe, he's 99 percent sure, but the unfinished business at his property on Bayou Boeuf has to be cleaned up, so he can't avoid riding through Vidalia on occasion. So far he's had no sense of danger when he goes through the town, but he keeps a sharp eye out, even so.

The place in Rapides Parish seems like it's melting back into the forest. Cornelius arranged for a surveyor so the fields can be identified properly in the parish records, and he wrote up a description of the place, its houses, furnishings, cabins, wells, barns, privies, pens, furnishings—all the things he could think of that a buyer would want to know. But with no slaves, no animals, no crops, it's a shell of a place. He hopes John can negotiate a good price, and soon.

Then he'll see about investing in the steamboat consortium John proposed. With the money he's already come into, plus the money that'll come in as soon as John finds a buyer, his main vocation will be managing his investments. He wants to help Malachi and Jenny and the others find their people before things get too far along with the *Euphonia Carson*. Once construction begins on the steamer, he'll want to be nearby every day until it's launched at Natchez-Under-the-Hill. Euphonia can christen it herself. It'll be her namesake.

When he gets back to Natchez, he calls Malachi and Walker Jackson into his office. "We need to make some plans," he says. "This finding everybody's kinfolk is getting to be a big project."

"Yes sir," Walker says, sitting forward in the straight pine chair. "I'm here to help you with all of it."

"There's going to be some travel involved," Cornelius says. "I'd rather not be gone more than I have to, with my businesses being here in Natchez."

Mal says, "I need to find my brother in Virginia. My mammy too, if she's still alive."

"Now, some of this is going to be easier than others," Cornelius says. He takes out a sheet of paper and draws two lines down the page, making three columns. "Let's make a list of everyone so we can lay it out and decide how to start. Then I can see how to go about it."

In the top left corner he writes, "Esther." At the top of the middle column he writes, "Her daughters Helene and Theresa." At the top of the third column he writes, "Where located" and in smaller script below that, "as far as is known." He writes "Louisiana" under that.

"Esther's girls," he says. "That's going to be hard."

Going back to the first column, he writes "Malachi." He reads it out loud.

"Yes sir," Mal says, leaning forward.

"Mother and brother," Cornelius says, writing. "Virginia."

"Albemarle County," Mal says.

Cornelius writes "Albemarle." Then he continues on the next line, "Dancy; husband; Texas." Cornelius sits back and looks at the listing. "She told me she wants to find her husband. But I won't put her on the list just yet. The women's husbands went to Texas, and it'll be hard to find them. Texas is a big place."

Then: "Jenny; brother Kofi."

"I know where Coffee's at," Walker says. "That's the name he goes by now. He's at Windrush Plantation, down by Bayou Sara."

Cornelius is surprised. "Oh. All right, that's a big help." He writes it down.

"Jenny'll be glad to know where he's at," Walker says.

"Who else?" Cornelius asks. "Cassie got anybody?"

"We can ask her," Mal says. "I ain't never heard her say."

"What about you, Walker. You got anybody?" Cornelius asks.

Walker shakes his head. "No sir. I just got my mammy up at Vicksburg, and my brothers and sisters are up there, too. I can go up there whenever I want. It ain't that far." After a minute he says, "What about May? From what I understand, Jenny picked her up off the dock in New Orleans. She got any family we ought to track down?"

Cornelius frowns. "May's my ward," he says. "But you're right. I should go down to New Orleans and try to find out. It wouldn't be right to keep her away from her family, her blood kin, if she's got any. That might be wrong."

"That would be wrong," Mal says.

"It depends on who her kin is," Walker says.

Cornelius writes "May" on the next line, and puts a question mark behind her name.

They sit in silence for a minute. Then Walker asks, "Which one of these we gonna do first, sir?"

"Mal, I'll go with you to find your kin, but let me start with Jenny, since Walker knows where her brother is, and he's close by. I'll need to find out who owns Windrush Plantation."

"Her name's Missus Aulie Aikins," Walker says. "She's a widow-woman."

"Well, I can write to her and get some news about Kofi. Coffee. I told Jenny a long time ago I hoped she'd find her brother, and now maybe she will. Then sometime I'd better get down to New Orleans and make some inquiries about May. And then, Mal, let's you and me head for Virginia."

"Yes sir."

"After we get back I'll need to find out where Helene and Theresa are. The auction house might have records of who bought them. And I have my business here to run, so I can't be spending all my time chasing down kinfolk. So everybody has to be patient. We'll start with Jenny's brother. Walker, you come with me down to Bayou Sara. Don't say a thing to Jenny about where we're going, though, in case we can't find him."

"I already told her where he's at," Walker says.

But Cornelius has stood up, closing the meeting.

The road to the main house at Windrush Plantation is little more than a path winding through deep woods, and when the road dips through some low places where streams cut across, moss hangs down so low the men duck to keep it from knocking their hats off. When they pass by a pond, its glassy surface reflecting the open sky, they see snakes everywhere, lying on the vine-covered tree trunks and hanging down from the branches. A huge log lying across the road begins to undulate slowly, and the men pull their horses back just in time to keep from being thrown.

The plantation house itself is so large and so white that it seems unreal, sitting as it does in the middle of this jungle. The very woods whisper with animal life.

A slave boy is sitting on the porch when they ride up to the house. When he sees them he gets up and goes to the door.

"Missus, there's some company," he calls. Then he disappears inside.

As Cornelius and Walker climb the steps to the broad gallery, Walker thinks he's never seen so many columns on one house. Four columns is a good number, he thinks, like they have at Carefree, or six if you really want to get fancy, but this house is surrounded by columns. He counts twelve across the front and it looks like they go clear around all sides of the house. Why so many columns, when there's nobody around but slaves and gators and snakes to see them? It makes no sense.

A gray-haired woman comes to the door.

"Yes?"

Cornelius takes off his hat and introduces himself and Walker.

She nods. "I am Aulie Aikins."

"I'm sorry to trouble you, ma'am, but well, we're here on some business. A mission of mercy. One of my slaves"—*former slave,* Walker thinks, but he knows it's easier if Cornelius doesn't ruffle the waters—"she has a brother she's trying to find. His name's Coffee. Or Kofi. And we understand he's here with you. We aren't trying to disturb you, ma'am. We're just trying to help Jenny find her brother. She'll be much better satisfied if she knows where he is."

"Oh. I see. Well—"

Walker sees her hesitate. *I'd hesitate if it was me,* he thinks, two strangers showing up, asking nosy questions.

The dark face of a teenaged boy appears over the woman's shoulder. She studies Cornelius's face and looks at Walker, who's standing behind him on the step. Then she says, "Well, here he is, right here. Coffee?"

The boy steps around her.

That's got to be Jenny's brother, Walker thinks. *Same dark skin, same round face, bright smile.* The boy nods at Cornelius and grins at Walker.

"But my lands, he's been here since he wasn't more than a little boy," Missus Aikins says. "Nearly ten years, I'd say. My husband Mister Aikins brought him here that long ago, and I took him in. He's been part of our family all that time."

"Yes, ma'am," Cornelius says. "He's got a big sister. Her name's Jenny. She's been with me all that time, too. And she's been heartbroken not knowing where her baby brother's at." He looks at the boy and then back at the woman. "Would he remember his sister?"

She turns to the boy, who nods. "I remember her. Abena."

"That's not the name we know her by," Cornelius says. "We call her Jenny."

"Is she all right?" Coffee asks. Cornelius hears the proper inflection in the boy's voice. Missus Aikins has trained him well.

"She's well. She has a daughter, Rosabel. We live in Natchez now."

"Natchez?" Missus Aikins says. "Oh, my. I was there once. It's a big city to me. Living here in the country, we don't travel much. In fact, I don't travel hardly at all since Mister Aikins died, five years ago, except I go to see my sister in Jackson every year. Coffee goes with me. What part of Natchez is it you live in, Mister Carson?"

"We live on the east side, in a house called Carefree."

"That sounds like a big place."

"It is."

Missus Aikins puts her hand to her chest. "Oh, I hope you ain't come to take Coffee away from me. It frightens me to think that. I'm hardly able to think how I could manage without his help. We have others here, about ninety in all, but he's special to me. I practically raised him. Mister Aikins had no patience for him, and he'd beat the boy for no good reason, but now Mister Aikins is gone, so—"

"I didn't really come to try to buy him away from you," Cornelius says. "I mainly wanted to find out where he is, to see if he's Jenny's brother for sure, and to give her some news about him, and maybe give him some news of her."

"I could never sell him. I know it's silly, to be so devoted that way, but I didn't have any children of my own, and my heart has to stay the way the Lord made it. And he's only sixteen. That's too young to go away."

"Missus, I don't want to go away," Coffee says, steppin' back. "Long as I know Abena's all right, that's all I got to know right now. Maybe someday I'd like to go see her, but I don't need to right now."

She pats his arm and turns to Cornelius again. "Anyway, he's got a friend here he won't want to leave." Her eyes twinkle. "Her name's Harriet. She's our ferrier's daughter."

Coffee grins. "Yes'm."

"Tie your horses and then come on in and have some refreshments," she says to Cornelius. "Coffee, ask Lorene to bring us some iced tea. And see if Harriet wants to show herself too. Lorene can bring some tea for Walker out here on the steps."

"Yes'm," Coffee says, grinning.

Cornelius and Walker go down the steps to tie the horses. Walker says in a low voice, "She oughta get some of them ninety slaves to clear them snakes off her roadway. Else she ain't gonna be visitin' her sister no more."

Cornelius chuckles and goes inside. Walker sits down on the steps, fanning himself with his hat.

"Your real name's Abena?" Cornelius asks Jenny three days later when he and Walker get back to Natchez.

"Yes sir," Jenny says. She's lain Rosabel in a wicker basket hanging from ropes on the back gallery. The breeze is mild, and the baby babbles as the cradle wafts gently. Then the rhythm soothes her and Cornelius knows if he leans over to look at the baby her eyes will be half-closed.

Jenny fans the baby with a folding fan and turns around to look at Cornelius. "How'd you know my real name?"

"Your brother Coffee told me."

She steps away from the cradle. A long minute passes. Cornelius looks down the slope of the hill to where the pond reflects the sky.

Then she says in a low voice, "I ain't heard anybody say my real name in all these years. You found Kofi? Is he all right?"

"He's well. He's on a plantation down by Bayou Sara. Windrush, it's called. And he has a girlfriend. He lives with an old lady and takes care of her, I imagine. And she takes care of him. I could tell he's your brother. There's a family resemblance."

"I want to go see him."

"I can't take you there right now. I've got other business to tend to. But we can keep up with him. I'll write to Mrs. Aikins and make sure he's doing all right."

Jenny stares across the yard to where Jane and Margaret are sitting under the oak tree, knitting and talking. Jane's cane is propped against the tree trunk. After a moment Jenny says, "This is an old lady he lives with?"

"Yes."

"How old?"

"How would I know? She's old. Gray hair," Cornelius says, irritated. *Why would you care? Here I've found your brother for you, and all you can do is ask daffy questions.*

"If she's old, she might die," Jenny says.

"Anybody might die."

"If that old lady dies, what's gonna happen to Kofi? She'd die and we wouldn't even know about it. He'd be sold off down the river and all you'd know is you ain't heard from the old lady for a while. Don't you think you better bring him back here?" She points at the brick floor. "So we can know for sure where he's at?"

"He didn't want to leave. He has a girlfriend."

"So what? I had a boyfriend once, and we saw how that turned out." Rosabel frets, and Jenny gives the crib a gentle push. "I ain't tryin' to be impertinent, sir. But I don't want to lose him again, now that I just found him."

"I don't want you to lose him. All right, I'll get back down there again to talk to Mrs. Aikins about buying him out, soon as I can. But in the meantime, I'm leaving in a couple of weeks to take Mal to Virginia. We're gonna see if we can find his brother and his mammy, if she's still living. I think I'll try to get to Georgia too, if there's a way to do that. I wouldn't mind seeing my mammy's grave there behind that church we used to go to. Then I'll be back, and I won't go off on too many more trips. Just one for Esther, maybe, to see if I can find her girls, but that might be hopeless. Then if y'all don't mind, I'd like to get back to managing my business."

He turns and goes back into the house to his office. And what's on the papers spread out on the desk, and standing up in file folders in the drawers, will keep him there for the rest of the afternoon.

It's nearly sunset when Cornelius stands up and stretches his legs. He walks out of his office, just in time to see Jenny come out of her room and head out the back door and down the steps. She doesn't look around to see him. When he gets to the back door he sees her striding away down the hill toward the road. She's wearing a shimmering red dress and her hair is pinned up. He walks out to the kitchen where Esther sitting at the table with Rosabel in her lap.

"Where's Jenny going?" he asks.

"She's gone to town. I told her I'd watch Rosabel this evenin'."

"I think Jenny could mind her own baby."

"I don't mind doin' it, sir."

He goes back out. Esther gives the baby a cracker to gum on and listens for the sound of the back door closing as Cornelius goes back inside the big house. She shakes her head, even though there's nobody but sweet Rosabel to see.

Cornelius don't understand much of anything, Esther thinks. *He's a kind man, but he don't understand a young lady like Jenny at all.* What she'd like to say to him, if she could ever be so bold, is sometimes a young lady doesn't want to just be mamma all the time, feeding the baby and changing its diaper. Sometimes she wants to put on a fancy dress and bite her lips red, and go into town big as you please, with her bosom hanging almost out and her skirt swinging.

But Esther knows she won't ever be bold enough to say that.

Just before sunset Cornelius sits on the gallery with Euphonia. May comes out to sit on the step below them with her spelling book. When the girl lays the book upside down on the porch to think about something else for a minute, Cornelius can just make out the words *Byerly's New American*

Spelling-Book on the brown cover. Coella has taken to giving the girl reading lessons, and Cornelius thinks this might be the same book that Stephanie learned to read from, in this same house, so many years ago.

Euphonia gazes across the lawn where the shadows are growing longer. "I like it out here in the evening," she says.

Cornelius thinks how quiet it is tonight. Traysa's little boy George is not running around underfoot for once, and Jenny's gone off to somewhere in town. May's sitting there frowning at her speller. Thomas is here with two toy soldiers, which he marches against each other on the floor until they crash. Then he sets them up for another battle. Esther comes around the side of the house carrying Rosabel; she sits down on the step next to May, and Rosabel wriggles off her lap and toddles across the porch, holding her arms out for balance. Her head's a crown of tight brown curls, and her face is wide. Just the color of café au lait, Cornelius thinks.

"She's learning," he says, meaning Rosabel walking.

"She is," Esther says.

When Rosabel reaches the edge of the porch, Cornelius reaches out and takes her arm so she doesn't get too close. She looks up at him indignantly. He pulls her back and hoists her up onto his lap and fishes into his pocket for a piece of soft divinity candy he bought in town yesterday. He unwraps it and breaks off a piece, and the girl puts it in her mouth and sucks it, making loud smacking noises.

As it gets darker the grown-ups sit in silence and the children quiet down too. A light breeze stirs the moss. Cornelius thinks, yes, this is peace. He's a man with responsibilities, but he's meeting them. He's freed all his slaves. Not one person on this place is in bondage now.

Except for me, he thinks, a stray thought. But then, he's the most fortunate of men. He'll be a steamboat builder; that's the kind of enterprise he can really get his mind around. He'll build a fine steamer, better than the sorry ones that often pull in at Natchez, sagging in the middle and looking like they're gonna blow up any minute. His steamer will be splendid, with a dozen staterooms and a dining room with white tablecloths and silver candlesticks and waiters serving the finest wines. A floating palace. *The Euphonia Carson.*

He looks over at Euphonia, but she doesn't look at him. She's gazing out toward Natchez, where the newfangled street lamps which the city's recently installed are winking on, one after the other, down on Main Street, as the lamplighter makes his way.

CHAPTER TWENTY-SIX

ON THE LAST FRIDAY in November, Willie Joe Haynes was buried on a day of pouring rain, but even so a hundred people stood around the open grave to watch him lowered. Eston Ferris, the new sheriff, stood at the back of the crowd so he could study the mourners. He didn't know most of these people, being new to town; he just came in from Alexandria a week ago, hired to be Haynes' deputy, and then two days ago he unexpectedly had to step right up to take Haynes' place. Concordia Parish couldn't be left without a sheriff, and everyone knew old Willie was in failing health these past few months. When Eston met Sheriff Haynes for the first time just a week ago, he was surprised at the man's pasty sallow face, his purply eye sockets. But Willie wasn't ready to retire, and two days ago it was a heart attack that took him.

Looking around at the mourners, Eston thinks, who's the criminal here? They all look like respectable Baptists, as much as you could tell in a driving rain, and swaddled as they are in capes and shawls and huddling under umbrellas. Standing next to him at the back of the crowd is a short black man, well-dressed in a dark green jacket and creased pants and holding a child-sized umbrella. The man's been following the service closely, praying when it's called for and shaking his head dejectedly as the minister talks about the futility of following the things of this world, and how all is vanity anyway. And nodding when the drenched pastor says Willie Joe embodied that creed, always faithful at doing his job, making the world a better place for the citizens of Concordia Parish.

Opening his eyes during the prayer, Eston notices that the man's polished shoes are no bigger than a boy's, and water's beginning to cover the tops of them, because he's standing at a low spot on the grass. Eston's own boots aren't being flooded, because he knows not to stand in a low spot in a cemetery; it's probably some old grave that never got a marker. But it's only a passing thought; the rain's running off in a torrent from the brim of the wide hat he's wearing. He wants to get in where it's dry.

When the miserable service is over, he turns to go. But the little man is looking straight up at him, almost as if he's going to introduce himself. But the rain picks up again, and Eston lopes toward his horse without looking back.

A few minutes later he unlocks the sheriff's office to see what kind of mess Willie left for him. He wants to get the place set up as it should be, and it's plain Willie wasn't doing much the past couple of months. But he, Sheriff Eston Ferris, intends to start in making big changes tomorrow morning, first thing.

When he met with Willie a week ago, these same papers were strewn across the desk just as they are now. Next to the desk is an overflowing wastebasket. Eston swears under his breath. Willie didn't know a thing about running a proper sheriff's office. Here in the wastebasket are papers filled with all kinds of private business, information that shouldn't be made public. Willie didn't even bother to tear the pages up. When the trash got burned these papers could blow up and down the street easy as anything. Might as well let every perpetrator and their relatives and friends know all the sheriff's business.

Eston sits down at the desk, which is scarred and nicked from all the years Willie sat here. He opens the top drawer where a faded newspaper is folded to a headline, "Nat Turner Finally Captured and Identified." Eston glances over the article and crumples it up and sets it on top of the overflowing wastebasket. No need to keep such an old article; the Nat Turner uprising was more than a dozen years ago. He doesn't need to be reminded, because no insurrection will get by him in this parish. The slaves here will know their place.

He shuffles through the papers on the desk and then stares at the faded wallpaper on the wall opposite the desk. Two daguerrotypes, each the size of his palm, are tacked up there. One of the dim images is of a young white man, the other a slave girl holding a white toddler. The child's image is a blur, as kid's pictures usually are, since they won't hold still, and what he can see of the black girl is mostly the whites of her eyes. The picture of the white man is clearer.

Eston considers. Willie looked at these photographs every day. They meant something important to him; maybe an unsolved case, or two cases.

He'll go through every drawer, every file, and find the records of all the old unsolved cases. It was just like old Willie to let things dangle, but he, Eston Ferris, is a different kind of sheriff, young, ambitious. Nothing will be left dangling while he's sheriff. He'll clear everything up. Every perpetrator will be brought to justice. He's not like Willie, who'd been here so long and who everybody knew from way back. He's new to Concordia Parish, but before long he'll be known, too. Every loose end Willie left will be tied up.

A light knock at the open door interrupts his thoughts. He looks around, surprised to see that the same small man he'd noticed at the cemetery is standing in the doorway.

The man comes into the office snapping his umbrella closed. "Sir," he says with a courtly half-bow, "I'm sorry to disturb you. But I've come to ask you if you might have any odd jobs I can do for you here. I used to do jobs for Sheriff Haynes. He was a fine man. I hated to hear he'd passed. He'd often find me some job to do, sweeping out the office or such like."

Eston shakes his head. "I don't have anything like that. I'll find a woman to take care of the sweeping."

"Yes sir." The man glances around the office. "Well, thank you, sir." Then he bows again, backing out through the door.

After he leaves, Eston thinks, first thing tomorrow I've got to get a deputy in here to sit at that desk in the front office, so people don't just come barging in whenever they feel like it. He thinks about the intruder who was just here, whose umbrella dropped spots of rain on the floor. That little squirt did odd jobs for Haynes? Well, considering the mess Willie left, if that little man was helpin' out, he wasn't worth much.

At three o'clock on the same day, Euphonia dresses for a funeral in a black crepe dress with a high neck and covered buttons running down the front, and she fastens her favorite string of pearls around her neck. Miss Dolores made this dress for her last year, not long after she came to Carefree; it's a funeral dress, but fortunately there haven't been many occasions to wear it. But today a big funeral is taking place at St. Mary's church: Elenora Landerson, who died after the birth of her sixth child, from a bleeding that wouldn't stop as it should have. The last child of the Landersons' was a girl, now two weeks old, a perfect little specimen who'll never know her mother. Life can be cruel that way sometimes. Euphonia thinks of John Landerson, now with six children to raise, all younger than nine years old. Well, he has lots of slaves who can help, and one with a new infant of her own, so she can feed little Dolly.

She turns away from the mirror and pushes a tortoise shell comb into the twist of her hair. She pins a black hat, peaked and feathered, on the top of her head, and then she steps back to look at her reflection. She looks pretty good for a woman of forty-two, she thinks. Even if today she's only headed for a funeral.

She goes downstairs to the parlor, where Cornelius is talking to May, conversing about something serious, no doubt; he has a way of discussing a child's topics in the most grown-up manner. The girl's filled out in the months she's been here. Her hair no longer looks like it's going to leave her completely bald, even though there isn't much color to it; it's just the color of dust. May's cheeks are full now, and she even looks a little round-faced. She's wearing a blue plaid calico dress this morning, and Coella has tied a grosgrain ribbon in her hair; it hangs down her back. The girl sits on the chair opposite Cornelius, her feet dangling above the floor.

Euphonia stands in the doorway for a moment, watching. The fire is banked, and Cornelius is wearing his black suit with the string tie. That's a pretty scene, she thinks, the tall man and the little girl, conversing like two grownups, here in the parlor where the gilt sconces flicker against the silk-papered walls.

Euphonia walks into the parlor. "You go on to Miss Coella, now," she says to May, and May slides off the chair and runs out of the room, her feet slapping on the floor. "Daniel's brought the barouche around," Phony says to Cornelius. "We should be going."

Cornelius stands up and reaches for his black hat. They go out to the front of the house and Cornelius takes Phony's hand to help her up into the seat. Walker Jackson comes up behind him.

"Sir," Walker says. "Sir. I need to speak to you for a moment."

Something about the man's voice sounds urgent. Cornelius glances at Euphonia and then steps away from the barouche. He looks down into Walker's worried face. "Yes?"

"It's about the new sheriff in Vidalia," Walker says in a low voice.

Cornelius shakes his head "No" and turns away. "Tell me later. I'm overdue for a funeral."

He puts his hat on and climbs up onto the seat and sits opposite Euphonia. Daniel shakes the reins. Walker watches them drive away down the hill until the only thing he can see as they drop below the curve of the hill is the top of their black hats, two crows.

What Walker wanted to say to Cornelius was that the new sheriff in Vidalia has a face like a ferret. Sharp and shifty-eyed and ready to bite. He's gonna want to make a name for himself, and you better hope the first name on his list isn't Cornelius Carson. Or Jenny Cornelius. But Cornelius is figuring his lawyer can save him from any trouble, and maybe he can. A rich man, all kinds of things can save him. It's just that today, Cornelius's lawyer is sitting in a church with his wife about to get buried, and he's got all those children to see about when he gets back home. He's not going to be thinking about heading off a sheriff's warrant.

And hanging on the wall in the sheriff's office in Vidalia are two pictures, one of Cornelius and one of Jenny. That sheriff will come looking for them. Well, he tried to warn Cornelius. But Cornelius is rich. Why would he listen to little ole Walker Jackson, anyway?

But Jenny'll listen. She's got a better head on her shoulders than she had back when she was just out of slavery. She's smart as anything. If that sheriff comes sniffing around, the thing Jenny can do is make herself scarce. She can't be nabbed if she can't be found. And Walker'll tell Esther and Malachi and Dancy and the others: the only person you ever knew here named Jenny left a long time ago. Nobody's heard from her since.

As he walks back to the Dependency, he thinks he'll go up to Vicksburg to see his old mammy. It's been a while since he's been there, and this might be as good a time as any to head up there. For one thing, he wants to see Governor Alexander McNutt. Just lay eyes on him. The governor is a mild-faced man, a handsome man, Walker remembers that, and he lives in a fine Vicksburg house, corner of First and Monroe. When Walker was still living in Vicksburg, he used to go there to sell peas out of his mammy's garden. The people there probably thought he was just a kid coming up to the back door with a basket of peas, even though he was already a grown man. He remembers one day when old Mrs. McNutt herself came to the door. She turned to the cook and said, "Euvala, let's buy some of this boy's peas. These are the prettiest peas I seen all summer. I mean *They are pretty.*" Why he remembers that one day and what the old lady said, he doesn't know.

He's got a pistol. Whether he'll ever fire it or not is another matter, and he's not supposed to be carrying a gun, being a black man. But what about being a *tiny* black man? Does the law make an exception for that? But it can't hurt to carry a weapon, when you're out on the roads. A free man can get snatched, so he's got to have a defense.

When Alexander McNutt's law partner Joel Cameron got murdered, back about the time Walker was selling peas at the kitchen door, McNutt claimed it was a freedman and some slaves that did it. He wanted the case to go to trial right off, and he hired a famous lawyer named Prentiss to try the case. Prentiss was such a talker, people just got caught up in what he had to say. Oh, they loved to hear that man talk. But Walker knows better than to love what a man says. The freedman that got hanged was his cousin Mercer Byrd. Mercer tried to tell them it was McNutt who did the murder, but the noose was already tied to the tree branch. And after the hanging, McNutt up and married the widow Cameron. Now Mercer's been dead all these years, and Alexander McNutt is the governor of this whole state of Mississippi.

Walker's heard that the people who own Camellia Run, a big house on the other side of Natchez, are gonna start renting out rooms. They're telling people the house is haunted, that it's got a ghost who comes down the stairs every night just at two o'clock. They're probably thinking who ever pays to stay there will pay more, just hoping to see the ghost.

Ain't that ridiculous? Walker thinks. Do grown people really believe that? Shoot, if people want to see a ghost, they don't need to stay in the fine houses here and pay those big prices. They ought to come out to the dependencies. That's where the ghosts are.

But right now he'll go talk to Jenny and explain the seriousness of the situation. Jenny might go around in a red dress sometimes, but she ain't gonna do anything foolish, not with Rosabel to take care of. And right now Missus Landerson's funeral's about over, and it won't be long before the pore woman is lowered into the ground. He needs to hurry, take the old buggy from behind the barn and hitch up Old Dun. Cornelius won't mind. He's got new horses and that new barouche, and Daniel likes to drive it. Cornelius and Euphonia look so good in it when they drive around Natchez. And Dun ain't much of a horse. He won't be missed.

He'll take Jenny and Rosabel and they'll head straight on up to Vicksburg. He's always needed a family of his own, and now he's about to get one.

He opens the kitchen door, and there sits Jenny nursing Rosabel, just as he'd hoped, and Esther standing at the fireplace stirring the ashes. Esther looks around when he comes in, and says nothing. Jenny looks up and smiles. She's so pretty, when she smiles like that.

He pulls up a chair opposite her, their knees almost touching. He can smell her breath, the gumbo Esther cooked earlier today.

He leans as close to her as he can. "Jenny, listen. The sheriff is coming for you. *Today.* Your picture's hanging in his office and he knows your face. You could swing from a rope, girl. They're crazy over there in Vidalia, and this sheriff's crazier than the last one. Right now he's sittin' at Miz Landerson's funeral at Saint Mary's, watchin' Cornelius out of the corner of his eye. But the funeral ain't gonna last that long, and once it's over, Cornelius is on his own. There ain't nothin' I can do for him. But you can get away. We'll head on up to Vicksburg."

"What?"

"That sheriff's got a warrant out for you. He's probably already sent it over to Adams County, and now he's just waitin', like a spider. We got to go."

"How we gonna get to Vicksburg? That's a long way."

"We'll take the old buggy. Cornelius'll understand. Don't worry about being fancy, just grab your clothes and the baby's stuff. We got to make tracks."

Jenny looks at Esther, who stands next to Walker. She sees fear in the older woman's eyes. She jumps up and hands the baby to her. May comes in to the kitchen and Esther puts her arm around the girl's shoulder.

Jenny kisses May quickly on the forehead and then she runs out of the kitchen, up the back steps and into the big house. She goes to her room and pulls Sophronia's big satchel out of the chiffarobe and stuffs her dresses and Rosabel's clothes into it. Walker's right; they have to go. The sheriff will never know she was here. Cornelius will understand, and Miss Phony'll be glad.

An hour later Jenny and Walker are driving fast into the rolling hills north of Natchez. The road is a tumble of ups and downs, muddy in the bottoms, but on the hills the sandy soil is drying in the sun. Walker keeps Dun trotting as much as he can, wanting to put distance between them and Natchez. Jenny sits next to him, Rosabel on her lap.

He watches the woods. They're riding along like any proper couple, and no sheriff's deputy has shown up to tail them. If Esther and the others back at Carefree keep their mouths shut, which he thinks they will, that'll throw the sheriff off the trail. The sheriff's got pictures, but Jenny doesn't really look the same as she used to look anyway. She used to be skinnier, back before she had Rosabel. And when she took that picture, she was a lot younger. Now she's still not very filled out, but her face is a little more round. She still has that sweet look she always had, but she's more knowing now. How could she not be, an experienced woman like she is now, with a baby and all? But he's saved her, brought her out of danger. The lawyer might see to it that the sheriff won't come for Cornelius; but he could come for Jenny, if he finds out where she is. It's the way things are now, with everybody so worked up.

They won't stay in Vicksburg long. It'll be wonderful to see his mammy and his brothers and sisters, but as long as he stays in Vicksburg he'll always be just little Walker to them, even though he's a grown man, just like he was back when he was selling peas at the governor's kitchen door.

Somewhere there's a place where a man like him, little though he is, can live a life without always looking over his shoulder, where there won't be a slave-catcher hiding in every thicket of trees up ahead. And where he and Jenny and their baby Rosabel can travel around any time they want to, and they won't have to be in hiding. It'll have to be in the free soil, and after they leave Vicksburg that's where they'll head.

"I think we'll buy us some land, have a farm somewhere," he says to Jenny. "Maybe in Indiana or Wisconsin Territory. That's free soil."

She looks at the road ahead. "That would be better. They wouldn't have ghosts there."

"Oh, there's ghosts there, sure enough," he says. "The only difference is, up there the ghosts are beatin' on tom-toms."

"They are?"

"We'll probably be able to hear 'em some nights when it's quiet. There's ghosts everywhere. Anywhere you go, it's bones all the way down. Don't worry about 'em. You don't bother them, they won't bother you."

He reaches over and covers Jenny's hand with his own. Rosabel's fallen asleep, with her full belly. *His little family*, he thinks. He loves this.

He can hardly wait to get to Vicksburg. His mammy's always glad to see him, and she's getting awful old. What'll she think when he comes in the door with Jenny and Rosabel?

Won't she be glad?

Won't she be surprised?

ACKNOWLEDGEMENTS

WRITING *Jenny is Free* has been an intensive labor of love for me for the better part of a year. But while writing is a solitary endeavor, no one accomplishes anything without the explicit assistance of others. My primary debt of gratitude goes to my husband David, who has never doubted the worth of the project, and who has been endlessly encouraging, serving as a proofreader and patient sounding board. My family and friends have been very supportive. Professor Mark Spencer, Dean of the School of Arts and Humanities at the University of Arkansas at Monticello, offered invaluable advice and input. Many people who read *Spinning Jenny* told me they were eagerly waiting for the publication of *Jenny is Free* so they could find out what happened to Jenny, Cornelius, Esther, and the other characters. In a project such as this, tenacity and determination may be what count most. In the midst of this project there were days when Jenny, Cornelius, Malachi, and the other characters seemed to dance upon the typescript before my eyes. I hope they danced for you, too.